T

A contra
wrecked
enough t
profit. Bu
by which
through t
whom Ni
The nece
tional ru
bankrupt
the powe
mination
task of g
tracted da

THE MANASCO ROAD

by

Victor Canning

THE BOOK CLUB
121 Charing Cross Road
London, W.C. 2

*This edition by arrangement
with Hodder & Stoughton Ltd.*

Made and Printed in Great Britain by C. Tinling & Co., Ltd.
Liverpool, London and Prescot.

PART ONE

Chapter One

THERE had been only a few people on the plane from Barcelona. They walked ahead of him now, all hunched against the evening drizzle, their long, oblique shadows thrown back to him by the floodlights on the face of the airport buildings. The wind lifted the edges of a coat of a woman ahead of him and the lights put a hard, steel polish on her nylons.

He followed her up the steps into the hallway. Purgatory, he thought. Airport waiting halls, full of people going up or coming down. Maybe the real purgatory was better lit. Here the current oozed sluggishly through the lamp filaments. His eyes went round the place looking for her. Lining the shadowed benches was a still fresco of waiting figures . . . an old man, his feet up on a cardboard case, a shabby parcel tied to the handle; a young peasant couple, hand in hand, the boy's face wary and distrustful; a Guardia Civil leaning against a pillar picking his teeth; a woman staring at a *Compagnie de Navigation Mixte* poster. . . .

Maybe she's in the bar he thought. He went across to the right, the grit on his shoes from the wet runway grating on the tiles. There was a smell of cigar smoke and scent and coffee and cognac. A pilot he knew beckoned to him but he shook his head.

She wasn't there. Usually she would be standing in the waiting hall, in her long white coat, bare-headed, the soft pale hair looking as though it had just been brushed . . . and then there would be the good moment when she saw him and came eagerly to him. . . .

Smiling at his disappointment, he went out into the drizzle, into the forecourt of the airport. Five or six taxis stood there, their curved roofs shining under the rain, the little bunches of scarlet and gold ribbon at their radiator caps and mirrors drooping like seaweed. There will be sun tomorrow, he thought. Hard, chromium-plated sun and everyone will forget the rain. A driver got up from a running board and came towards him. His face was like old cork bark and the drizzle silvered the shoulders of his suit.

"Taxi, señor? Palma?" The touting tone vanished as the driver recognised him. "Señor Thorne. . . . Welcome, welcome. . . ."

"Hullo, Jaime. Have you seen my wife around?"

"No, señor. She has not been here."

Thorne handed him his baggage ticket and waited while he went to collect his big case.

Jaime drove him into Palma, one hand on the wheel, the other on the horn, and talking all the way. Thorne only half listened for in imagination he was ahead, in the flat at the top of the old building behind the Cathedral and the Almudaina Palace.

The wheels sang on the wet road. A tram came up into the headlights. Buildings began to gather round them. Jaime's voice came back to him. The bullfights had been lousy. The *Guardia Civil* had picked up a fishing boat down near Cabos Salinas with nearly two million cigarettes aboard. . . . And Thorne was thinking, it is good to come back. It is good to have something, someone, to come back to.

On the far side of the Piazza de España he made Jaime stop. He got out and went into a flower shop. An old woman with twisted, puffy hands sold him twelve roses; apricot coloured, like the ones his father used to grow at the villa. The old woman took an age arranging the flowers and his impatience showed. Handing them to him, she said, "If it were me, señor, and forty years back, you could have come without the flowers and been welcome. A man has only one gift a woman needs." She held his hundred-peseta note up to the light and jerked at it with a sudden movement of the puffed hands to prove its worth.

Jaime took the car rattling and clattering over the cobbles up the hill to the Cathedral. Thorne sat in the darkness, holding the roses in his hands carefully.

"This car should have fallen to pieces years ago," he said.

"Packard, nineteen twenty-eight. Old cars are best. Like wine——"

Jaime broke off to curse a man who came out of a side turning on a bicycle. He drew up outside the house. The street light and the rain veneered the baroque stone facings and the tall, narrow entrance with blue and grey gleams.

Jaime wanted to carry his case up but he paid him off and took it himself. He went in out of the rain, hearing the car draw away, and up the dark stairs. The last flight, unable to withhold his impatience, he took at a run.

He opened the door with his key and in the dark hall dropped his case to the ground.

"Katey! Hi, Kate!"

He waited for one of the doors to open, for a yellow patch of light to fall across the darkness. But there was no movement.

"Kate!"

The darkness filled with the echoes of his voice.

Hell. She was out. That meant that she hadn't got his message that he was coming back. He switched on the hall lights.

The place was full of her. There was a sherry decanter on the sitting-room table. Wine flies had drowned themselves in the dregs of two glasses. An air mail edition of the *Daily Telegraph* was crumpled on the floor by the window. She was untidy, used things and threw them down. Untidy because she had all the time in the world to be orderly. He folded the paper neatly and then fixed himself a glass of whisky. The clock in the hallway struck ten. He went through into the bedroom, carrying his glass. Face down on the end of their bed was an open book and perched near it a large ash tray. He had a sudden picture of her lying there, reading, and for a second or two there was a keen

A*

sense in him of the time on her hands, the twenty-four hour padding of each day. On the dressing table was a sealed envelope addressed to their daughter. He picked it up, felt the bulk of the long letter inside and read the neat, meticulous script; Miss Julia Thorne, Hawkhurst School, Kent, Ingliterra. . . . The autumn winds would be turning cold in England now. He pictured Julia wrapped in a green school cape and the end of her nose shining.

He went into the bathroom and began to run a bath. Another book was open on the shelf below the mirror. She read three or four at a time, propped open about the house. A girdle, damp from recent washing, hung on the expanding rail of his shaving mirror over the basin.

He stripped, whistling to himself as the bath ran.

The long mirror above the bath showed a tall, easy-going figure, no flabbiness, the brown skin hard and polished. He stopped whistling as he ran a hand over his chin, wondering if he should shave. Travelling always brought the stubble out. He decided to let it go. Kate would take him as he was. With the thought he smiled and the whistle began again, gently. . . . Suddenly he was reminded of his father; the old man had had a Red Indian look, the planes of cheek flesh like hard teak; a stern face until the smile came into the blue eyes and the mouth twisted, spilling over with humour. . . . Everyone said he was like his father. At thirty-five he didn't mind looking like him, but he hoped that was as far as it would go. While he lived he had loved him, but the old man had left his children few illusions . . . browsing always on the slopes of bankruptcy, one mad scheme after another financed with other people's money. The old devil had had charm. Must have had to have carried on the way he did. He raised his hands, scratching at the soft brown short-cut hair. . . . Well, he'd done a little better than the old man. He was a little higher up the slope than his father had been . . . but not much. Enough though. Enough to buy Kate a new dress when she wanted one, to give her a good time. . . . He leaned forward, grunting and touched his toes. There were two of Kate's hairgrips on the floor. He picked them up. Holding them, and thinking of Kate, he said contentedly to himself. Well, I may not be a successful man, but at least I'm a happy one. He reached back and touched the wood of the door for luck.

He got into the bath and lay back, finishing his whisky. He lay there and he knew what it was to be content. It was something a man had to live long to discover. He'd had it for ten years. Knowing it was waiting for him when he came back after a week, a month or two months . . . a wife and a child. Always there. Until he had met Kate he had never known what that meant, never been sure what he was coming back to find.

It was eleven o'clock when he got into bed. He read for a while, taking up her book and going on with it from the place she had left open. He got the impression that the people in it were wearing themselves out over trivialities, that their whole trouble could have been blown apart with one honest sentence.

*   *   *   *

When he woke up, the light was still on and she was standing by the side of the bed. She must have been shaking his shoulder for her hand was outstretched between them. The loose silver chain on her wrist was still swinging, the soft, pale hair was a little forward and the edge of the coloured silk shawl over her bare shoulders had slipped. For a moment there were no words in him. Only the thought. This is Kate. This is her, always. The frightened girl with fifty pesetas to her name in a Barcelona café, the woman who met hunger in him . . . the thing which went beyond a body and a personality. She was right. You couldn't say it any other way. Everything was right; the shape, the look, the feel, the pattern she made in his mind and his eye.

He grabbed her wrist.

"You devil. Why didn't you come to meet me?"

"Devil yourself. Why didn't you let me know you were coming?"

"I did. Through Peroni."

"He's away."

"Blast him." He could feel the pulse beating in her wrist. "Where've you been all the evening?"

"With the Stanways. It's their last night in Majorca."

"Come and be forgiven. . . ."

He pulled her down and she lay across him, her hands framing his face, the fingers hard on his flesh. Then they moved pulling at his short brown hair. She turned her head away, laughing as he searched for her mouth. The pearl drops of one of her ear-rings swept across his face.

"You'll ruin this dress."

"To hell with the dress."

"To hell with you."

He held her as she laughed and struggled. And then the laughter was suddenly gone as he found her mouth and the struggle in her turned towards him eagerly.

Later, much later, in the darkness he was awake again. The morning was coming. He could hear the distant *put, put* of a motor boat down in the harbour. Cut against the patch of sky through the window he could see the ornate stone-work along the edge of one of the Cathedral pinnacles. Somewhere in the towers a jackdaw swore lazily against the coming dawn. Out in the country the bullock carts would be moving and the old lorries shivering and spitting with uneven life as they were loaded for the town's markets. Pimento, aubergine, young lettuce, tomatoes and stout sticks of fennel and celery, and on the fish quays the shapeless grey-black spread of octopus, and the jew-fish and gropers, the golden dories and the steely blue bream. . . . I love it all, he thought. The sun and the hard smells. Here I am and here I belong.

He lay there content with the darkness and warmth and the nearness of Kate. His hand was on her arm as he listened to her breathing. Once she stirred and spoke in her sleep.

"Nick," she said, "Oh, Nick, Nick. . . ." She sounded as though she were pleading with him and that was a thing she had never had to do. Tomorrow, he thought, he'd turn all the papers over to Peroni. Then he'd pack the car and take her up to Perada. It was still warm enough to bathe and lie in the sun. He saw her pale hair against the sand, the dark rock pines running up to a sky as blue as her eyes.

He lay there watching the sky lighten. The rain was gone. The daws on the Cathedral began their morning fights. A door slammed somewhere deep in the building. After some time he knew that she was awake, too.

He lay there in the darkness, cushioned by the silent communion between them, knowing she was awake, aware of the change in the rhythm of her breathing. The stillness which was between them and the waiting spirit in their minds reminded him of his brother. For this had been the moment of their confidences, the early morning gloom and the world poised between the last grumble of sleep and the rawness of waking. Hector was dead now . . . no one knew how or where for certain; drowned, it was thought, as a prisoner of war after leaving Singapore on a Japanese ship. But in these quiet moments he still lived and his voice came out of the bed-shared darkness of their boyhood.

"Nick?"

"Yes?"

"Awake?"

"No." For that had been the ritual.

And then after a while.

"Nick?"

"Yes?"

"You know what a black sheep is?"

"Of course." A little scornful. Weren't there scores of them in the flocks around Gerona and Palafrugell; scraggy, dusty, sorry sheep.

"No, not that. A black sheep in the family." And now the moment of doubt, for Hector was older and when scorn came into his husky voice with "No, not that" you knew you were on the edge of something new. "It's father. He's the black sheep in the family. That's why we live in Spain."

He could remember still his sense of disappointment. Hector had made more fascinating and disturbing discoveries for him. This one had seemed flat, still to be understood.

"I like living in Spain. . . ."

He smiled to himself as he lay there remembering it, remembering Hector trying to explain. And now out of the darkness came Kate's voice, forming a similar pattern, as secret and loved as Hector's had been.

"Nick?"

"Yes?"

"Awake?"

"No."

"Then what are you chuckling about?"

"Was I?" He put his hand on her bare shoulder and she took one of his fingers in the way a small child will.

"A dark chuckle."

"I was thinking of Hector and the time he tried to tell me the old man was a black sheep."

"Oh."

She was silent and he wondered what she was thinking. She hadn't known Hector and she had met his father only once. All that was shut away from her. Could that make a woman jealous, to be shut out of part of a man's life? When she told him things from her past, laying out the small fragments of happiness and memory he was always jealous, wanting to have shared it with her.

She said slowly, "Nick . . . just how well off are we?"

"We eat. I manage to pay most of my bills. What do you want? A new dress?"

"No, not that."

He smiled to himself. An echo of Hector's scorn was there. She reached out to the bedside table and found matches and a cigarette. Just for a moment in the flame the room swayed into life. She drew on the cigarette and he saw the pink glow moulding her arm exotically against the gloom and he remembered her in cabaret just before they were married, dancing, arms raised against the shadows with the rose-pink of table lamps on her. He reached out, took the cigarette and drew on it. As he handed it back she went on:

"I mean how would we stand if you sold up?"

"You mean quit?"

"Yes."

"I don't know. I suppose Peroni would give me about two thousand quid for my share. If he could find it. We never have much cash reserve, you know. It's mostly good will and a bank overdraft. Where's this leading?"

"Nowhere." Her voice was flat, the word just a dull sound.

"Come clean, Kate."

Almost as though she hadn't heard him, she went on. "I've got three pounds a week from those shares——"

"Two ten. They were three."

"Julia's growing."

"It's a habit of the young."

But she didn't laugh. He waited, knowing something was coming, but not disturbed. She had to come at it her way and he knew how to be patient. At the same time he could usually see well ahead of her through the maze, working out in advance the path she would take. But this time he was lost.

"You like it here?" she asked.

"Of course. Don't you?"

"You like Spain, or the Spanish? Or that business of yours? Or the weather? Or the cheap wine? Or what is it you like?"

"I like it." He was frowning in the dark, puzzled.

"All of it?"

"I suppose so."

He could feel her head half nod against the pillow as though she were telling herself that this was what she had thought, that it was as she expected and not to be argued or beaten down, and now the beginning of disturbance was rising in him.

Abruptly she said, "Sometimes I feel if I hear anyone else say '*Buenos dias, señora*' or '*Hasta la vista*' or any word in Spanish, I'll scream. Just scream. And shout 'God Save the Queen!' or . . . or something."

He propped himself up on one elbow and took the cigarette from her.

"What on earth's got into you, Kate?"

"I don't know. Maybe it's the change of life."

"At your age?"

"Then maybe I need a change of life."

He put his arm round her shoulders and kissed her.

"Then you shall have it. We'll pack the car this morning and go up to Perada for a while."

"Perada!" And then as he kissed her again she added a Spanish adjective to Perada and he drew back laughing.

"Kate!"

"Well, that's how I feel. I don't want to go to Perada."

"Then somewhere else. Where do you want to go?"

"I want to go to England."

"To England?"

"Yes. England."

"Well . . . I don't know. We might arrange a trip around Christmas time, perhaps. Yes, why not. . . ." The last phrase was to himself almost. She was close to him, she was with him still, her face resting against his arm, but there was a newness in her which couldn't be explained by any of the obvious thoughts that came into his mind.

"Yes, we'll take a trip at Christmas and pick Julia up and go off somewhere together. . . . Brighton, Cornwall . . . anywhere you like."

"I don't want a trip. I want to go back to England to stay."

"Who doesn't? But we've had all this before. We can't go back for good without something behind us. You know that."

"I know."

"Then why bring it up?"

"I don't know. It was just a nice thought."

It was much lighter now and he could see her face clearly. She wasn't looking at him. She was staring straight ahead of her and her face showed nothing except the gentle bleakness of early morning, the familiar nakedness of a face without make-up. He leaned over and, wishing he could give her all the things she wanted, kissed her shoulder.

* * * *

It was six o'clock when Domingo Peroni telephoned from the office. This was no surprise to Thorne. Domingo had no idea of time. He did things when he felt like it or when he had no further excuses left for avoiding them.

"Nick?"

"Yes."

"Can you get down here right away?"

"Is it necessary?"

"Yes."

He got up, grumbling, leaving Kate in bed and deciding to shave when he came back.

"Domingo should have a wife," said Kate drowsily. "It would give him a respect for regular habits."

For offices they had two rooms on a third floor over-looking the *Paseo Generalissimo Franco*. Walking down the hill from the Cathedral he had a glimpse of the harbour. The Trans-Mediterranean boat from Barcelona was just coming in. The early morning wind made a dry, brittle sound in the top-hamper of the palms. The sky was hard and clear like a blue diamond and the sun was warm on his back.

Turning up the *Paseo* he was thinking about Kate wanting to go to England. Well, who didn't really? Even the old man had always hankered for it, though he had never said so. Well, he'd like to go too. But not without a bean in his pocket. He could have done more about that if Kate would have let him. But she was a hell of a girl for honesty.

Tangier, for instance. Six or seven years before he had been over there for three months. Those were the days when he and Peroni had been really tight for money, when the rashness and piracy of his war years were still with him and a few risks hadn't seemed out of place. Mediterranean business life always had that tinge . . . a little bribery, a dark night, and a fast boat to get around Customs interference. But when he'd come back she'd given him hell. She couldn't accept the risk he took so lightly. So, he'd given up the Tangier trips and the lucrative business of importing American cigarettes. A pity . . . her view was too English. That way they could have been in England years ago. She just didn't understand the Spanish. Getting on the wrong side of the law out here was just awkwardness, bad manners . . . all you had to do was to pay the right tribute and fill the outstretched palm. Since that Tangier trip he had been a reasonably honest business man. Peroni was always grumbling about it.

He turned into the hallway of the office building. Their board in the stair recess read *Peroni and Thorne, Importers and Exporters*. It didn't mean much, but they managed to survive and even flourish a little by snapping up the marginal tit-bits. So long as there were lions an active pair of jackals wouldn't starve. Going up the stairs now, remembering Kate's conversation, it struck him strongly that ten years was a long time in which to have got nowhere in particular. The groove was too worn and too well known.

On the third floor landing a woman was scrubbing the floor. She looked up at him and smiled but her right hand with the brush went on moving, filling the dark passage with a soft hissing. Down below, he thought, her old man was still in bed, waiting for her to finish and bring his coffee. Protect our comfort and keep our wives docile—the motto on the arms of the Lords of Creation.

He went through into the office.

Peroni's room was a mess; papers and samples all over the place. The hard sun shafts falling through the window showed up the dust. The Domecq calendar over the fireplace, all legs and skirt and a girl's face split with white teeth behind a glass of brandy, was askew and hadn't been torn off for two months.

Peroni had an electric coffee percolator bubbling on the desk and he was spreading peach preserve on a roll with a silver paper knife. The smell of peach was strong.

"Nick! Welcome. Have a good trip?"

"Reasonable. We might make two hundred quid out of it."

"Not bad. But we're going to do better than that. Coffee?"

"That's our motto. We're always going to do better. You got me down here at this hour for that?"

"Sure."

Peroni began to pour coffee into the two cups that sat on the blotter. He handed the one with a saucer to Thorne.

He was a plump man, in danger of coming apart at the seams. There wasn't a grey hair in the thick curly crop on his head, though he could give Thorne ten years. He was alive and overcharged; happy, generous and not to be trusted.

He sat back in his chair and sipped at the hot coffee. "Only got back late last night, Nick. Too late to disturb you. But at last we're in. Strictly honest business, and over two thousand quid to be made in a month. Like it?"

"Get down to details." But he did like it. Who wouldn't? He'd just spent two months or more working hard to scrape up an extra two hundred quid.

"It's your kind of job, Nick. Remember, just before you went away a ship ran aground up north, near Puerto Regano?"

"I do. An old French tub, due for scrap. She was on the Palma-Marseilles run when I was a boy."

"That's the one. Don't ask me why she went aground. Maybe the crew was drunk, or maybe the owners wanted the insurance rather than the scrap value. The point is we've got a chance to buy the cargo, salvage it and sell it to Vargiu at a fat profit."

"Elisio Vargiu?"

"I know he's a crook. But he's also my mother's cousin, and there's a contract he can't break—so long as we deliver within the month. By laying out just under two thousand pounds we'll be able to sell the stuff for four. It's from heaven!" Peroni kissed his fingers and then prolonged the gesture to lick peach jam from them.

Thorne stood up. It could be from heaven, and it could be from some other place. One thing was certain; it could never be a simple, uncomplicated deal. Not with Vargiu and Peroni in it. However, he was used to that kind of maze. Two thousand pounds profit had a bright ring to it.

"Where would we get two thousand pounds to lay out in order to make four?"

"One way and another I've scraped just enough. I've put up every bit of security, or asset, we own."

"We'll have operating costs."

"Credit—and they won't be big. Nick, this could be a turning point. The cargo belongs to the original shippers in France. It's up for auction and I can get our bid taken."

He didn't ask how Peroni could get his bid taken at a public auction. Any office boy in Spain could answer that. Somewhere, far back in the darkness of his mind a light had begun to wink, though he wasn't paying much attention to it just yet.

"What is the cargo?"

"Steel frames for doors and windows, wash basins and bath fittings. All hardware. Nothing the sea can have hurt."

"Why doesn't Vargiu bid at the auction and then salvage the stuff himself?"

Peroni waved his hands. "Can you imagine it? Vargiu's got a contract for the new airfield installations and the barracks they're going to build outside Palma. It's all this American aid, strategic expansion programme. His hands are full. To him, this little cargo is unimportant. But he is my mother's cousin and he would like to help me."

"Not if it costs him a cent."

"Maybe—but it doesn't, Nick. So long as we deliver by the end of the month it's all right. If we don't—then the deal's off. He'll start making up wooden frames and buying the other hardware locally. He's got a big job on his hands, Nick. We can't grumble at a time clause."

"Will he stick to it? I'm not saying anything against your family, Domingo—but you know Vargiu as well as I do. Will he sign an agreement to take this stuff if we deliver on time?"

Peroni smiled. "I am no child, Nick. He has already done that. I had to have such an agreement before I would dare bid at the auction. It is all here, signed and sealed. What do you say? Shall we bid for it?"

Peroni sat there beaming at him. His fat, smooth face had a plastic bloom so unlike flesh that—Kate had once said —you felt that on the back of his neck you'd find a stamped warning that patents were pending for the product.

He didn't answer right away. Not because he didn't know what to say. He knew that it was a risk which neither he nor Domingo could resist taking. They'd do it because it was in their nature to do it. On the surface it was a straight-forward as anything could be out here. The light at the back of his mind was a fine glow now. Normally he and Domingo worked like blacks on small commission deals, taking anything that came, making their bread and butter from a few steady lines. But this was something big. This wasn't buying up umbrellas and straw hats, tourist junk, highly coloured towels that fell apart in a month, carved corks and Manacor costume jewellery, or shipping Majorcan ware to America where they saw nothing of the fancy Fifth Avenue profits. With the money he could make from this there was a lot he could do.

"You've got a report on the condition of this boat and the cargo?"

"Sure, Nick." Peroni began to search among the mess on

his desk. "Everything, including the cargo manifest. She's practically high and dry. Here." He handed a bunch of papers across, and then went on, "What do you say, Nick? Is it a good thing? You're in?"

Thorne nodded. "It's a good thing, and I'm in. But I'll bet there are snags. There always are. Anyway, I'll go up and have a look at her today."

Peroni stood up and extending his plump little arms did a slow *gavotte* around the desk. Outside a tram car rattled by and a flight of pigeons went past the window, flecking the sunlight on the floor with rapid shadows.

"Nick, you do me good. For a time I am worried because not always can I be sure of you. Now I can tell you."

Thorne looked up. Here it came.

"Tell me what?"

"That already I have done it. The auction was the day before yesterday and I bid and got the cargo."

Thorne didn't say anything.

"You are angry, Nick?"

"No, you old rogue. But I hope you're not holding anything else from me?"

"Nothing, Nick," Peroni put his hands on the lapels of his jacket and pulled them apart as though he would expose his innocent heart to the world.

Thorne stood up. "Now I'll tell you something." It was out of him almost without his knowing that he had to say it. If everything went right this would be a quick haul. "My share in this business is worth about two thousand. Half-share in the cargo profit will be another thousand. When this job is done, I'm clearing out. I'll take my three thousand and you can look for another partner——"

"But Nick——"

"Save it, Domingo. We get on fine. But you could do better with someone else. Someone who won't mind the cigarette and penicillin deals. . . . Someone who doesn't have a wife like Kate."

He had expected Peroni to fight it, but he was mistaken. The man drew his hand across his face and left it a rather solemn mask. He nodded his head and then said gravely—

"I've seen it coming for a long time, Nick. Maybe, clearer than you. Born in Spain, raised in Spain—and you love it. But here, Nick—" with his index finger he tapped his heart, "Here, a man always wants to go back, for one reason or another. I understand, Nick. But this job first, eh? Otherwise we go broke." He smiled as though the prospect were delightfully remote.

Chapter Two

SHAVING with the door open into the bedroom, he thought it over. He hadn't said anything to Kate yet.

With three thousand pounds in his pocket he could take Kate to England. Stanway, who ran an electrical components factory there, would let him take up his long-standing offer to buy himself in. Kate had raised this England project before and he had laughed it off or even got bad-tempered about it. Money was the thing. You had to have that to go back to England. And now here it was . . . if the job came off. He wasn't prepared to tell Kate yet. There was no point in raising her hopes too soon.

Wiping the lather from his face he called, "Come on, you lazy slut. Get out of that bed."

"What for? I like it here. Come and join me."

"I'm a working man. Domingo wants me to go up to Puerto. I'm taking you and we're leaving in half an hour."

"Is it business?"

"Yes."

"Oh. . . ." The sound made a hole through which all her interest escaped.

"Don't you want to come?"

"I want to be with you, yes. But I should have thought your first day could have been free." Her voice sounded far away.

"I can't put it off."

He stood there, wondering whether to tell her. It would bring her to life. But it wasn't the moment. When you'd lived with someone as long as he had with Kate; when you loved someone, it was easy to tell when the reception between you was bad. She kept fading and going away from him. He began to clean his razor with a small towel.

Even the silence between them was awkward. He found himself waiting for her to say something and when she didn't he said casually:

"How were the Stanways?"

"Who?"

"The Stanways."

"Oh, them. Just the same."

In the silence that followed he could hear the tiny rasp of an emery board as she lay in bed doing her nails. Maybe, he decided, that was the trouble. The Stanways were off to England that morning after their holiday. They'd stirred something in her.

"Where'd you go last night with them?"

"Around. He's getting quite a pot."

"He can keep his pot. I'd like his bank balance." He laughed but it was only a sound. Something had slipped into her voice when she had said, "Oh, them. Just the same." He frowned at himself in the mirror.

"Come on, you've got to get ready."

"All right. I've got all the time while you get the car."

Damn it, he thought, what's happening? Usually when he got back there was laughter and horseplay between them, a quick bullying full of love. She went off like a beer bottle that had been shaken before opening. . . . But not this morning. Everything was flat.

He laid the razor down on the shelf under the bathroom mirror. As he did so he knocked over the book which she had left propped there. It fell to the ground with a crash and took with it a small bottle of nail solution. As he picked them up, she called:

"Don't break the place up."

"Books all over the damn place."

She laughed. The sound brought her back.

Putting the book on the shelf and smiling to himself at his sudden irritation he noticed the ear-rings she had been wearing when she came in. They lay on the shelf as she had taken them off and tossed them down. He remembered the cold touch of the pearls on his face as he had pulled her down to him. He picked up one of them now. There was a little cluster of bright stones and then three pearls hanging from them.

"Haven't seen these before," he said.

"What's that?"

"These ear-rings. They're nice."

"Oh, those. . . . I got them in town. They're only cheap costume pieces. But attractive. Be an angel, Nick, and run my bath."

He walked to the bath, put in the plug and turned the hot tap. But in one hand he still held an ear-ring. It was in him now, the real disturbance. If she hadn't asked him to run the bath, asking it quickly, throwing it in to cover what should have been unimportant enough to stand by itself, then he might never have known, might never have looked a second time. You can't live with someone for years and years and not come to know the nuances of truth and evasion, he thought. Not with Kate, anyway. And now he felt himself abruptly ruthless and practical. Trouble, he told himself, was best faced. Suspicion though it made you feel dirty and ashamed, was best confirmed or proved false. He didn't believe the Stanways had kept her company last night. And he didn't believe the ear-rings were cheap costume pieces. He and Peroni had handled that kind of stuff from Manacor for a while and there was a difference in feel and texture, in the look and the settings, which he had come to recognise. What the hell was Kate playing at?

He went through into the sitting-room. The first thing he saw was the silver tray with the sherry decanter and two glasses. There should have been three glasses. Both the Stanways took sherry and so did Kate.

He stood there, lost. He went back into the bedroom. Kate was in the bath singing gently to herself and momentarily the sound eased the sickness in him, warming the numbness which was as confusing to him as a sudden pain to a child.

He went into her. She looked up, hair-turbaned and five or six coloured flannels patch-worked about her body as she soaked in the water. How often had he teased her about the number of flannels she used in a bath? She said, "Darling, have I told you how nice it is to have you back? Even though it means I'll have to keep the flat tidy. And I love you. Come and give me a kiss."

He went over and bent down and kissed her shiny forehead and it was right. It had to be right, he told himself. The thing was between them, the thing that was as proper to them as a bud to a branch.

Going to the mirror to straighten his hair through which she had run wet fingers, he said, "I'll get the car. Better pack a bag with some nightclothes for us. We may have to stay. I'll blow the horn when I get back."

She nodded, raising a flannel in one hand and squeezing it so that a cascade of water ran over her breasts.

He went out. In his pocket were the two ear-rings. In his mind was the picture of her lying there, the long brown body, chequered with the reds and greens and yellows of flannels, her eyes shining, and her lips pouting to take his kiss.

Yesterday, he thought, I was looking forward to coming back; knowing Kate would be there and with her the whole parcel of things loved and sure. It was always one of the high moments in his life with her. Coming back in the old days had always been uncertain. You went away from a villa by the sea and you came back to scruffy rooms in Barcelona or Madrid. Sometimes the old man was all over you and sometimes he hardly spoke and you seldom saw him. With Kate you knew what waited and that was good.

Until today. Walking in the sun he was tempted to do nothing about it. Put his head in the sand. But he knew he wouldn't. It wasn't his way.

He turned into a coffee bar, and after ordering he went across to the telephone. He called the Hotel Victoria. The Stanways always stayed there. The clerk told him that the

Stanways had left for England on the afternoon plane the previous day.

He drank his coffee and ordered another. Another would keep him there longer. There was a reluctance in him to move, as though he could see the pattern laid out ahead and didn't want to follow it.

Behind the bar a waiter switched on a radio. A fat tenor voice turned asthmatic by the regular hiss of the Espresso machine filled the place. Go to hell, he said to himself. One hand in his pocket was fingering the ear-ring. He told himself, he wasn't like that and Kate wasn't like that, and the whole thing was just bloody fantastic.

The tenor drove him out into the sunshine. He got his car from the garage and went into the town. He could have gone into any jeweller's shop and had the ear-rings valued, but he was well known and aware of the idle talk that could easily be drawn out of a simple action. Lepesco was the man for him. Lepesco would think the whole thing was part of some business transaction.

Lepesco was a Hungarian, a refugee in Spain from some youthful political indiscretion made long before the First World War. Seventy now, he cherished the idea that some day revenge would overtake him and he would be assassinated. Meanwhile, he lived happily and was a first-class craftsman, cutting, polishing and setting, and keeping the questions some of his work raised to himself.

From the shadows of his workshop he nodded over his bifocals at Thorne. Then his eyes went beyond him to the door and the three steps up to the street level. Any day it could happen.

Thorne knew what he was thinking.

"Don't worry, Lepesco. You'll die in your bed."

Offended, the old man said, "Shut the door. There's a draught."

Thorne pushed it behind him and took out the ear-rings. He dropped them on to the square of green baize.

The old man picked them up and looked at them through his glass.

Thorne said, "What do you think of them?"

Lepesco put them back on the baize.

"If you're going to start shipping these, you're going into a different class. This isn't artificial Manacor stuff. The pearls are real and the setting is small diamonds."

"Price?"

"Five or six thousand pesetas."

The price moved him. Where had Kate got ear-rings that cost more than fifty pounds? He picked them up and slipped them into his pocket.

"You're right, Lepesco. Out of my class."

"The setting is French," Lepesco said, "and from that, and the way the stones are cut, I'd say they weren't made in the last twenty years. Anyone who says otherwise is a liar."

"Thank you, Lepesco."

"God be with you. Goodbye."

Lepesco's life was barren of *au revoir* or *hasta pronto*. For fifty years he had lived expecting every moment to be his last.

Thorne shut the door on him. Greeted by the sun and the movement of traffic, the crowding of colour and life along the street, he thought, he's safe in his world of fantasy. He's got a secure shell about him, and the years add gentleness to his madness. But he, himself, now stepped out into a fantasy that offered no security. Slap into it, he thought.

*   *   *   *

He blew the horn outside the flat. After a while Kate came down with a suitcase. He jumped out, took it from her, and dropped it into the back of the car.

She was wearing a green linen suit and with the gentle morning breeze playing across her hair she looked young and crisp like a lettuce leaf, looked the way that added an extra inch to a man's height from pride to have her by his side.

Fantasy, he told himself; sheer, bloody fantasy. This kind of thing just couldn't happen between them.

As they drove across town she chatted away at his side, and listening to her he told himself there couldn't be anything wrong. How could there be. Not between Kate and himself.

". . . It took me ages to find a pair of stockings without a run in them. It's absolute hell the way they go. . . ."

She flexed a leg, stretching it out ahead of her and he saw the long, sweet shape, and underneath the polished gleam of nylon the shadow of a small scar where she had fallen from a rock a year after they were married and had cut herself badly. She wasn't really a boating, climbing, outdoor girl . . . she was clumsy and timid and he loved her for it. He knew the scar, knew her body, thought he knew her—but did he? Deep inside there had to be a Kate that was kept just for Kate. Everyone had to have that.

He took the main Inca road. They could reach Puerto in under two hours and his first idea was to have lunch there and talk to her afterwards, but ten minutes in the car with Kate chatting away told him that he could never hold his peace that long. Whatever there was to know he wanted to have it quickly.

"You're very silent, Nick," she said after a while. "Brooding over the job? Has Domingo landed you with a sticky one?"

"Could be."

"Domingo's a pirate type. Not a pirate king. He's not swashbuckling enough for that. But he'd make a good pirate cook . . . the captain's right-hand man for dreaming up devilry and wickedness." She laughed. "Can you see him with a patch over one eye."

He said suddenly, "Kate, dear, I want to have a talk with you."

"Talk away then."

"Not while I drive."

He saw her look across at him curiously and he smiled,

but it was as though he hadn't smiled in years and his cheek muscles were stiff and awkward.

He found a track, bordered by fig trees and he pulled the car into it. Ahead of them a dog began to bark at a hidden farm. To their right a couple of women were hoeing across a field of artichokes whose tall leaves cut the pale sky in stiff, heraldic patterns. He sat with his brown hands spread on the wheel and he stared at the smooth metallic green of the fig trees. How the hell did a man begin a thing like this?

"Kate, dear. . . ."

"Yes, Nick?"

That part was easy. But what now? She sat there, silent waiting for him. She was no longer just his wife, his woman and ten shared years of living together held as common property between them. She was suddenly Kate; a person with thoughts he would never share; with emotions, maybe, that could never be stirred by him, a part of herself held away for herself. It was easy to forget that in marriage. You knew about it in yourself, of course . . . but you forgot about it in the other partner.

Her voice low, and now clearly concerned, she said, "What is it, Nick darling?"

"It's us."

"What on earth do you mean?"

"I think you know what I mean."

"But I don't, Nick."

He half-turned and stared at her. She met his look with a little frown and he tried to tell himself that he could be wrong; that there was nothing in all his fears. But he knew Kate, knew that if she had decided on a certain way to handle a thing she would stick to it until she was forced to change her pose.

He pulled out his cigarette case and opened it. Kate took one and as he held his lighter to her he wondered why so much of his embarrassment should be in his body, making his hands awkward and clumsy.

"Don't beat about the bush, Kate. You weren't with the Stanways last night——"

"But I was."

"No, Kate. They left yesterday afternoon. I phoned their hotel and found that out."

He saw the expression on her face change. With a nervous movement she jerked her cigarette into the road ditch and the movement sent a shiver of sunlight over her bright hair. Then she stared straight ahead of her, watching the two women hoeing along the artichoke rows. He saw her lips begin to tremble. Fleetingly there was in her face all the uncertainty and forlorn beauty which he had seen that day long ago on their first meeting in Barcelona.

He put his hand gently on her arm and said, "Let's go and sit under one of the trees over there. It's too hot in this car."

He went round and opened the car door for her. With his hand on her arm they walked to the shade of a tree and sat down.

She said huskily, "How could you know?"

"There were only two sherry glasses out on the tray." He took her wrist, holding it firmly. "Let's get one thing straight, Kate. I love you. You're the only thing that matters to me. That's why I want the truth. It's not only the Stanways. It's this as well."

As he spoke he took out the ear-ring and dropped it into her lap.

She didn't touch it. She just looked down at it and there was an echo of innocent surprise in her voice as she said, "But why on earth should this say anything? They're just a pair of cheap costume pieces. I could have bought them anywhere for five hundred pesetas."

"Really, Kate!" He kicked at the hard ground with his heel. "You don't expect me to believe that?"

"But I do——"

"Well, I don't! And anyway, you never bought them— did you?"

He knew what was coming and he could feel his body taut, each muscle strained against an invisible pull.

"No . . . no, I didn't . . ." she said miserably.

He stood up, his body restless, and anger spreading in his mind. "A man gave them to you?"

She nodded.

He shut his eyes momentarily. She was telling him this. His Kate. He didn't want to be angry. It wouldn't help. But there was a fury in him that he held down like a secret agony.

"Are you in love with this man?" He couldn't help it, his voice was loud and angry.

"No, of course I'm not." She came to her feet quickly, "If I were it would be easy. I wouldn't have tried to keep anything from you. I'm in love with you. That's what makes the whole thing so bloody . . . makes me feel so horrible!"

"You mean if I hadn't found out you wouldn't have told me?"

"Of course not. Why should I make you wretched as well as myself. . . ? I want to forget it. . . ."

"I don't understand you." He breathed deeply, feeling the sun-warm air filling his lungs but giving him no relief against the stifling fury in him. "You wanted to keep it from me—and yet you leave things about. Damn it—they're worth at least fifty pounds! A man doesn't give a woman a present like that because he likes the colour of her eyes. If I get near him, I'll kick his guts out!" he shouted, and inside him there was a warm, astringent uncoiling of fury.

"But he told me they were a cheap pair that had taken his eye in a shop——"

"Taken his eye!" he cried. "And you'd taken his eye, too! Any shop girl in Palma would only have to have them in her hands to know their value. And you come bouncing back from him wearing them and promptly get into bed with me."

B

She faced him, as angry as he now. "You make it sound beastly," she said.

"Well, isn't it?" He moved away from her.

"Please, Nick—" She caught at his arm. "Let me try to explain. Don't judge me until you know everything."

"I know all I want to know."

"You don't. We've been married ten years and you still don't know. Two or three times every year you go away for a month, two months, and you know nothing about the Kate who gets left behind. What happens to her? Do you know what happens to her? You think you do, but you don't. I'm a nice feeling in your mind, someone who's going to be there when you come back—but you don't miss me as I miss you."

"Of course I miss you."

"Not in the way I do. You've got your work, and you like it. You don't get so bored you could slash the flat pictures or let the bath run over just to have something happen. I get bored and bottled up."

"But damn it, you've got friends and you belong to clubs. And you've had Julia to look after."

"It's not always enough. Not for me, anyway. . . . I suppose I'm like that. I need people . . . a special person. I can't stand by myself like you. I miss you far more than you miss me——"

"That's not so."

"But it is, Nick. That's the whole point. I know you miss me, but it's not in the way I miss you. . . ." She broke off for a moment and he could see the beginning of tears in her eyes. "It's so difficult to explain and I know I'm not doing it well . . . but try and be patient, Nick dear. Don't you ever while you're away find yourself thinking of me and suddenly find yourself full of. . . . Oh, God, how can I describe it? Nothing to do with sex. Just an awful ache. Usually I just sit and think about you, read your letters again or day-dream. . . ."

"Well, I can see that. But hundreds of women put up with that without——"

"Of course they do! So do I. But just this once everything went wrong. You like a man, you dance with him . . . talk to him. And that's how it stays——"

"Then why not this time?"

"Maybe because I was too sure of myself. I knew it couldn't happen—and then suddenly the thing was out of my control. Do try and see it, Nick. It just wasn't me at all. It was some traitor in me. It can happen like that. One half of you can't believe it, and the other half is a complete stranger to you. . . . No, I can see," there was a rising trace of exhausted bitterness in her voice, bitterness that belonged to her, not to him, " . . . you don't know what I'm talking about."

"All I know is that I miss you, just as much as you miss me. But I don't go round jumping into bed with other women——"

"Neither do I with other men!" Anger came into her voice swiftly. "It happened once and I hate myself for it. I can't put the reasons down in black and white for you. Maybe no one could. It's just a horrible trick that life plays now and again. Maybe because you get too smug and so sure that this kind of thing can't happen to you. . . . All I know is that, although you're the only person in the world I love, it happened. . . . Almost as though it were a punishment for being too happy, too much in love."

"Who was he?" His anger was still there, but he had it well under control now. Just listening to Kate, full of confusion as she tried to explain, touched him sharply. He couldn't understand why it should have happened. Not in black and white. Nothing ever was black and white in this kind of business. But he caught the echo of truth in her words. Human beings weren't perfect. Put too much strain on them and they cracked. But why was one more than another picked to take the unbearable strain . . .? There was no answer. It had to be accepted, endured. . . .

"Tell me who he was." As though it made any difference, he thought.

"He's an American. He works in the Military section of their Embassy in Madrid. He was over here for a month on some job and I met him at the Yacht Club."

"Where is he now?"

"He flew back to Madrid this morning."

"And his name?"

"Ray Asherton."

"What do you mean Ray? Raymond?"

"Yes."

It was odd how deep that went, the use of a nickname. She was right, there was a whole life belonging to her that he knew nothing about. He could follow her, could understand what she had explained. He wasn't a fool. But understanding wasn't acceptance. The thing between them wasn't entirely subject to reason and logic. He knew the passion that could be roused in her by him. He could understand the hunger that waited there while he was away. He shut his eyes, as though to blind his imagination, and the effort drove pain through him.

"I don't know." The dull words were the nearest he could come to expressing his real despair.

"You don't know what?"

"What I feel. You can't take this kind of thing in in five minutes and know your mind. The only thing I feel like at this moment is giving you a damned good hiding and going over to Madrid and—Does this bastard think he's in love with you?"

"Yes. But he knows quite clearly how I feel. I shan't see him again and the whole thing is dead."

A cart drawn by a gaunt, hungry-looking mule came down the lane. A labourer, lying stretched across the floorboards, tipped a straw hat from his eyes and nodded to them. A faint "*Buenos*" died in the hot air.

Thorne watched the cart creak and lurch towards the main road. He was no young man in love for the first time, no starry-eyed romanticist. He was old enough to know how to take the unexpected blow, how to cover up and ride the

pain until strength came back. He could ride this one out.
There was too much between Kate and himself, too much
love and understanding even to think of throwing everything away.

He put his hand on her arm. Suddenly his grasp tightened
and he jerked her towards him roughly. Her head went
back and he saw that her eyes were full of tears. She began
to say something but he cut her short, his voice curt and
hard with emotion:

"All right, Kate. All right. It's over. Let's get away
from this damned place."

He slid his arm round her shoulder and began to lead her
away. Her shadow marched with his across the rough track.
In the distance the low hills, their rough grey flanks studded
with dark green cactus palm patches, arched their backs
against the sky. It was hot and he could smell the sweet,
unmistakable odour of irrigated earth.

The sight of the hills with their strips of cork oak reminded him of his father. As a boy he'd gone with him on
mule back into the hills around Gerona to see the charcoal
burners and arrange for the collection of *bruyère* roots for
the pipe factory. The old man had loved Spain and the
Mediterranean. So did he. He and Hector had danced
sardanas through the streets of La Bisbal at an age when
other boys were learning the first cricket strokes at prepara-
tory schools. A hunk of bread, smeared with a rubbed
tomato and dressed with oil and garlic, had been to him
what Bath buns had been to other boys. The old man had
made him look after himself. Beginning so young, he saw
now, he had developed a form of selfishness. And Kate
had suffered from it.

That she should be there. That she should give love.
That was what he had asked from her. But she was right—
never while he was away had he asked himself what happened to her. He'd taken it for granted that she was there,
waiting for him. It had never occurred to him that in her
loneliness and hunger another man could wake, even

transiently in her, the response which he had always imagined was uniquely his.

He opened the car door for her and as she moved to it and close to him, he pulled her to him and kissed her. He could feel her tremble with the uncertainty of him in her, and he held her tighter.

"Nick," she said, as he let her go. "Nick . . . will it be all right?"

He touched her cheek with the back of his hand gently. "Don't worry, Kate. We'll be all right."

Chapter Three

THEY reached Puerto Regano in time for lunch. The port was no more than a collection of villas and a few hotels strung along the road that skirted the wide bay that lay between the capes of Liquera and Perada. A few fishing boats were drawn up on the beach and the yacht basin was a plantation of bare poles. The holiday season was dying and there were few people about. The whole place seemed to be settling down into a long sleep.

They had lunch at the Hotel Margarita and there was little talk between them. Both of them still had a lot to say but the time hadn't come for it yet.

Over his coffee in the tiled lounge, while Kate leafed through a magazine, Thorne went over Peroni's papers. For the moment the heart had been taken out of this trip. He was in no mood to tell Kate about it, to point out that if it came off they could go to England. At the moment they weren't travelling anywhere. Just going round and round like a couple of leaves caught on the slow circle of a whirl-pool.

The ship had gone aground on the north side of the Perada peninsula. Thorne knew the coast. Great cliffs went up two or three hundred feet, cut here and there by a few unprotected inlets. The position of the ship was marked on a map in the papers. To reach it he would have to take a rough road that ran over a low shoulder of hill behind the town and then fell away through a narrow valley to the north coast. It was about a four-mile walk. If the track weren't wide enough to take a lorry they would have trouble getting the stuff out. He saw that at the entrance to the valley there was a farm called Cala Boquer and beyond it, almost at the end of the valley and not far from the ship, another house marked, but unnamed, on the map. The track went as far as the house and he thought it was a good bet that it would carry lorries. If it wouldn't it would mean shipping the stuff right up around the Cabo de Perada and off loading into trucks at Puerto Regano. That could cost money. He decided to walk. He had plenty of time and he felt he could use it to sort some of his thoughts out.

Even so, he gave Kate the chance to come with him. Maybe, she didn't want to be left alone.

But she said, looking up from her magazine, "No, Nick. You go by yourself. I shall be all right here." The magazine dropped to her lap and for a second her right hand was free, half-raised towards him. He took it and squeezed it.

He went out of the hotel and along the road at the back of the strung-out villas. A couple of lorries passed him, heading for the naval seaplane base at the far end of the port. In the hot, still air he could hear the sound of a sea-plane taxi-ing across the stretch of water by the great grey hangars. To his right the hills went up in a green-mottled sweep of grey rock. They looked raw and primitive as though they had been tumbled together by an unskilled hand.

The track from the road to Cala Boquer ran between stone walls that hedged fig and almond orchards. A boy with a handful of goats was driving them across red, fresh-turned stubble and shouting when they reached up to crop the lower branches of the trees.

The track rose to Cala Boquer, skirted the edge of an unkempt garden and then died in a wide farm courtyard. A couple of women were pounding at their washing on the edge of a stone trough. They stared at him but said nothing. One of them was good-looking and young. As she turned and watched him cross the yard, the water dripping from her wet hands on to the front of her black apron, he remembered Kate asking him if he had ever wanted another woman when he had been away from her.

What man, away from his wife, hadn't, he asked himself? It was taking the step beyond that which started the real trouble. Everything depended on what kind of arrangement you saw marriage as being. Personally, he was damned old-fashioned. If you couldn't say "No" to yourself the whole thing just degenerated into chaos. . . .

A dog came barking out of one of the stable doors. As it circled him he swore and swept his arm at it. Behind him he heard the women laugh.

Harassed by the dog he went through the wide gate and shut it in the animal's face.

The track now, although still wide enough for a lorry, was across natural rock with smooth shoulders of boulders just thrusting through it. It would give the springs of any lorry hell. It went up in two tight turns and then through a narrow defile in the hill slope. For a while it was cool out of the sun.

Beyond the defile the road ran rough and stony into the valley. The valley walls were high, going up through miserable rock-strewn pastures and fallen rubble to steep rock faces. Above the crest of the right-hand wall a kite circled. Some sheep moved, searching for pasture, on the lower slopes and there were three men stacking stones from a field into a bullock cart just off the road. The place was hot, barren and not worth bothering with.

The valley bed sloped upwards for about two miles and from his map Thorne saw that from the top of the slope it began to fall away to the sea for another mile. Dark across the skyline he saw the uneven trail of a stone wall.

When he reached it the track, though it ran on, was barred by a gate. The gate was padlocked and topped with a strand of barbed wire. Wire ran the whole length of the wall. He saw that the wire was new as were also the chain and padlock on the gate. There was a board to one side of the gate with a notice which read—*Villa Ermano. Propiedad Particular*. The board was new, too.

Just for a moment he thought of Domingo Peroni back in Palma. Domingo could shut his eyes easily to difficulties other people might have to tackle.

B*

He rested his elbows on the gate. Away ahead the track dipped out of sight towards the sea. He could see a great wedge of it, blue and sparkling like a holiday poster and a great corner of unpleasant-looking cliff. Off to the right, a mile away there was a line of eucalyptus trees, some umbrella pines and the corner of a white building showing through them. Above the trees the hillside had been terraced to make a large garden.

He stepped back from the gate. He would have to get permission for lorries to use the track. To do that he had to reach the Villa Ermano. This wouldn't be the first locked gate he'd climbed over.

He was straddled on top of the gate, about to lift his foot over the strand of wire and jump when from his right came the report of a gun. The spread shot hit the track two or three yards inside the gate and a quick cloud of dust and stone chips billowed into the air.

Thorne jumped back on to his own side of the gate. As he landed he fell. He picked himself up, cursing.

Away to his right he saw that a small bamboo-slatted hut had been built against the wall. Walking from it towards the gate were two people. One of them was a young man and the other a girl. The girl had a shotgun crooked under her arm. With them, ambling along with a false demureness, was a black Alsatian dog. They came leisurely down to the gate and stood there looking at him.

He didn't like the way they were looking at him. Both of them were enjoying it too much. But of the two only the girl was smiling. She wore a yellow cardigan over a white blouse, red canvas trousers and white sandals. The skin of her neck above the open blouse was brown and the sun caught and flashed on the gold chain she wore. Her dark hair was short and untidy and as she stood there she slowly raised a hand and ran her fingers through it. The movement was full of insolence and it touched Thorne off.

"What's the idea?" he demanded angrily. "You damned nearly filled me full of holes."

"I didn't see you," she answered. He had spoken in Spanish, in Catalan, but she used pure Castilian. "There were some quail on the road."

It was cool, too damned cool, and all the time her eyes were going over him and telling him to go to hell.

"There wasn't a quail in sight. And anyway you must have seen me standing on top of the gate."

"There were quail," she said. "Six of them. My eyesight is very good."

"Is it?" Thorne snapped. "Then your shooting is bloody poor. You didn't get one of them."

She laughed and scuffled the ground with the point of one sandal. "It's Guido's gun. I'd forgotten it pulls to the right."

Good-looking, he thought, and insolent and behind it all the smell of bigger trouble which warned him to keep his temper.

The young man said, "You shouldn't have been standing on top of the gate." He was about twenty, thin and with a weak, good-looking face. He had the girl's dark hair and Thorne guessed they were brother and sister and much of an age. He could place them both, wilful, arrogant, spoilt by their parents, plenty of money . . . the kind you saw in a clique in the better cafés.

"It's locked and I wanted to get by," said Thorne.

"You speak Spanish. Surely you read it?" The girl tipped her head towards the notice.

Holding on to himself, Thorne answered, "How am I supposed to let people at the villa know I want to visit them? Shout?"

"Didn't you read the notice down at Cala Boquer?" said the girl. She wasn't looking at him. She'd broken the gun and was taking out a spent cartridge case. "It says visitors to the villa are asked to call there. They telephone through. That's the line up there." Her head came up and she nodded towards the foot of the valley wall. Against the greyness poles stood up at intervals. But Thorne wasn't interested in the poles. She was looking at him now and smiling still. But the smile had lost its insolence. Her expression was full of curiosity and frankness as though it had suddenly occurred to her that he might be of interest.

"There's no notice down there," he said.

"That's right, Juana," said her brother. "I'd forgotten. They haven't put it up yet."

"And it looks as though this has only just gone up." Thorne pointed to the board. "In Puerto they told me you could walk right up through here." They hadn't but it was worth trying.

"So you could," said the girl. "Until a few days ago. But the holiday crowd made a nuisance of themselves and we've had to stop people coming through." She was still looking at him as though she were making a mental catalogue. No smile now. Just sizing him up, clothes and body. And something told him that she wouldn't make any mistake. She'd price his white linen suit to a peseta and judge his weight within a few pounds. There was no doubt in him that, given a chance, this was a girl he could heartily dislike.

"All right," he conceded. "There were six quail on the road. You didn't see me. And I had no right to climb on the gate. Now let's start again. My name's Thorne and I'd like to make a call at the villa."

Guido laughed, but it died quickly as the girl turned and frowned at him.

"Why do you want to call at the villa?" she asked.

"To see the owner."

"You can't. He's not there."

"When will he be back?"

"In a month, I think."

"Or maybe, two months," added Guido.

It was no good losing his temper. They were enjoying themselves, but they weren't fooling. He'd lived in Spain too long not to know the signs. Somewhere along the line a palm was going to be extended. This gate had never been locked against tourists. The season was practically over. Any Spanish villa owner annoyed by them wouldn't put the fence up now. He'd wait until the beginning of the next season.

He pulled out his map. Going closer to the gate he handed it to the girl.

The black Alsatian, resenting his movement, growled unpleasantly.

"Quiet, Eduardo," said the girl.

The dog sat back and panted, grinning, all tongue and teeth, at Thorne.

"Perhaps you'd help me," Thorne said. "I really want to get over to this beach called Agua Gelida. As it means passing over this property isn't there someone who could give me permission in the absence of the owner?"

She took the map and looked at it. Then she shook her head.

"There is no one who would dare give such permission in my uncle's absence."

He wasn't annoyed now. This was the game, the old, old game and he decided to play it.

"Can I get in touch with him? You know where he is?"

"No. He goes off and doesn't say."

"Maybe in Madrid, maybe in Buenos Aires," said Guido.

"I see." He put on a smile, but not because he was warming to these two. There was a way in and, if it had to be bought, a little patience would show it to him. He fished a pencil from his pocket and held it out. "Perhaps you'd be good enough, señorita, to mark on the map the extent of your uncle's property."

"Why not?"

She took the pencil and moving to the wall put the map on a flat stone. As she bent over it, marking it, her hair fell forward over her forehead. She pushed it back and the movement was unexpectedly childish. . . . It hadn't been many years ago, he thought, that she had been a schoolgirl at a desk and hair tipping into her eyes as she wrote. Her teachers must have had their hands full with her.

She handed the map back. She had drawn a line across the valley to indicate the stone wall. From each end of the wall a line ran back to the sea following the ridges of the high crags that enclosed the place. But at the sea the line curved back in a small semi-circle to exclude the Agua Gelida beach.

"In other words," said Thorne as he studied it, "there's no other way to approach the beach by land except over your uncle's property?"

"That is so," she said.

"You can reach it by sea, of course. It means going round Cabo de Perada," said Guido.

Thorne folded the map and put it in his pocket. Without a trace of anything he really felt in his voice, he said, "Thank you. You've both been very helpful. If you should come across your uncle's address, I'm staying at the Hotel Margarita. I'd be glad to have it."

He began to turn away. They weren't going to let him through, and he understood quite clearly that he was going to have to buy his way in. Only a fool would start to bargain now. First of all he wanted to talk to someone in Puerto. Before you greased a palm it was advisable in any country to know something about the owner of the palm.

The young man, Guido, was lighting a cigarette, all his interest apparently gone. But the girl had rested her elbows on the gate, the shotgun crooked between them and she was rubbing her chin gently on the stock.

"You did say your name was Thorne, didn't you?"

He swung round at the question.

"Yes."

"Nicholas Thorne?"

"Yes." And then he added speculatively. "It seems I was expected?"

She nodded. "You were. But I must say, I thought you'd be different."

For a moment he was tempted to try and get some explanation from her. Then he decided against it. She wouldn't give anything away. She was just enjoying herself at his expense.

He turned away without a word.

As he began to walk back down the valley he knew that she was still there watching him.

*　　*　　*　　*

He didn't go back to the Hotel Margarita. He went to see Johnny Manchester. Johnny had a garage off the main street with a yard that backed on to the open space in front of the church. He was called Johnny Manchester because he had spent ten years as a bar-tender in Manchester and had come back eventually to his birthplace to buy a garage out of his savings. Thorne and Peroni had hired lorries from him in the past and, in the early days, Johnny had manned a motor launch for them. Both he and Thorne had turned more or less respectable at the same time. Thorne because of his wife and Johnny because of a duodenal ulcer that forced him to drink milk every two or three hours. Long sea trips interfered with his milk supply.

Thorne walked through the garage and found Johnny in the yard. He was sitting on the running board of a jacked-up lorry watching his son, Rigo, change a wheel. Johnny did a lot of watching, for his son was a strong twenty-two and Johnny a wise sixty-odd.

Very slowly Johnny stood up and shook Thorne's hand.

"Welcome, señor," he said. Then he sat down again. He was hard and brown and twisted like an ancient olive tree. Every movement he made was deliberate and awkward as though his muscles had long ago contracted and dried as hard as leather. His shoulders were permanently pulled forward. He was like an old goat, used to hard pasture, and lost to all surprise because he knew everything.

"Nice to see you, Johnny." Thorne nodded to the son who was sweating with tyre levers to get a cover off.

He sat down on the running board.

"I saw you drive in with your wife," said Johnny. "Business or pleasure?"

"Business," said Thorne. "As though you didn't know. Domingo and I have bought the cargo of that French boat out at Agua Gelida."

Johnny nodded and stared at the junk in the yard.

"In Manchester once. . . ." It was a favourite opening. "A man sold me four five-pound notes for a pound. I was drunk at the time."

"We were sober."

"That makes it worse, señor."

"You've still got a motor boat, Johnny?"

"Such as it is, señor." Johnny scratched at the grey stubble on his chin.

"You could take me round to Agua Gelida this evening?"

The old man shook his head. "The engine is in pieces. Tomorrow, the day after, maybe we will get it put back."

"One of your friends? There are plenty of boats about."

"Oh, yes. Plenty of boats. But many of them are under repair. Some go out fishing tonight and can't be had, and the others. . . . He smiled at Thorne. "You know how it is, señor. The tourist season is ended. The boatmen feel lazy after so much work, and there are many jobs to do."

Thorne was silent. Any other man, he thought, not knowing the form might give up. But this was the pattern. Each brick in the blank wall a familiar one. The blank wall could be spirited away but you had to follow the rites and pronounce the magic word and the word had to be bought.

"No boats," he said quietly. "Barbed wire along the wall and the gate padlocked. Who owns the Villa Ermano?"

"Señor Casares Manasco."

"Rich?"

"Stinking," said Rigo looking up suddenly. And in the

word, thought Thorne, all the old punch and violence that went on surviving from the Civil War.

A priest went across the open space to the church with a schoolboy on either side of him and his trailing robe edges sent little puffs of dust into the air. In the distance where the grey line of road snaked up to the Perada peninsula the bare crests of the mountains were biting into the dying sun.

"He's away, I hear."

Johnny shook his head. "He's there."

"Sure?"

"In this place, señor, if a mouse forsakes the church for the bakery we all know it. He's there."

"What's he like?"

"He's a man who can carry two water melons under each arm and still have his hands free."

"What's his business?"

"Name something," said Johnny, "and you have it."

And again the son looked up from the wheel and said brutally, "Silk, steel, plastics, wines and other things for which it is hard to find polite names."

"Rigo," said Johnny, indicating his son, "is at the age of political bitterness. Señor Manasco is a business man. He will always talk business—though he may be hard to approach."

"Now you mention it—I think I have heard of him." But as he said it Thorne was aware that Johnny had said what he had to say in his last sentence. Everyone knew everything about everyone else here. Everyone would know that he knew Johnny and would come to him.

"He keeps in the background," said Johnny. "The young cubs play in the sun, but the dog fox lies in the bushes. Señor Peroni is well?"

Thorne stood up. "Señor Peroni is my friend, but right now I hope he's in a great deal of pain."

"Rigo," said Johnny, "it is time for my milk."

Rigo straightened up and Thorne, after saying goodbye to Johnny, walked back into the garage with him. He stopped for a moment at the street and Rigo stood with him. The young man pulled out a crumpled packet of *Peninsulares*, and lit himself a cigarette.

"You don't like Señor Manasco?" asked Thorne.

Rigo, the sun half across his body, his singlet marked with grease, screwed up his dark eyes and spat into the roadway.

*   *   *   *

There were two things now. This, and Kate. Watching her, talking mechanically as they had dinner, it was hard to keep his mind clear. All he was conscious of was a sense of sudden complication, and resentment. The two things had dropped out of the blue. But the boat business was a practical difficulty. Given a free run, it shouldn't have roused more than a working bloody-mindedness and a shrewd decision. Señor Casares Manasco might be stinking rich. But that wouldn't stop him from holding out his hand. He hadn't any doubt that Señor Manasco had already settled the figure. . . . and he knew that it would be only just a little more than reasonable. Their profit of two thousand would carry it easily.

Up there, facing the girl Juana across the gate, Kate had gone from his mind. But down here, moving like a couple of pasteboard figures through dinner, monitored into different positions again for brandy and coffee, the job dropped away and there was only Kate. When he had walked back to the car with her after their talk and he had said, "Don't worry, Kate. We'll be all right," he had meant it. There was too much between them, too much love and understanding for it not to be all right. What he hadn't seen then because everything was crowded on top of him was that forgiveness was more than a matter of words. A man could turn the other cheek but that didn't mean that the shock of the first slap in the face was miraculously gone.

He fussed around with this, raising only embarrassment

in himself and making conversation with Kate harder and more artificial. They could have been two people forced to share a hotel table, trapped again in a corner of the lounge over their coffee, and both of them sighing with boredom at the effort of making talk.

She went up to their room before him and he knew she was escaping. Escaping but expecting to be rescued. And that was it. Here was the whole thing, the whole act of forgiveness, stripped of words, fined down to a practical gesture . . . the real truth lay in the body. For the first time he realised that the banner of night flew high over most marital defeats.

When he went up finally, Kate was in bed reading. . . . She'd tied her hair back for the night and her face was free of make-up, shining. In the soft light she looked about fourteen; lost in the large bed, sitting up and waiting for him. She smiled and her eyes held the brightness of a new shyness that reminded him of their early days. . . . In Barcelona of a morning he'd sometimes gone into *Los Almendros* to watch her rehearsing . . . the old piano echoing among the piled chairs, and Kate in a cotton blouse and tight trousers. At the end of a month he'd just walked in and pulled her out, jealous of the men who watched her, jealous of the designed, professional movements of her body and the slow smile . . . loving her and damning the delight in other men's eyes. Married, they had come to Palma where he had set up with Domingo. And damn him, too, for good measure at this moment.

He went into the bathroom and began to fiddle around.

Kate called, "What is the job up here, Nick?"

"There's a French boat aground at Agua Gelida. Domingo and I have bought the cargo."

"Is it big? Lots of money?" She was putting the clock back. He could hear the brightness in her voice, and it hurt him. She was trying. Let it be right. Let's pretend that nothing has happened. Kate chatting away while he cleaned his teeth and got ready for bed.

"Could be. Or it could bankrupt us."

"Not if you're handling it, darling."

At any other time he could have enjoyed a grumble about Domingo and the job and taken her encouragement. But the job was miles away now. There was only Kate in there waiting for him. And for this moment his experience was a dead loss and his own good sense suspect. Grimly, he wondered how a newspaper heart-throb column would handle it. As grimly, he put it baldly in his mind, seeing it as a telegram. *Today learned wife unfaithful stop Inform make love or not this night stop We love each other stop.*

Make it reply prepaid, he decided, as he leaned over the hand basin and stared at his own face in the mirror. Hard, yes, he looked hard. And a little savage. He scowled at himself.

"How long will it take?"

"I don't know. A month maybe. I can't tell yet."

She was waiting for him, and he knew she was nursing and calming her own anguish. No telegram would help. A man couldn't tell what he would do. He could imagine the ambiguous answer of the world, the buttered, journalistic phrases that didn't help a damn. . . . *Well, of course, in a situation like this so much depends on the personality and temperament of the two people concerned. Gentleness, understanding and true forgiveness can fortify and repair the breaches in the great citadel of love.* . . . Oh, for Christ's sake, he cried to himself, a man called Raymond Asherton has slept with my wife. I'm as jealous as hell. I'm hurt. And if I'm hurt, I'd like to make someone else suffer. . . .

He went into her, dressed still, and sat on the edge of the bed. Her hand came out from the covers and found his.

"Nick . . .?"

"There's trouble over this job," he said quickly.

"What kind of trouble?"

She half-turned towards him and the movement bared her shoulders so that he saw the brownness of her breasts and the faint shadow of the nipples through the silk of her nightdress. He remembered their first night in Barcelona, both of them full of the hungry wantonness of love, neither of them strangers to it, but the past then had been wiped away in the completeness of their possession and submission. But this was now. Seeing her body, his imagination escaped him, and fighting to control it he began to talk. . . .

"I've got to go out. I've got to get over to Agua Gelida, and the only way to do it quickly is now . . . in the dark. . . ."

As he talked he knew he was a fool, that he should have taken her and held her, buried his face in her breasts and cursed and loved her. He wanted to do it, even now, but he couldn't. He sat there, hearing his voice going calmly over the business details, laying them out for her understanding, when he should have been bruising and crushing her with the angry love in him.

Chapter Four

JUST before he got to the farmhouse at Cala Boquer he heard the sound of horses ahead of him. At the farm a dog began to bark. He went through a gap in the wall at the top of the avenue and stood behind a fig tree. The moon was thin behind a grey wash of clouds. The fat, web-fingered leaves made a skirt of shadow round the tree.

The sound of hooves changed from the sharp clack on the hard track to a soft *thump, thump* as the horses took to the grass verge under the trees. Two Civil Guards went by and the air was thick with horse and leather smells. He let them pass well away towards the port before he moved on. Night walking around the coast was not encouraged. You could be as innocent as a daisy but if you were abroad after two and the guards picked you up they might make you spend a couple of days in custody to give them a feeling of having achieved something. Cigarettes, nylons, and now—with the trouble in Africa—a forwarding depot for arms . . . a man could make a fortune on this island if he knew the ropes.

He stayed off the road and skirted wide round the farm to keep the dog quiet. The guards probably came through each night like clockwork, but if the dog barked twice it might start trouble. He went down between the low, bushy rows of a field of cotton. Some of the seed was already bursting and in the darkness the night looked as though it were losing its stuffing. The ground rose and he began to pick his way through small boulders.

He stopped on the shoulder of the hill, above the narrow defile entrance to the valley, and looked back. There were a few lights in the port and to one side of the bay the beam of the lighthouse flailed away at the water. Looking back at it he knew that he was really running away.

Sure, he had to do this job. If he wanted to get by the *Propiedad Particular* sign the night was the time. And if he wanted to come to reasonable terms with Señor Casares Manasco he had to show him that he was ready to be unreasonable in his insistence on an interview. All good reasons. . . . Meanwhile Kate would be lying in bed, wide-eyed. . . .

He stumbled as he turned to go on and he cursed silently. He moved down from the shoulder of the hill into the valley. He kept away from the track. He'd put on canvas shoes and he made little noise. It was warm and here and there, clinging to the hollows of the ground were milky puddles of mist. The night was so still that when a sand-piper got up from a tuft of grass ahead of him its flighting cry seemed to cut like a diamond across glass. He found one word to describe the bird and hoped no one was abroad to hear the noise the thing had made.

When he reached the wall he turned in its shadow and went along to the gate. It was still padlocked. On the far side steam still rose from a pile of horse dung. Señor Manasco could shut his property up, but he had to give a key to the Guardia Civil.

He went along from the gate and climbed carefully on to the wall. Balancing on the top he stepped over the single strand of wire and jumped. He landed lightly but on loose stones and for a moment the night held the sound of their sliding. He stayed, crouched, and then from away beyond the gate he heard a dog bark. A torch flicked on and then came the sound of voices. He got up and, bending low, began to run towards the left-hand side of the valley.

Behind him someone shouted and the dog barked again. They were coming from the small bamboo shelter he had seen that afternoon. He fancied he heard the girl's voice. Blast them, he thought. They'd guessed what he might do. They'd enjoy every moment of this. If the black Alsatian took a piece out of his arm, or decided to make a night of it and tear his throat out they'd laugh their heads off. Someone—the girl probably—out of sheer *joie de vivre* loosed off with the shotgun and the valley clattered with echoes like a house collapsing.

He ran hard then, taking a slanting line across the valley bottom towards the sea and climbing all the time up the loose rubble slope that rose to the hills. He came off the rubble and struck a small pathway. His pursuers were about two hundred yards behind him. They came on, noisy and shouting, and their line was good. Probably they had the dog on a leash and were letting it make the chase for them.

The path dipped suddenly, lost itself in a spread of bushes and then by the pale light of the clouded moon he saw that he was in a small quarry. The rough face of grey rock went straight up and horned back on either side of him.

He found a footing on the rock and began to climb. He was twelve feet up when he heard them enter the quarry. The torch beam swung in a great arc across the bushes. He climbed fast, feeling for holds in the dark. The torch came across the bushes and then, when it was almost at the foot of the rock face, began to slant upwards. He drew back into a recess and waited. The light came up to the crevice, struck spark gleams from the felspar in the rough spurs and then passed him.

Down below he heard the young man Guido say, "He must have turned back."

A man's voice, uneducated, a little blown said, "He can't have gone up there, señorita."

Juana answered, "Eduardo wouldn't make a mistake."

Thorne leaned out a little. The torch was still on and he could see them all, foreshortened, dwarflike. Juana had the black Alsatian on a leash, a gun under her arm. Guido stood by her and lit a cigarette and the match flare reddened the thin grass and earth for a second. The other man leaned forward and took a light. He was thickset and momentarily a patch of baldness showed in the torchlight. The torch went out. They were all breathing heavily.

"Anyone who goes up there in the dark is asking for a broken neck," said Guido.

"Of course he's up there. It's not such a difficult climb. I'm going after him."

"You're mad."

"Señorita, it is dangerous. . . ."

She made an angry little sound. "You men, you're always worrying about breaking your necks. He's probably sitting up there now somewhere, listening to us and laughing. I don't like to be laughed at. I should have let Eduardo off the leash."

"Let's give it up and go to bed," said Guido and his tone showed that he was tired of the whole thing.

"Go to hell if you like."

Leaning over Thorne saw the torch flick on. The girl handed the leash to the other man, slipped her shotgun across her shoulders and went to the rock face.

"We'll come and collect your body in the morning," said Guido.

Thorne drew back as the two men turned away and the girl began to climb. He stayed where he was. The girl was starting to climb a few feet to the right and with luck she would go up past him without discovering him. He was ready to make a climb if necessary, but he saw no reason why she shouldn't take a little exercise if she felt like it. He heard her going up to his right and she was going quickly, too quickly. But then she was the kind who took risks and got away with them. The day she broke her neck the gods would be sleeping. But that wasn't likely to happen for many years. They were far too interested still in her capers to nod off. She stopped once or twice and flashed the torch around. But she was well past him now.

He sat there and waited. In the distance he could hear the dying sound of Guido and the other man moving away across the rough ground. They were talking in low voices to one another. Then the sound died. Above him, now and again, he heard the fall of a stone and then, as she went higher, the silence came back to the valley.

After a time he lit a cigarette and, cowling it with his palm, smoked. The grey mist pools deepened and the moon blanketed by cloud still slipped behind one of the far crests and left the valley in darkness.

He gave her an hour and then he came down. He made a line along the foot of the valley wall towards the beach. He took his time, going very carefully. As he went he was thinking of the two. Brother and sister they might be but there was a world of difference between them. Guido was all right for short bursts, but the moment he was checked the heart went from him. He lit a cigarette and lost interest. But not Juana. She kept on and he could sense that any obstacle became a personal affront, a challenge that stirred her temper.

*   *   *   *

For the two hours before dawn he sat on the dry sand of Agua Gelida beach, his back to a boulder and waited for daylight. A morning wind was stirring, clearing the sky of cloud. Thirty yards away the sea shook a lacy skirt trimming and he could just make out the grey bulk of the grounded cargo boat. It was very close inshore. Getting the stuff on to the beach shouldn't be difficult and—once the road was open to him—lorries could come right down to the beach edge. The sooner he saw Señor Casares Manasco the better. He didn't smoke as he waited. The girl might easily come down to the beach looking for him and he wasn't in the mood for her company.

He'd been there an hour when way out in the bay he caught for a moment the low beat of a motor-boat engine. It was coming in towards the beach and at first he wrote it off as a fishing boat. Lobster pots were set all along this coast and the boatmen were out early lifting and re-baiting them. Then the engine note ceased. A little later he heard the stir of feet in the sand on the far side of the beach, and then unmistakably the grind of a keel on shingle and the single thump of an oar or a foot against boat boards. Then quite plainly he heard a man's voice and a sudden smother of laughter.

He crawled round his boulder and lying close to the ground raised his head so that anyone passing across the beach would be silhouetted against the paling stretch of sky above the far crests.

Five minutes later he saw three hunch-backed figures coming slowly across the beach. They moved obliquely across the sand, their feet plugging into its looseness, and passed within ten feet of him. He heard them suck and grunt at the air with their labour and the living frieze they made had no strangeness for him. Years ago he had taken part in the same ritual, taken on the hump-back of contraband case and sack himself. The bowed form and awkward gait of the first man was familiar. It was Johnny Manchester.

They went up from the beach and the night swallowed them. You couldn't get it out of your blood, he thought. A duodenal might stop you from going to sea, but the mind and the blood itched for the chance to do authority in the eye. Every Spaniard was the enemy of authority. Laws were made to be undermined. . . .

Slowly the dawn light seeped over the hills behind him and filled the bay. The beach was a flattened semi-circle about a hundred yards long. It was soft sand, strewn with driftwood and dried lengths of bamboos. Backing it was a small broken cliff with the fresh green of growing bamboos and rushes springing up between the boulders. On the far side of the beach, below a clump of bamboos there was a dark channel across the sand where the fresh-water spring that gave the beach its name worked its way to the sea. A wide cut in the cliff led up to the track to Cala Boquer, but the height of the low cliff cut off all sight of the valley. At the foot of the cut was a squat shack made of bamboo, packing cases and odd lengths of plank, bleached and worn rough by the sea. To the side of the shack was a small rowing boat and a pile of lobster pots and boxes.

Seaward the narrowing sides of the valley ran out in lofty, dark cliffs, pinching in at the mouth of the small inlet. The sea was a sombre, restless mauve from the cliff shadows still across it.

The French cargo boat lay about two hundred yards out from the beach and almost broadside on to the left-hand run of cliffs. Between her starboard side and the cliffs was a narrow channel of water about fifty yards wide. She sat there on an even keel, but low in the water, a black, bulky shape with high, flaring bows pointing towards the beach.

Thorne eyed her from the water's edge. From the report on her he knew she was holed low down on the port bow and that the forward and after hatches were partly flooded. She carried a single stack, high and old-fashioned, with two bands of purple and white painted round it. The bridge work was squat and a dirty mustard colour. The name *Doria* was plated to the bows and long, pointed streamers of rust, like stalactites fanged downwards from each letter. She sat out there, black and rusty, like some gigantic old fish kettle. How she'd ever come in through the narrow bay entrance and settled herself in here he couldn't think, but no doubt anyone with a knowledge of marine insurance could have found a dozen answers.

He dragged the row boat down from the shack. There were no oars, but he found a long thin piece of plank from the junk outside and used it over the stern to ferry himself out. The sun came up over the valley behind him as he went out and the black cliffs were suddenly transformed into bright planes and slopes of gold and crimson with here and there the hard green of pines marking the gullies. He went round to the stern and found a small steel gangway lowered over the side, its foot in the water and thick with a mat of drift and seaweed. He tied the rowing boat to the lowest step and went aboard.

Stacked on the after hold covering was a pile of long timber lengths about two feet square in section and held in place by wire hawsers that ran down to shackles set along the

sides of the framework of the hold covers. Forward there was
a similar pile on the other hold but here the wire hawsers
had snapped and the timber baulks were spilled across the
deck. To get into the holds all the timber would have to be
moved. If he knew it none of the steam winches would work.
That meant sweat and muscle and rigging up some kind of
hoist.

He spent half an hour going over her. She wasn't a big
boat, not much more than five hundred tons, a disreputable
old hack, worked too long and little money spent on her.
The engine room had a foot of water in it and there was just
enough movement on the *Doria* to keep it sloshing to and
fro. At some time, he saw, there had been more movement,
for great fans and tide marks of oil marked the bulkheads and
the machinery was covered in a greasy scum. Everything
that could be taken had been stripped. The galley was
empty, not a saucepan or a spoon left, and the crew's
quarters forward were bare except for a few magazine
pictures pinned by the bunks. Only the cargo in the two
holds would be untouched and he saw why. To get at it
below decks meant going through water, while from above
decks the timber baulks blocked anyone from raising the
covers. On the bridge behind the wheelhouse was a small
saloon which the captain had used. Somebody had tried to
unship the table which was bolted to the floor and had given
up. The bunk that ran down one side under a long plate
glass window held a couple of empty wine bottles and an
old copy of the newspaper *Baleares*. He could imagine the
scene a day after the crew had gone off with their belongings.
Every lobster boat within ten miles had gathered about her
and she had been picked clean. Somebody had gone right
through her carefully unscrewing all the brass door catches
and hooks and there wasn't a light fitting left intact. In front
of the engine telegraph there was a splintered stump of
mahogany which had once carried the compass binacle.

He went forward and sat on one of the wood baulks and
lit a cigarette. The sun was warm now. The run of water

along the *Doria's* sides made a gentle, soothing sound. There was no doubt about it. It was the kind of job which, normally, he liked. Peroni had guessed right about that. And there was a profit to be made. But he had the feeling that it was not going to be straightforward. The physical difficulties could be faced . . . yet something about the whole set-up made him uneasy.

Inland, above the low cliff of the beach he saw the morning breeze run shivering through the tall eucalyptus trees around the Villa Ermano. He had a good view of it from here. A pink wall with a tiled pent to it ran around the seaward side. Terraces with vines, a patch of azaleas, and a flaring red run of tall geraniums and through them a glimpse of the house and a forecourt. . . . Against the bare backcloth of the valley mountains the place looked as though it had been dropped there by accident.

An iron gate in the wall opened and he saw Juana come out and begin to walk down towards the beach. She was a small white figure in the distance.

He got into his boat and began to row ashore. It was time he saw Mr. Casares Manasco and got things straightened out.

*   *   *   *

She stood at the top of the cut and watched him pull the boat ashore. He abandoned it halfway up the beach and turned and walked towards her. He'd been up all night and he felt dirty and in need of a shave. He climbed the rutted slope to the top of the low cliff and she stood, unmoving, in his path.

She had a half-smiling, half-insolent look of appraisal on her face. I could be a prize bull, he thought, and she a judge, ticking off my points as I go round the ring. But no matter how he made out he knew he wasn't going to get a first. And because she watched him like that it made him awkward from the outside right through to the marrow, and the awkwardness did nothing for his temper. She didn't move out of his way and he was damned if he was going to walk around her.

He stopped a yard from her.

"For a girl who's been rock climbing all night," he said, "you look remarkably fresh."

She hadn't expected the remark and for a moment he had her off balance. He saw her look down at the spotless sweep of her white skirt and one hand hovered for a second towards her hair. Thrust into the short curls above her right ear was a single head of pink geranium. He could see her coming down the garden path and picking it off, and it had been put there, not for exotic elegance, but as a child idly picks a flower and thrusts it through a buttonhole.

"You are now," she said arrogantly, "standing on the boundary between the beach and my uncle's land."

"And now," he stepped forward as he spoke, "I am on your uncle's land."

She held her place but her right hand dropped to the skirt pocket of her dress and she drew out a tiny automatic, so small that he could see only the black mouth of the muzzle like the entrance to a wasp's nest.

"Get off our land!"

He laughed.

"What a girl you are. Shotguns, automatics, barbed wire and a black guard dog. I should think there are times when even your uncle gets tired of you."

He moved up to her side and his face was close to hers and he read in it dark anger signs which he would have been a fool to ignore. One jibe too many and she would fire.

"I don't like you," she said coldly. "Get off our land."

He shook his head and walked by her and as he did so he said, "I'm going up to see your uncle. You can shoot me in the back if you must. But he wouldn't approve."

He walked on, not looking back. If she fired it would be at the path close to him; to scare him, to give herself the pleasure of his anger. But no shot came and he went all the way up to the wrought-iron gate in the wall without looking back because he knew she would expect him to look back, to betray some sign of uncertainty.

An iron bell pull hung at the side of the gate and he tugged at it. Somewhere in the house he heard the harsh jangle of the bell. Then he turned and looked back. She was sitting on the edge of the low cliff, looking out to sea and smoking. Her back was to him.

A short, bald-headed man in a green baize apron and a blue-and-white striped shirt came to the gate.

Thorne handed him his card and said, "I'd like to see Señor Casares Manasco."

The man began to say something but he cut him short. "I'd like to see Señor Manasco." He stepped through the gate. The man hesitated and then with a shrug turned towards the house. Thorne followed him.

There was a little forecourt, overhung by one of the house balconies. A great bank of bougainvillaea sprawled over it and down the supporting pillars. Lemon trees growing in large earthenware jars flanked one side and there was a small pool in the centre with a lead statue of a rearing unicorn. Through the archways in the far wall which was footed by a long bed of canna lilies, Thorne could see the cliffs and the bright waters of the narrow bay. The servant left him and he waited.

It was a good spot. Just the kind of place he would have liked to have had for Kate and Julia. They'd lived too much in flats with other people's furniture. . . . A swallow-tailed butterfly came looping across the courtyard and hovered clumsily over a patch of morning glory whose flowers were raising blue trumpets to the sun.

The servant came back and led him around the side of the villa that faced the full blaze of the morning sun down the valley. There was a cane table and two chairs on a tiled terrace. A man sat at the table with a breakfast tray. The fold marks in the white cloth were knife-sharp. The servant withdrew. The man poured coffee into his cup, reached for a cigarette and then, without hurry, looked up at Thorne.

He wore a rough fisherman's shirt and dirty white trousers. His feet, poking beyond the table, were bare and brown and looked as hard and knotted as *bruyère* roots. A fly couldn't have landed on his face without touching a wrinkle. His hair was a coppery red, dry and lifeless-looking, and cut so short that the pink of the scalp glowed through it. Without a word he lit his cigarette and then pushed up a pair of bifocal spectacles to rest on the bony ridges of his eyebrows. A dry, sapless man who could have been any age from forty to seventy; a small man with pale blue eyes and a hard, little trap of a mouth almost lost in his wrinkled skin . . . a man, Thorne felt, who could make years of experience in others amount to no more than a child's first steps in the world . . . and a man clearly who at this moment hated his guts. The little blue eyes were on him, blinking, going over him, missing nothing.

Thorne said, "Señor Manasco?"

The man nodded.

The black Alsatian walked out from the room behind the terrace, raised its head curiously at Thorne and then dropped heavily on the sunlit tiles, stretching out in the warmth.

"You make it very difficult for anyone to see you, Señor Manasco."

Manasco wiped his mouth with a napkin and said shortly, "Not everyone—just you, Señor Thorne."

"May I ask why?"

Manasco gave a sharp, intolerant grunt. "You know why. Don't waste my time on that kind of talk."

"But I don't know why. I just want to talk some simple business with you. I almost got a bullet in my back."

"You deserve one." The words were brittle, like the sound of dead leaves stirred by a quick wind.

"Perhaps you're mistaking me for someone else?" Thorne was being patient. He had to be. He wanted something from this man.

Manasco stood up. He was a short man, but in his move-

C

ments there was a cocky, bantam-like thrust, full of fight and confidence. "There is no mistake. You're Señor Thorne?"

"Yes."

A small brown hard hand beat at the air impatiently. "I know all about you and your partner, Peroni. Inside somewhere I have a twenty-page report on you both. You're here and I know why you're here. Frankly you're not the kind of man I care to deal with, but just now it is necessary. However, let us make it quick."

Thorne stirred angrily.

"I don't like the way you're talking to me, Señor Manasco. You've obviously got something wrong."

Manasco turned his back on him, walked to the edge of the terrace and began to pick dead flower heads from a box of geraniums that topped the wall.

"I've got nothing wrong. And I talk to you the way you deserve." He swung round, the stubby fingers of one hand teasing at a flower head. "Now get this clear. You got that cargo out there"—his head tipped stiffly towards the bay—"by a dirty trick. But the thing you didn't know was that you had to come across my land to reach it and to cart it away. Well, you're never going to shift it because I won't give permission for my road to be used. Instead——"

"Wait a minute. What dirty trick are you talking about? You've got something pretty badly mixed up here."

For a moment Manasco stared at him, the blue eyes hooded, almost closed as though he were trying to see in and through Thorne. Then the small mouth opened, snapping, fishlike, and a short, contemptuous sound marked the angry wave of his hand.

"If you don't know, your partner does. But I think you know."

"Are you calling me a liar?" Thorne stepped forward.

Manasco stood his ground but he snapped his fingers and the black Alsatian was on its feet, head lowered.

"There are a lot of things I could call you, but I don't intend to waste my time on you more than is necessary. I'm going to teach you and your partner a lesson. You don't get that cargo. I'm going to have it. I'm going to transport it to Palma and sell it to Vargiu and make the profit you and your partner fancied you were going to have."

"You are?"

"Yes. I'll give you two thousand pounds for it. What you paid. My offer stays open exactly three days. After that—if you won't sell—well then you can go to hell and the cargo can rot out there for ever because you'll never move it."

Thorne was silent. This man was in a rage. Just why he couldn't guess, but he already had a very shrewd idea that the answer might rest with Domingo Peroni.

"You don't like my offer?" Manasco's head came up, his neck was lean, the flesh loose like a turtle's.

Despite the anger and confusion in him, Thorne smiled. Manasco was loving every moment of this. This was his life, to fight, to break and make . . . big business or little business, no one ever got the better of him.

Thorne shrugged his shoulders. "No, I don't like your offer. If it comes to that I don't like you, and quite definitely, Señor Manasco, I don't intend to hand over my chance of a nice profit because you've got some bee in your bonnet."

"Three days. Just phone my agent—Manuel Rodriguez—in Palma. And in future, Señor Thorne, don't make dirty business deals until you're big enough and ruthless enough —and clever enough—to bring them off."

Thorne was past anger now. The whole thing was out of perspective. He put his hand in his pocket and felt for his cigarettes. Domingo would have to explain. . . . He reached to the table and picked up a silver lighter and without hurry lit his cigarette. Manasco watched him.

Thorne said, "You've got the advantage of me, Señor Manasco, because I don't know what the hell all this is about. But I'd like to make one thing clear. If you were more my age and you'd talked to me as you have done I'd have knocked your teeth out."

"You have three days." Manasco moved towards the door of the room behind. "Guido!"

From inside the room Guido came out on to the terrace. He wore an American shirt decorated with a design of pineapples and palm trees and he had his hands in the pockets of a pair of white shorts. He looked young and easy and he was smiling.

"Guido, go down and unlock the gate for Señor Thorne." Manasco's voice was abrupt, full of authority.

As Guido passed him Thorne said, "He was listening?"

"He was. He has a lot to learn."

He turned and walked into the house, leaving Thorne standing at the head of the terrace steps. Guido called to the dog and it went down the steps past Thorne.

Thorne joined the procession and the dog dropped back until its nose was almost touching his right hand.

They went in silence down the valley road, their positions unchanged. Guido unlocked the gate and held it open.

Thorne passed through and then paused. Guido stared at him and the skin between his eyebrows puckered giving his handsome face a sullen look.

"What am I supposed to have done? Do you know?"

Guido made no answer. He pushed the gate shut and then began to fasten the padlock.

"Do you know, or don't you?" Thorne asked curtly and he could feel his anger coming back. They'd treated him like dirt and they wouldn't even say why. He was supposed to know.

"Of course I know!" Guido's head came up and his face was defiant. Too defiant, Thorne felt, as though he were forcing himself to it.

"Then tell me."

They faced one another over the gate. Thorne kept his eyes on the young man's face, waiting for an answer. Slowly the defiance went from Guido. He blinked and his mouth moved weakly, marking some inner embarrassment. Suddenly he turned away and began to walk back towards the villa.

Chapter Five

IT was still early when he got back to the hotel. Kate was up. She was in her dressing gown and sitting at a little table by the open window having her breakfast in the sun. He came in feeling dirty and unshaven, and angry at the trouble on his hands. Whatever Domingo Peroni had been up to it had been enough to make Manasco blazing mad. But if he thought he was going to do them out of their profit. . . . In that moment as Kate turned to greet him he was glad that so far he had said nothing about pulling out and going to England if this job came off.

Kate smiled at him and the movement of her head and shoulders, the quiet beauty of her face reached into him, thrusting past his anger.

"Nick, darling. . . . Lordy, you're in a mess! What have you been doing?"

Warm, concerned words without a trace of hesitation . . . last night, he knew, not forgotten, but discarded. That was one of the things he loved in her; she was always ready to push disappointment into a dusty pigeon-hole; always ready to try again.

"Domingo's sold me a pup, I think. I could wring his blasted neck!"

She laughed. "I've heard you say that so often. You couldn't wring it, anyway. It's rubber and would just spring back."

She poured him coffee in her own cup and brought it over to him. He bent forward and kissed her on the cheek as he took it. She smelt good, womanly. . . .

Her face was close to his. He saw the fine lines at the corners of her eyes and the faintest touch of lingering fatigue shadow under them. He'd married a girl and he now kissed a woman. There was no holding back the seasons. But with the years he loved every new Kate that came, girl, woman, mother. . . .

He said, "We've got to get back to Palma. Peroni somehow has bitched this whole thing up. I've got to get the truth out of him. Why I trust that man as much as I do I can't think." He sipped at his coffee and he knew, and didn't mind, that she didn't care a scrap about his business just now; she was content to have him there.

Kate said, "You've scagged your coat. Here, on the shoulder." She put up her hand and touched the cloth, and he knew she wasn't touching the cloth, she was touching him, wanting him.

"I had to do a bit of climbing." He put his cup down on the table. "If Manasco thinks he can stop me. . . ." He was talking for himself, not for her.

"Take it off. I'll fix it while you're bathing and shaving. You look terrible with all that stubble." She moved behind him and her hands were on his shoulders. He slipped the jacket off and she turned away slightly, dropping it on to the bed. Suddenly the previous night seemed a long way off . . . a kind of stupidity. Turning back to him the movement drew her fair hair loose across her neck and with the swing of her body the dressing gown opened.

"Who is Manasco?"

"A very angry man, though heaven knows why."

She laughed and her head came down to him. The falling line of her chin and throat had a quick, vivid loveliness. Manasco and the night's business dropped from him, and he felt the anger in him sweep into a new channel, become an unnamed strength. This was the morning, this was Kate, the sun was shining. . . . He put up his hands roughly and held her under the arms, feeling the softness of her small breasts against the heel of his palms.

"You're not caring a damn about Manasco." His hands were fierce on her.

"No, Nick. . . ." Her face was lifted to him, the eyes shut as though the hard grip of his hands were tearing her with sharp pleasure. "No, Nick, I don't care about this job . . . about anything but us. . . ."

"I ought to thrash you! I ought to cut your heart out . . ." He shook her.

"Do anything," she cried, "but don't be a rock. Don't be cold, Nick. . . ." Her fingers were on his arms and she shook at him. The movement brought them together and the moment her body was against his the violence broke in him like a dam collapsing. He picked her up and as he carried her her lips were over his face.

As he flung her on to the bed one hand reaching for her caught at the yoke of her nightdress and the thin silk ripped. She lay there, half-naked. The blood thundered in his head and the hunger in him was like a swordthrust as he threw himself down and gathered up the fierce offering which, open-eyed now and smiling with love, she waited for him to take.

Long afterwards, as she lay calmly in his arms, she said, "That nightdress cost me a thousand pesetas."

"Cost me."

"You then."

She smiled and then sighed. He felt her body flex and stretch in his arms and he knew what the movement meant. She was content to know that the love between them had begun to heal the wound in him.

But as he lay there thinking, he knew that the thing was still to be lived with; he had to get used to the new Kate, the woman who had been able to turn away from him, no matter how briefly, and no matter where the fault lay or how it was shared. For a long time he knew that there was going to be the shadow of a third person hovering anonymously near them. He could not shut his mind to the presence, couldn't will it into limbo . . . it had to be endured until it went of its own accord.

"What are you thinking about, Nick?" Kate asked

gently. With one finger she scratched at the stubble on his chin.

I'm just thinking, he told himself, and that's the trouble. I don't want to think. But for her, he laughed and smacking her fondly on the bottom said, "That I should be getting off to Palma. Rome's burning. . . ."

"Let it. . . ." She raised herself above him, looked deep into his eyes and then her lips came down softly.

*   *   *   *

Domingo Peroni was sitting at his desk when Thorne entered the room. He sat full in a patch of noon sunlight, his wide white forehead glistening with sweat, his arms limp on the desk. Like a jellyfish, thought Thorne; hopelessly stranded on a beach.

Seeing Thorne, Domingo raised his hands a little from the desk and then let them flop back. He rolled his eyes and gave a long sigh.

"You know?" asked Thorne curtly.

"Yes, Nick. I know. I found out after you left. We are in the soup."

Thorne lit a cigarette. "Let me have it straight, Domingo. No hedging. And the truth. What have you done to get a man like Manasco stirred up?"

"Nothing, Nick. Absolutely nothing. . . ." Domingo heaved himself out of the chair and waddled towards the window, his shoulders sagging.

"You've done something. I could be lying up there with a bullet in my back or my throat ripped out by an Alsatian. Nothing! From the way Manasco acted you've done plenty."

Domingo turned. "Nothing, Nick. You think I'm fool enough to cross a man like Manasco? I know my place. Why even the government would think twice about stepping on his toes. Oh, it is all most unfortunate. . . ."

"Come on—tell me what it's about!" said Thorne impatiently.

"It's the boy."

"Guido?"

"Yes. Guido Iesu Sebastian Manasco. How was I to
know he was a Manasco? I act in good faith, Nick. Would
I send you on a job like this, if——"

"Domingo! Just give it to me plain. What did you do
to the boy to get his uncle stirred up?"

"Nothing, Nick. I will swear any oath you like. I did
nothing."

Thorne smacked the edge of the desk. "Don't keep on
saying 'Nothing.' Something happened. Manasco's put
Peroni and Thorne on the black list. You know what that
could mean. Already he's said he won't let us get to the
cargo, but that he'll give us two thousand quid for it and
take the profit we hoped to get. A fine offer. And all because
you did nothing."

Domingo sat on the windowsill heavily and rubbed at his
eyebrows with the tips of his fingers. He looked deflated
and dejected.

"All right, Nick. . . . I tell you the truth. Absolutely the
truth. I went round to Madame Paradiso's place some days
ago. . . . No, not for what you think. She is my friend and
sometimes I call in for a chat with her and the girls. This
boy is there and he is very drunk. Naturally she is embarrassed because he is so drunk. You know how strict she
is——"

"She's a grasping old hag. But just stick to the facts."

"Neither of us know who this boy is. Just a boy . . . a
nice Spanish boy, except that he is very drunk. If I'd known
he was a Manasco. . . .!"

Thorne began to have some idea of what might have
happened.

"He was talking, I suppose?"

"Yes, Nick. He was talking about this cargo auction.
It was the first I have heard of it. From this boy I learned
that he was down here to bid——"

"On his own account?"

C*

"Yes. He kept on about that. His uncle wants him to be a good business man and this was his first deal. If I'd known that he was a Manasco! Is it my fault if he's young and gets so drunk? If you're in business you must not get drunk and talk. Someone takes advantage. It is recognised. Business is business."

"So you kept him away from the auction. How?"

Domingo stood up. Slowly he pulled himself together and a severe dignity crept over his face. "There is a story going round the town that I drugged him. This, I learn from Manasco's agent here, is what Guido swears happened. But this I swear is not the truth! Not the truth!" Domingo smacked his fist into his open palm.

Thorne looked at Domingo. He had known the man a long time. He knew his faults and knew his weakness. Domingo could lie convincingly. But one thing his pride would never let him accept was a false accusation. He was full now of temper and stiff indignation.

"You believe me, Nick."

"Yes. I believe you, Domingo. But Manasco won't. If Guido says he was drugged, then that's it. Why didn't he turn up at the auction?"

"Because nothing could get him away from Madame Paradiso's. He was so drunk . . . like young men sometimes are. He didn't come round until the next day. After the auction was over."

"In the meantime you'd been busy?"

"Of course. I am a business man. I went round quickly and found out about the auction. It seemed a good thing. I got Vargiu to agree to take the stuff—and then I decided to bid. The boy didn't turn up and the cargo fell in my lap. Nobody else was interested."

"Of course not. You've got to go across Manasco's land to get the stuff out."

"On the report and auction details there was no mention of the owner of the land. You think I would knowingly start something like this against a man like Manasco?"

"No, I don't. But it's a bad business. Guido, to cover himself, obviously went back and told his uncle that you'd had him drugged. . . . Nice boy!"

"But Nick, if we tell Manasco the truth, show him the boy is lying—then he will be different, maybe. . . . No?"

"No. He's in, and he's going to stand by the boy. Now he'll show him how to handle the situation. It may be small stuff for Manasco, but he won't pull any punches. If Guido's like a son to him and is going to take over some day—he must learn all the tricks. And you and I, Domingo, are going to pay for the lesson."

"You mean, Nick, that you'll take his offer? Give up the chance of all that profit. . . . Just because a boy gets stupid drunk and then lies about it. . . . Is this fair? Is this business?"

Thorne smiled, but there was no true humour in him. "All right, Domingo. You needn't shout. I haven't decided anything yet."

Domingo nodded. "That's right. That's it. I have great faith in you, Nick. Maybe there is some way we can outplay Manasco. For instance, couldn't we hire lighters and take the cargo out by sea?"

Thorne's mouth twisted wryly. "We could try, but I don't think it will work. Not if I know Manasco."

He picked up the phone and called a number. There were two salvage and navigation companies in Palma and he knew the managers of both. All he needed was a tug and a couple of lighters for a week's work once the cargo was free to be lifted from the holds. At this time of the year the weather would be reasonably good and it would be a simple matter to offload from the *Doria* to the lighters and tow the stuff around to Palma. But the rate for the job had to be reasonable.

The first manager listened carefully to his proposition and when he had finished, said—

"I'd like to help you, Nick. Could do in a couple of months' time. For the moment our books are full. We've got a big harbour job that'll take over a month."

"You could drop that for a week. I'd pay a bonus rate."

"Sorry, Nick. The Ministry wouldn't let us do that. This is a contract job. If you wanted a rowing boat even I'd be hard pressed to find you one."

"Don't tell me that. You know you could fix a week's delay in the harbour work. You can pay for it——"

"Nick," the word carried an echo of surprise, "are you suggesting I bribe a public official?"

"Why not? Or," the anger was clear in his voice, "has Manasco already bribed you?"

"Manasco?"

"All right. . . . You don't know him and suddenly you're full up with work."

He put the phone down and looked at Domingo.

"He acts quickly, doesn't he? He's beginning to make me dislike him quite a lot."

He picked up the phone and made another call.

There was no pretence this time. A sad voice at the other end said, "I was expecting you to call, Nick."

"You know what I want?"

"*Cierto*. The whole of Palma knows by now. You might as well ask for the moon."

"You could help me."

"Listen, Nick—I've got a tug and I've got lighters. But also I have a wife, a family and a nice business. My boy is doing well in the *Banca de Mallorca*; and my daughter —she is musical, you know?—needs a nomination for the *Conservatoire* in Madrid. They are hard to get without. . . . You want me to say more?"

"No. You've said enough."

"It is good of you to understand. I like you Nick—and Domingo. But he needs his head examined. Why does he have to stick a pin in Casares Manasco of all people?"

"Don't ask me."

He put the telephone down and walked to the window, biting at his lower lip. A pigeon got up from the roof opposite and with a lazy clap of wings sailed away down the

Paseo. Talking more for himself than Domingo, he said harshly: "We won't get a tug or lighters. Not in Palma. Not in Barcelona. Not anywhere. We're stuck with two thousand pounds of cargo we can't move. The only thing we can do is to sell it to Manasco at cost and watch him take the fat profit we'd marked out for ourselves unless——"

"Unless what, Nick?"

He swung round and came back towards Domingo. His face was hard and severe, his mouth drawn thin.

"Do you want to take his offer? Or would you like to fight him?"

Domingo blew out his fat cheeks gently. "I do what you say, Nick. . . ."

"If we don't take up his offer within three days he won't give us another chance. If we fight him, we could lose. You know what that means? We'd be bankrupt. . . ."

Domingo took out a cigar and bit off the end. "I do what you say, Nick."

Thorne began to move towards the office door.

"I'll call you back in a little while. This needs thinking out."

"All right, Nick. You do that."

* * * *

For himself it would have been a simple decision. With only himself to consider he would fight. Manasco was in the wrong and he was in the right. He didn't like being pushed around. It was better to fight back and lose than to give up tamely. For himself the money was unimportant. To finish up without a penny after a fight . . . that was all right. But he had Kate to consider and Julia. They only just got by as it was. To start all over again from scratch was asking a lot. . . . And there was a good chance that it would happen. Walking back to the flat he decided that he would put the situation fairly to Kate. He wouldn't influence her one way or the other, and he would accept her decision.

He found her in the kitchen preparing a late lunch. He took her by the arm, led her into the sitting room and sat her down. He fixed a couple of dry martinis, handed her one and then walking about the room with his own, gave her the facts, baldly and quickly.

"The point is," he finished, "what do we do? Take his offer or have a go at him?"

Kate didn't answer for a moment. She rubbed her finger gently across the rim of her glass. Her face was thoughtful and her right leg, crossed over the other, swung slightly.

"You want my advice?" she asked finally.

"No. I want your decision."

"Why my decision?"

"Because it affects you as much as me. I've said, we may end up bankrupt. We might have to take Julia away from school and bring her back here. . . . I don't have to point out all the things that might be."

"And you don't want to influence me?"

"No, Kate. I want it to come straight from you."

"All right . . ." she smiled. "Then I can ask some questions?"

"Fire away."

"Did Peroni have the boy drugged? Your honest opinion, Nick."

"No."

Despite her untidiness and easy-going nature, there was a hard practical streak in her that came out when she met a problem. She wanted facts before she gave her decision. He liked that.

"And Manasco won't let you use his road and is already stopping you from hiring lighters?"

"Yes."

"Have you got any idea how you'll get over that?"

"No. Not yet. Johnny Manchester at Puerto might help. But generally I haven't an idea."

"David and Goliath?" Her eyes were on him and he

knew she was gauging him, reaching to him, watching for every shade of thought and emotion in him.

"That's what it would be. Except that I don't think my chances are as good even as David's were."

"But you don't care a damn about that?"

She stood up, putting down her glass.

"My feelings don't count. It's your decision."

"Any decision I make must include your feelings, Nick, dear. Neither of us can escape that." She said it quietly, sincerely, and her hand came out and held his arm. "You don't like being pushed around. I don't like seeing you pushed around. If ever a man was asking for a fight at this moment, you are. If that's what you want, then I want it——"

"Keep me out of this. You say."

"I am saying. Can't you see that, Nick. I'm saying what I want. What I want for me and what I want for you. It isn't a question of money, is it? Or of pride being hurt if you take Manasco's offer. It's something else . . . something I can't find the words for yet. Except to say that you want a fight. But I've only got to look at you to see that it's important, that it's got to be. So I say fight. . . ."

He put his arm up and slipped it round her shoulders, drawing her to him. This was it then, and he was aware of a warm feeling of relief in him. Yes, he wanted a fight. Maybe it was the medicine he needed. That was putting it in words a little more clearly than Kate could—or would—just now. But he knew what she meant; knew more clearly perhaps than she did—though he wouldn't bet on that. By fighting he did something for himself and for Kate. The other thing was there, a shadow over everything . . . he had to fight, to smash something in order to prove himself to her. He'd lost stature with her . . . he couldn't escape that knowledge. When a thing like this happened between man and wife it could only mean that. There were a hundred different ways it could happen. But they all added up to the same thing. The man had lost something in the woman's eyes. And now he had to come back. As simple as that. Some men would beat the hell out of their women and come back. Some men would beat the hell out of the other man. . . . He didn't want either of those. He wanted something bigger and here it was right in his lap. He had to kill a giant for her; had to blind himself to the possibility of defeat and look always to the triumph of victory which would bring him back and hold her to him for ever. . . . And, by God, he'd do it.

* * * *

They drove back to Puerto late that afternoon. It was dark when he went along to Johnny Manchester's garage. The old man and his family lived in three rooms above the place. Along the sea front the lights were on in the bars. Although it was a warm night few people were drinking outside. Out in the bay a few fishing boats had their bow lamps lit and were on their way out for the night's work.

Rigo let him in. They went through the dark garage and up the stairs to a sitting-room.

Johnny was sitting at the table reading. On it there was a bottle of *malaga* and two glasses. There was an old, faded picture of Belmonte the bullfighter on the wall by the window, a Madonna in a niche in a corner of the room, and two unfinished lobster traps by the door. Johnny's wife, a quiet, grey shadow, brought another glass and then went and sat by the window, watching the street and knitting. Johnny filled the three glasses. Rigo sat down on a stool by his mother and, picking up a small car dynamo, began to work at it silently. He was a handsome, well-built fellow. Once, Thorne thought, Johnny must have looked like him.

"Why do you come back?" asked Johnny.

"To finish my business."

"Good, you are wise to finish it quickly."

"I am going to finish it my way—not Manasco's."

"If it could be done, you might be the man. But it can't be done, señor."

"You could help me, Johnny. We've worked before."

"No, Señor. If there were a chance, I might be with you."

"What about the other men up here? Can I get any of them?"

"No, señor."

Thorne paused. Kate should see this, he thought. Me, pushing over a brick wall. So far he'd only bruised his knuckles. He lifted the glass of *malaga* and drained it.

"But everyone around here can't be in Manasco's pocket?" he snapped his lighter to a cigarette, angrily.

"He has a big pocket."

"Full of pesetas," said Rigo.

"In the ship basin there's a big flat-bottomed lighter. I saw it when I got up here. They've been using it to take sand ballast across to the seaplane base but the work is finished. Who does it belong to?"

"Marla, one of the fishermen."

"Is he in the pocket, too?"

"I don't know."

"You used to have all the answers, Johnny."

"He still has, but he's careful with them now," said Rigo.

"My son," said Johnny unmoved, "is still young. You will forgive him, señor, if he seems to show disrespect to his father. As for this business, you are wasting your time."

"With a good, powerful motor boat and that lighter I needn't waste my time, Johnny. You've got such a motorboat."

"Señor Thorne, why do you not respect my desire for a quiet life? The boat is not for hire."

"Or any other boat?"

"Or any other boat."

Johnny's wife looked up and said sharply, "Señor Thorne's glass is empty."

"Pardon, señor." Johnny refilled it.

Thorne lifted the glass and nodded at Johnny across it. "Manasco has a good friend in you, Johnny."

He saw the lean turtle-neck stiffen and the old man's eyes, colourless under the shadow of the bushy eyebrows, narrowed.

"Manasco is not my friend, señor. I. . . ."

"He likes a quiet life, señor," said Rigo. "It is true that he is not always in his bed. But then old men find the night air easier to breathe now and then. But he is for quietness."

"Rigo has said it," Johnny nodded approvingly at his son. "Quietness."

"I know your father, and I meant no offence," said Thorne to Rigo. "It just is that I do not like to see good men live in the shadow of small men. . . ."

"Who does, señor?" said Johnny. "But then there are many things we do not like but have to accept."

"All right, Johnny. I have no more to say."

A car went by outside. Johnny smoothed the pages of his open book like a man soothing a cat to repay neglect. His wife's needles made a brittle sound in the silence of the room. I speak their language, Thorne thought, but I am not with them. They were three centuries behind, bonded people whose straw huts huddled against the castle walls . . . and in every castle was a Manasco.

He saw Rigo look up at his mother. The brown face and dark curly hair had the look of a fresh pastel drawing.

"No more to say," Thorne repeated. "But I am not finished with Manasco."

Again there was a pause between them all. Then he saw Rigo put out a hand and touch his mother without looking at her.

"But I have more to say," Rigo said suddenly. He put the dynamo on the floor and stood up. "I am of an age when I do not care for quietness. When there are some things which I must do, even at the risk of offending my father and my mother."

"You will not offend me, Rigo," said his mother. "A pocket is no place for a man."

"You will offend me," said Johnny. "But no doubt I shall learn to live with it."

"Then it is settled," said Rigo.

Thorne stood up. "Just what is settled, Rigo?"

"That there will be trouble," said Johnny. "But for once I shall watch it instead of being in it. Remember, Señor Thorne, he is my son. At times unsatisfactory—but my son."

"He is a man and has a right to make up his own mind," said Johnny's wife.

"There is no need to say all these things," said Rigo, putting his hand inside his singlet and scratching his chest. Then looking at Thorne, he went on, "The motor boat is mine. My father gave it to me a year ago. You will need things for our work on the *Doria*. Tomorrow morning they will be ready."

Thorne said, "You will work with me?"

"Yes, señor." There was a quality of stillness and strength in Rigo which was disturbing. Somewhere buried deep, Thorne had the feeling, there was a bitterness of which even Rigo was afraid. He turned to Johnny.

"You knew he would do this?"

"No, señor."

"Then if you tell me not to accept his offer. . . . I don't want to cause trouble in this family."

"There is trouble in every family. But Rigo's trouble is nothing to do with you. Maria," he looked across at his wife; "it is time for my milk."

Rigo slipped on a woollen wind-breaker, letting it hang open over his singlet.

"Let us go and talk to Marla. At this hour he may be drunk enough to do a deal for his lighter."

* * * *

They found Marla in a small *bar y comidas* at the far end of the beach. He was sitting with three other men at a table under a tall date palm. A few yards away the water washed gently at the shingle, lacing it with a thin edge of phosphorescence. In the bar itself a gramophone played a *paso dobles* whose noise shattered the night. Marla looked like a limp piece of old rope with a knot in one end for a head and untidy frayings of hemp for legs and arms. His complexion told Thorne that there was more *vermut blanco dolce* in his veins than blood.

Rigo introduced Thorne to the group and they sat down. Marla, after no more than a nod, went on describing a football game that had taken place in Madrid five years before. He used the salted almonds and anchovy-stuffed olives from the saucers on the table to mark the various players and movements.

Thorne waited patiently. Marla and his friends would know why he was there. Late that afternoon he had walked along the harbour basin wall and made enquiries about the lighter. The news would already have reached Marla. In this place it wasn't only that the fall of each leaf was known, but everyone knew even which side up the leaf fell. Marla described the final goal, flicking an olive from the table with his forefinger and then slumped back into his chair and wiped his face with his hand.

One of his friends said, "How well he tells it."

The other nodded. "Each time I see it all. It lives." He picked up an almond that had been a centre-forward and crunched it between his teeth.

"It is more remarkable," said Rigo pleasantly, "that it is well known Marla has never been to Madrid in his life."

"Quite," said Marla. "Remarkable."

"But then," said one of his friends, "Marla has a talent for describing things he has never seen. It is easy to describe something you have seen."

"Quite," said Marla, and he cooled his thirst by lifting a *poron* from the table and letting a thin jet curve through the air into his mouth.

"My friend, Señor Thorne," said Rigo, "must now be all

the more eager to do business with such a remarkable man. It is the matter of your lighter, Marla."

"It is a fine lighter," said Thorne, "and I would like to hire it."

"It would be impossible," said Marla, letting his head drop forward and squinting at Thorne. "Tomorrow I am going to Palma and then to Barcelona. I have a friend there who gives me a job. You will understand that I do not lightly leave Puerto, but on the mainland I shall see more football matches. Also I am tired of fishing and stupid holiday people. The lighter is therefore, only for sale."

You couldn't take a bet on how much truth there was in that, thought Thorne. Marla might be moving, or he might have no further use for the lighter and want to sell it, or . . . God knew what dark and satisfactory reasons lay behind his creased forehead. All he knew was that he was going to have to buy the lighter. That in itself was an unexpected triumph. With a motor-boat and a lighter he could laugh at Manasco. But with his money as tight as it was, he knew, too, that the bargaining would take some time. Fortunately, before he had left Palma he had drawn a reasonable sum from Peroni for expenses.

It was midnight before the deal was made. He had paid more than he wished but less than he had expected.

He walked back along the front with Rigo and they went out along the sea wall of the harbour to look at the lighter. It was tied up in a crook of the wall alongside the small seaman's shelter. A big, flat-bottomed old scow with plenty of draught . . . and as ugly as hell, he decided, to handle in anything like a sea. However, with luck the weather would be good to them. Twenty trips with it and they might well have cleared the cargo, bringing it round to Puerto and then shipping it on to Palma by lorry. Domingo could look after the lorry end.

"Be here at six, Rigo. We'll tow it round tomorrow."

He walked back to the Margarita with a wary kind of happiness in him. So far he was doing well, and because for the moment he could relax a little, he was aware of the tiredness in him. He went up to their room and entered quietly. Kate had gone to sleep reading. Her bedside light was on and a book lay sprawled on the floor. She moved and muttered a little to herself. He picked the book up and for a moment he stood looking down at her . . . her face was relaxed and he could read the tiredness in her, too. Without make-up, without the stimulus of knowing she was being watched, it was a gentle face. He bent down and kissed her as he turned off the light. What the hell did it all matter, he thought . . .? When you love you must be big enough to accept all that love brought: the good and the bad. And just now it didn't seem to matter.

...

Kate smiled ...

Chapter Six

RIGO was waiting for him at six. He'd brought his motor-
boat around from its moorings lower down the beach and
already had a tow rope on to the bows of the lighter. It was a
powerful, twelve horse-power motor-boat and, so long as it
was allowed to take its time, would pull anything that
could be loaded into the lighter.

Piled in the stern of the motor-boat was a jumble of stores,
ropes, blocks and pulleys, a couple of crowbars, and some
food and wine . . . all preliminary necessities which he and
Rigo had settled the previous day. Not until they were on the
Doria could they tell exactly what they would want. Kate
came down with him. Looking over her shoulder as they
stood on the edge of the quay, she said, "Is that the girl?"

Thorne turned. Sitting on a loose stone block by the
shelter was the girl, Juana. She wore jeans and a pink shirt
and she was smoking.

"That's her," he said. "She must have got up early."

"News travels fast," said Kate.

From the motor-boat Rigo said stiffly, "She was here when
I came."

Juana got up and came over to them. She threw her
cigarette into the sea and the gesture held a suggestion of
contempt for them all.

She looked at Thorne and she said, "You are wasting your
time."

Thorne shrugged. "Kate, this is Señorita Manasco."

Kate smiled. "Good morning, señorita. No gun today?"

In the boat Rigo laughed. The girl's eyes narrowed, and
she gave Kate the kind of look a woman uses to strip another
of her vanities.

"You look sensible." She made it insulting. "Tell him

87

he is wasting his time. Tell him he is only going to run into trouble. . . . He and that Puerto muscle-boy who wants to help him."

Kate smiled.

"You don't want me to tell him that," she said. "You want him to go on and run into trouble. If he walked out now you'd be disappointed—and so would I."

She turned away from the girl. "All right, Nick. Let's go and collect our window-frames and washbasins so that Juana can have some fun."

Juana walked away from them. Not leaving them but suddenly no longer with them, as though they were so many scribbles on a slate which she had in one sweep swept clean.

From the boat Rigo, bending to start the engine, said, "What is wrong with muscle? I have a brain, too."

"You have to have money, also, Rigo. Otherwise you don't exist," said Thorne.

"You're both wrong," said Kate. "With a girl like that you have to have a No for her Yes. She'll marry the first man who spanks her bottom—and the Lord help him and give him strong wrists."

* * * *

Rigo had the wheel. Thorne watched him handling the weight and pull of the lighter. There was something deliberate but sensitive in Rigo's movements and to the smallest action he gave his full attention. One of the hardest things in the world, he guessed, would be to make Rigo change his mind, or to turn him from something he had settled he wanted. There was a great comfort in that.

They ran out towards the mouth of the bay and the Cabo de Perada. Close on their left hand the steep face of the peninsula went up through crag and pine to the high grey bare ridges. Up by Perada itself the cliffs broke back and dropped to a long crescent of sand, close fringed with trees, the white and pink walls of villas showing through the trees.

Meeting the open sea as the lighthouse on the point came up
on the port hand, the wind freshened a little and an awkward
chop began to slap at the bows of the motor-boat. According to the wind and the sea the run round to Agua Gelida
might take three hours. Thorne sitting with Kate was
silent. In his mind he was figuring out the possible cargo
loads from the *Doria*.

Without looking back Rigo said, "There is a story, señor,
in Palma that you and your partner stopped Guido from
going to the auction."

"That we drugged him?"

"It has been mentioned."

"Well, we didn't."

"That is what I think. He is wild when he drinks."

"You know him well?" asked Kate.

"Both of them. When I was a boy my father was their
boatman at Ermano. We played together." He bent forward
and eased the throttle back. They were around the point
and had the wind astern. The grey cliffs were still on their
port hand as they began the run down the other side of the
peninsula. But the cliffs were higher now and barer and the
sea running free pounded against their feet, sending up
great spouts and jets of white water.

"Well, you won't be playing with them now," said Thorne.

Rigo turned and smiled and the sun over his brown skin,
the muscle moulded against the thin singlet, the lift of the
dark, curly hair gave him the appearance of a magazine
drawing, glossy, coloured and filling the eye.

"We finished playing when I was fourteen, señor. Like
that." He snapped his fingers. "The curtain comes down and
I am my father's son, and they are Manascos." He said it
without bitterness. But a long way back, Thorne guessed,
there had been bitterness, and the confusion and anger of a
boy wondering what had hit him. He, himself, had played
with Spanish boys, all kinds, and the play had gone on into
mature friendships. The only time he had ever been thrashed
was by his father for a breach of good manners towards a

fisherman's son. And the old man when it came to thrashing —like everything else—never went in for half measures.

He saw Rigo bend forward to the throttle. As the engine speed picked up there was a jerk as the slack came up on the tow rope to the lighter. He looked back, seeing the small, broken bow waves smacking against the broad snout of the lighter. Little fans and sprays of water went high and drifted inboard. Suddenly, he stood up so that he could get a good look into the lighter. Three inches of water washed over the bottom boards.

"Ease up, Rigo."

"What's the matter?" asked Kate.

"The lighter's taking water."

They drifted and he pulled the lighter slowly close up astern of the motor boat. He climbed aboard while Rigo held the two boats together. Splashing through the water he went aft and inspected the bilge cock. It was secure.

He straightened up, frowning. There was nothing like enough sea going for the lighter to have shipped three inches of water. Then he saw that the water was running in fast from the bows. He went forward, bending low. Three feet back from the bows, and on either side, four holes about half an inch in diameter had been drilled just above the water line. Coming out of the bay and rounding the point the steady smack of water on the bows had sent water inboard through the holes. With three inches of water aboard the lighter was sitting lower in the sea. All the holes were now below the water line and the sea was spurting in through them.

He shouted to Rigo to find him something to plug the holes and seizing a dipper began to bale. The water was pouring in.

Rigo tossed him a lump of tow. He called to Kate, "You come aboard and bale while I get these holes fixed." He caught her hand and helped her. "Quick now." Kate began to bale, tossing the water over to the windward side so that most of it came back inboard.

"Throw it out the other side," he called sharply. He looked at the cliffs half a mile away. Agua Gelida was too far to make. There was a lot of iron in the construction of the lighter and once she filled she might go under. At the best she would go under to her gunwales and wallow in the sea like a dead weight. To tow her to Agua Gelida would probably tear the stern out of the motor-boat.

"There's a little beach." Rigo's hand waved towards the far cliffs. "If we get her in she could be beached in shallow water."

"Get going then, I'll see what I can do here."

He started to plug the holes with tow, twisting the stuff up into tight wads and forcing it into the holes. But the tow was soft and useless. After a little while in the water it went limp and the pressure of the sea outside forced it out. He went from one hole to another, renewing the plugs, but he knew that he was fighting a losing battle. The motor-boat was labouring along now, Rigo pushing her as fast as he dared, but the water was rising fast . . . faster even than Thorne would have imagined from the eight holes in the bows.

He went aft and, as he had suspected, found that the lighter had been given the same treatment there. The thing was riddled with holes, all originally just above the water line.

He heard the baler bang against the gunwale and then a quick cry from Kate. He turned to see the baler drifting away. A wave took it and it capsized and sank.

"Oh, Nick——"

She'd hit it against the side and it had been jerked out of her hand.

"Damn it, Kate. Why do you have to be so ham-handed——"

"I'm sorry, Nick."

"It's all right. Baling couldn't save her anyway. That bloody girl's done a real job!"

He stood with the water creeping up his legs and watched

the cliffs come closer. There was a narrow runback between the tall crags and a patch of sunlight on the beach and the gentle slope of hill coming down to it. High up on the hillside, as his head came up each time from plugging a hole, he could see a handful of dark ponies grazing across the thin cactus palm and myrtle bushes. The lighter jerked and wallowed behind the motor-boat. One moment the tow rope would be slack and the next it would sing like a harp string.

The sun sparkle went from the water as they entered the dark shadow of the cliffs. The sea smacked at the base of the cliffs and the air boomed with the noise.

Closer in there was an ugly swell running and now the lighter, with only about four inches of freeboard left, was lifted and swung with it and once or twice the long edge of a wave came curling inboard.

He reached out and took Kate's arm to steady her. "Get ready to jump," he warned her.

The engine beat increased as Rigo turned on more power to counteract the swell and to pull the lighter's heavy nose in line with the beach. The lighter lifted with a sluggish movement, water seethed and swirled down its length and the tow rope parted. The loose end came back in an untidy swing, like the sweep of a gigantic cow's tail. It hit Thorne on the shoulder and sent him sprawling against Kate.

As he picked her up he heard Rigo shout. The lighter refused to lift to the next swell and the water swept over it.

Rigo brought the motor-boat round and cutting the engine ran to the stern with a new tow rope. He stood there, waiting to throw it. As it came through the air and Thorne grabbed at it, the lighter lifted and from the corner of his eye he saw the cliffs very close and a sudden boiling of white water.

"Jump for it, Kate!" he shouted.

The black flank of the lighter reared up like a clumsy sea-cow and then crashed down on a hidden rock.

Thorne went overboard after Kate and swam to the motor-boat. Rigo pulled them aboard. As Thorne stood up he saw the lighter smash down once more on the rock and then slide off it and out of sight. He looked at Kate, wet, her face full of misery.

"Well, that's that!" he said savagely.

* * * *

They came into Agua Gelida and made fast alongside the *Doria*.

Thorne went into the captain's saloon with Kate and they stripped off and changed their clothes.

"We couldn't have kept her afloat by baling, could we Nick?"

"No. She was full of holes. Don't worry about it." He put his hand out and touched her bare shoulder.

"It's maddening. Just getting in a boat brings out all the clumsiness in me."

Rigo entered with a flask of wine and three glasses. He poured wine for them. Then as Rigo put his glass down he nodded through the thick plate-glass window that gave on to the bridge.

Away on the little rise above the beach Juana still in jeans and a pink blouse, was standing watching the ship.

Thorne picked up his clothes and began to wring them out.

"Well, she's taught us one lesson. You can never get up too early."

As he said it, he had no anger. The thing had gone deeper than anger. It was now a militant hardness. If nothing hung on this at all now; if the profit involved concerned only a few pesetas he couldn't have been turned aside. He was suddenly remembering an army slogan which he used to meet with in quartermasters' stores. *The impossible we can do today. Miracles take a little longer.*

That suited him; he'd become a miracle worker too. And the only way to a miracle for him was by putting his head down like a mole and boring away.

"This afternoon," he said to Rigo, "we'll rig a tackle

from the forward derrick and try and get those loose timber baulks away from the fore-hatch."

They worked through the afternoon until the sun, dropping into the sea behind the cliffs against which the *Doria* lay so closely, cast a great purple stain of shadow over the water. The forward steam winch could be operated by hand and using this with a block and tackle rigged from the long boom of the derrick just forward of the bridge they got a rope neck round one end of a baulk, raised it and swung it outboard. When it was almost on the point of balance over the side they lowered it to the rail. Then, running out enough rope to take the fall to the water, they eased the baulk beyond the balance point with their crowbars. In the afternoon they sent ten of the baulks overboard and each time Rigo, stripped to his drawers, would dive over and unship the rope neck from the end of the baulk for the next lift. Working with Rigo was easy. He saw at once what was needed. Sometimes they were both at the winch, sometimes with the locking pawl over, they were both straining and sweating at a baulk. Once or twice Thorne had to shout warningly at Rigo as he took risks with the swinging beams. One of them only had to swing back or drop and a man could have been crushed like a fly. He kept Kate away from this work. There was nothing she could do. She went into the galley to put it in order and to sort out the stores they had brought with them.

There was a moment of satisfaction for Thorne as each baulk hung for a second off balance and then crashed into the sea. Rigo would go in after it and come back with the free rope, dripping with water, his large, handsome face and curly black hair shining in the sun. For Thorne there was a strange contentment in the work. The labour held its own virtue. A man was freed of thought or worry. For the time being his sights were lowered. There were just the baulks on the foredeck to move and that was all. Nothing beyond that merited attention yet.

As the light went they packed up and went into the cabin.

Kate had laid out a meal of fruit, cheese and wine for them. Eating, Thorne got out a pencil and paper and made a list of further equipment they would need. At this time of year the light went soon and he wanted acetylene lamps. If they rigged a couple of the powerful lamps which the fishermen used for night fishing, they could work in the dark. He handed the list to Rigo.

"You go back tonight, Rigo, and see what you can do about these things."

He looked across at Kate. "I think you'd better go with him. Somebody's got to phone Peroni. Tell him to scout around all the little fishing places and see if he can pick up another lighter."

"Yes, Nick."

"Now you've seen what the set-up is, you can bring stores out. There's going to be a lot for you to do out here." He grinned at her, and then turned to Rigo. "Keep an eye on that motor-boat, Rigo. We don't want any holes bored in that."

"Nobody will touch the boat, señor. I shall sleep in it." He stood up, slipping on his windbreaker. "But there is one thing."

"What is it, Rigo?"

"The lamps, señor. I can get them, but they will make it difficult. They are powerful, and at night they will light up the beach. From the hills up there one could see everything."

Thorne stretched on the bunk, easing his back muscles. "You're thinking of your father? Of his need for a little night air?"

Rigo nodded.

"Don't worry. I don't know how much night work we shall have to do. But Johnny only has to pass you the word and we'll take a night off."

"Thank you, señor."

"Is Manasco tied up with this smuggling too?"

Rigo shrugged his shoulders. "You have done this yourself, señor. You know that everyone in Spain is tied up with it, somewhere."

"Sure. But I bet it would be hard to trace the string back to Manasco."

Before Rigo left he got him to go ashore and bring out the small rowing boat. It belonged to Johnny. The Manascos had another boat hauled up under a bamboo-roofed shelter at the far end of the beach near the little spring of fresh water.

When Rigo went down to the motor-boat he stood with Kate at the top of the steps. He put his arms round her and kissed her.

"I'd rather stay with you," she said.

"I know. . . . Still, things have to be done."

He kissed her again, feeling her warm against him.

He watched them go off into the darkness, the beat of the motor slowly dying in the black gulf of the bay. It was a warm night and he knew he would be comfortable enough stretched out on one of the bunks in the captain's saloon. His clothes had dried during the afternoon. Rigo had left him some cigarettes and there was half a flask of wine. A man who wanted more would be pampering himself.

He sat on deck, smoking and relaxing. A light showed from the Villa Ermano. He had no doubt that every move on the *Doria* was watched from the house. Well, they could go on watching. If they knew what he was going to do now that he had lost his lighter, then they knew more than he did.

*   *   *   *

About ten o'clock he went ashore in the rowing boat to fill a can with water from the spring. He would need it for washing and drinking in the morning. There was a soft wind coming in from the sea and the night was clear. The stars looked as though they'd just had a sluice down and the hills running back to Cala Boquer were bone-grey under their light. Back at the Margarita, he thought, Kate would be going up to sleep . . . to take up her book for half an hour. And in England in the quiet Kentish countryside Julia would be sleeping . . . a sudden pang hit him as he thought of his daughter. He usually wrote to her once a week. He must find time tomorrow. . . . Out of sight, out of mind. That was something Kate had accused him of.

The boat ran up on to the beach and he got out and began to plug his way through the loose sand towards the spring. Driftwood and sun-dried sea-wrack crackled under his feet. The spring was on the far side of the beach, just below the villa. It came down from the low bank, through a narrow slide which someone had concreted into a gutter shape and then fell from a rusty iron spout on to the sand. A patch of feathery bamboos marked the foot of the bank, and a small path led through them.

He pushed through the bamboos and halted in front of the iron spout. There was no water coming through it and the long concrete gutter was dry.

"The bastards," he said softly to himself.

There was one thing about the Manasco family, he thought; they used everything. They would take what amounted to a sledge-hammer to his lighter, but they also had fun with their pin-pricks. Cutting off his water was no more than an irritation. In this country one used it only for washing and Rigo could easily ferry him round enough at a time to last a week. Yet because it was a small irritation it somehow made him angrier than the loss of the lighter had. One should have expected that. But this was childish.

With his water-can in hand he climbed the bank and followed the course of the little stream. It ran across a piece of cactus-studded ground and up to the garden wall of the villa. It came out under the wall through a large drain pipe. Thorne looked at the wall, at the roof of the villa showing over it and then at the terraced hill away to the left.

He moved along the wall which ran parallel with the beach. Where it met the hillside it turned back at an angle, but a rough, flat-stone wall sloped up the hill enclosing the garden. Thorne went up the side of the wall. The slope grew steeper and he was soon quite close to the cliffside with the sea a hundred feet below him. The wall finished at the foot of a bare rock face. He climbed over and found himself on a terrace path. In the starlight a row of almond trees stood, old and thin, running away in a tangled perspective. Underneath them were patches of pimento. He stood for a while listening. The lights were on in the villa below. The sound of the sea-wash came up to him like a muffled snore. Then to his left he heard the water.

It came out of a crack in the bare rock face in an untidy dribble. Immediately below the source a stone basin had been built and from it an iron pipe ran out into the terrace path and disappeared underground.

He took the stopper off his can and filled it. As he straightened up and rested it on the side of the stone basin to screw the cap on he heard a growl to his left. He swung round. Five yards from him at the head of the path coming up through the terraced garden was the black Alsatian, Eduardo.

Its hackles were up and it was coming forward, slowly, taking one step after another with a menacing delicacy of movement, and its head was lowered. As it moved it grumbled and growled as though it were rolling boulders round and round inside its stomach.

Thorne stood very still.

The dog stopped two yards from him. Thorne knew that he had only to move and the dog would be at his throat. Eduardo was gentleman enough, he guessed, to like to take his game on the run. They faced one another and the growling died down to a gentle noise, like a car far away being driven with the cut-out open.

He didn't know how long they stood, watching one another. But he knew that Eduardo was capable of keeping it up much longer than he could. Eventually he would have to move, and it needed only to be the drop of a hand, the flex of shoulders to set the dog in motion.

Beyond the dog, in the shadows at the head of the path by the wall, something moved, a white movement like the sweep of a bird's wing. Juana came out of the darkness and stood just behind the dog. Eduardo didn't move, but the growling went to a higher pitch as though the animal were saying, *Look what I've found. . . . Look. . . . Shall I tear his throat out or disembowel him . . .?*

Gently, keeping his voice on one level, Thorne said, "I never thought I'd be glad to see you. Call him off."

She laughed, and the noise was colder and less musical than the sound of the dribbling water behind him.

"I've only come to watch."

And she meant it. Watching the ring and waiting for blood to flow across the sand. She was dressed for the kill, too. *Haute toilette* for the death of a matador . . . only he didn't feel like a matador. . . . The white lace shawl was looped across her back and came through her arms to fall almost to the ground. The evening gown could have been green or red in the starlight and the tight bodice, strapless, pushed her small breasts high and left the bare, rounded sweep of shoulders and neck to flower nakedly from a firm calyx of silk. She'd brushed her dark hair upwards in a high elaboration of curls. He couldn't have wished for a more beautiful spectator at his throat-tearing . . . or more appreciative. Here was an *aficionada* who would miss no fine point.

"Call him off."

"You're trespassing. We keep him to guard our property. Would you have us train him for five years and then deny him his rights? It is your own fault."

She laughed again and Eduardo, encouraged, took a step forward.

"Call him off. If you don't I'll shoot him before he gets me."

"You've got a gun?"

"A man needs one around here. I don't trespass unless I'm armed."

"You wouldn't shoot a dog. Englishmen don't do that."

"Englishmen like to keep their throats in one piece. I'm going to count three and then shoot."

She did nothing for a moment. Then she stepped forward and her hand dropped to the dog's head, barely touching it.

"Eduardo. . . . Leave."

Exorcised, the dog stopped growling, lifted its head and was suddenly interested in nothing.

"Thank you."

He moved, feeling the stiffness break in him, and lifted his water can. He walked up to them and he saw the shine in her eyes and the tiny movement of a gold chain about her throat.

He tipped his head back towards the spring source.

"Whose idea was that?"

"Guido's. We've diverted it to the other side of the villa . . . for the garden."

"It wasn't worth it. We can always bring our own water round."

"Of course."

"But I don't mean to."

He was walking towards the wall and she followed him, her hand on the dog's collar.

"No?"

"No. If it isn't running in the morning on the beach, I'll get some gun-cotton and blast this wall . . . so that the spring runs straight over the cliff."

He lifted the can on to the wall and then climbed up, sitting astride of it for a moment. Looking down at her, not feeling anger now, feeling only an even level of obstinacy and determination which, instinctively, he guessed was matched in her, he said—

"You did a good job on the lighter."

She made a little movement of her head as though acknowledging a compliment.

Then she said, "That is only a beginning. You should accept my uncle's offer."

He shook his head and dropped off the wall. She came

close up against the piled stones so that only her head and shoulders were showing. Against the grey, ash-coloured hills and the long sweep of stars in the distant cleft of the valley end it was a portrait that would have stopped anyone at an Academy showing. She wasn't smiling and she wasn't frowning; she was just being, nothing in her face except herself. Nothing marred it . . . no line, no mark of years or passion passed into habit. It was youth and loveliness, the smooth, velvety immaculateness of newness. . . . He suddenly thought of Kate, sitting in front of her dressing table, patting at her face with lotions. He was abruptly, and angrily, aware of disloyalty.

He turned away from her and began to walk down the side of the wall. On the other side she kept him company. In the silence between them he had the uncanny impression that, momentarily, she had been aware of his thoughts and found some defeat in them for him.

At the bottom of the wall she stopped, before turning towards the villa.

"I don't believe you would have shot Eduardo," she said.

"You're right," he said. "But don't get the wrong idea. Only because I didn't have a revolver."

He saw her lips tighten then and the moment of anger pass across her face because she had been tricked.

He laughed, rubbing salt willingly into the wound, and went down to the beach.

* * * *

The next morning early, though he didn't need water, he rowed ashore. The spring was running. He sluiced himself off under the spout and was towelling his face when Manasco came out of the villa courtyard and crossed to the beach edge.

He stood six feet above Thorne and non-committally said, "*Buenos dias, señor.*"

"*Buenos. . . .*"

He had a red dressing gown, belted tightly about the waist, and the morning breeze took the ends of the robe and swung them about. His legs were bare, brown and skinny, and the short-cropped sandy hair was ruffled. He was a grizzled, fight-toughened memory-strengthened ex-flyweight champion of the world. In a moment the robe would be slipped off, feet scuffled in the sawdust and he would show the youngsters a thing or two.

"You should be sensible," he said.

"I am."

"You can't get this cargo out, and you know it, señor."

"That's your opinion."

Manasco laughed, but it wasn't intended to do anything for their relationship. Then in a meditative tone, a man prepared to be generous when he meets courage mixed with folly in a friend, he said, "I'll be frank. At our first meeting, I think I made a mistake about you. I apologise for the way I received you."

"You mean you're giving me a clean sheet on the drugging charge?"

"If you put it that way."

"But not my partner?"

"No."

"You think he did it without my knowledge and now I have to stand by him?"

"Señor Thorne, I do not wish to discuss the relationship between you and your partner. I am concerned only with you. I try to be a fair man. Hence, my apology. But it doesn't affect the main issue. I am prepared to buy the cargo from you for what you gave. And also to pay for the lighter. But this is the last time I make the offer."

Thorne rubbed the back of his neck with the towel.

"This boy Guido means a lot to you, doesn't he?"

"I have no son. He will inherit everything. I have much to teach him."

"You have." Thorne draped the towel over a bamboo and began to button up his shirt front. "To begin with let's get the facts straight. My partner didn't have Guido tampered with. If he had I would know it, and I wouldn't be up here now. I don't know what Guido told you, but the truth is he made a fool of himself. I should have thought the first thing you would have wanted to teach him was that it's bad business to cover mistakes with lies."

Manasco's pale blue eyes blinked behind his glasses and his mouth was suddenly pinched in as though he had bitten at some sharp fruit.

"Guido didn't lie."

Thorne shook his head. He bent forward and picked up his towel. The water came down the concrete slide in a thin run, undulating like a silver snake. He could feel his feet sinking into the cushion of wet sand.

"You made me an offer just now, Señor Manasco. I can't take it. But I'll make you an offer—to help you and Guido. Guido particularly. He's the one who needs help."

"What's your offer?"

"I'll sell you the cargo for what we gave for it. But in addition, in front of both of us, you must have Guido admit he's been lying."

"You know I won't do that." As he finished speaking Manasco cleared his throat noisily as though the sharp taste in his mouth still bothered him.

"And I won't sell without. I'm sorry about it, but there it is. You go ahead and teach Guido how to buy and fight his way out of a lie—and I'll get my cargo ashore."

"But not to Palma!" There was a snap in the old man's voice, like ice breaking.

Thorne shrugged his shoulders and turned away down the beach towards his boat. And that was that, he told himself. Because of Guido they were in the ring, seconds out. . . . And don't fool yourself Nicholas Thorne, he said, the old man knows all there is to know about fighting; Queensberry or any other rules.

As he pulled out to the *Doria* he saw Rigo's motor-boat come round the distant cliff point.

Chapter Seven

THEY spent the morning going on with the work of clearing the timber baulks from the forward deck. There wasn't anything that Kate could do to help them and she passed the morning arranging the new stores she had brought out on the motor-boat. At midday they broke off for the meal she had prepared. Afterwards Rigo went up into the stern and began to check over the acetylene lamps which they had brought out. He sat in the sun, whistling to himself while Kate and Thorne lay on a cleared portion of one of the forward hatch covers. The bay was now a great basin full of sunlight.

Turning his head a little Thorne could see Kate's profile, sharp against the distant cliffs. She wore denim trousers and a checked shirt.

"How was Peroni?" he asked.

"Pretty pessimistic. He's had no luck with any lighters. . . . What on earth shall we do if we can't find any?"

He rolled over, touched by the anxiety in her voice. Then he smiled, reaching out and running a finger down the back of her hand.

"Something will turn up."

"I'll bet that's what your father used to say."

"Something always did."

She was silent for a moment, then she said, "Nick, you do want me out here, don't you?"

He sat up. "But of course. Why do you ask?"

"Well. . . . I don't seem to be able to do much. And I'm not good at this kind of thing."

"Nonsense. Just cooking is a lot. And anyway, later on, there'll be more you can do. Besides I want you out here."

He stood up and reached down a hand to help her to her feet. As she stood close to him he put his hands on her shoulders, looking her full in the eyes. "You're not worrying, are you? About the other thing, I mean?"

"Perhaps. . . ."

"Then don't. The whole thing is clear. We both understand it. We both know that it will take a little time for us to put it into its place. But that's all. Just time." He squeezed her shoulders affectionately.

But working with Rigo on the baulks that afternoon he was thinking about her. It was just a matter of time. That was the truth. But it was easy to say that without bothering to examine what time meant. Time really was only the wrapping around a sequence of days and the days had to be lived through with their actions and their thoughts. At first you had to watch yourself carefully. If Kate got too sensitive and anxious about them it could make him irritable. He knew that. Nothing stirred you up more than having someone you loved over-imagining effects, reading more into little incidents than they contained. Kate and the baler, for instance. And her feeling that she couldn't help much. She scared easily. . . . He smiled as he remembered the fear in her at their first meeting in Barcelona. She had been little more than a schoolgirl when the war came, a stage-struck doctor's daughter who had gone into ENSA. After the war she had done cabaret work in a small troupe touring Europe. Then a crooked manager had stranded them in Barcelona without a penny. When he had first seen her she had been sitting in a café, nervously pulling the paper-wrapping off sugar lumps . . . scared and trying not to show it. When an argument had started with the waiter over her change he had gone to her table. In ten minutes she had been a different girl, no longer alone . . . and already he knew that she was the one.

Sweating on a rope with Rigo to get a baulk shifted, he knew something else, too. He had to watch himself. Every so often when he saw Kate, or thought about her, the shadow of a third person fell between them . . . and imagining another mouth on Kate's, imagining and fighting off the pictures in his mind brought a red anger into him . . . making him want to shout and strike. Thank God, he had this job. He had a fight on his hands. He could always forget the shadow by thinking about Manasco. That made it easier for him than for Kate. She just had to sit it out without any relief. . . . There was nothing he could do about that.

Late that evening, after their meal, he strolled forward with Kate. He leant over the bows, smoking, and she was close to his side. A dozen or more of the timber baulks floated alongside. That afternoon the idea had come to him that if they lashed the timber baulks together they could make a raft alongside on to which they could off-load the cargo from the forward hold. Once they began to bring the stuff up there wouldn't be deck-room enough to stack it all. With a running tackle from the *Doria* to the beach they could ferry the loads ashore. . . .

He lifted his head towards the Villa Ermano. It didn't look as though they would get any lighters. That left only the road. With all the stuff finally stacked on the beach it could be lifted in a day by twenty lorries. If only he had the use of the road. . . . What was it his father used to say? Before you chop down the trees you must first clear the underbrush to get at them. . . . He decided then to get the stuff stacked on the beach.

"There's a boat," said Kate.

Thorne saw the Ermano boat come out from the shadows on the far left of the beach. Juana was rowing in it alone. She pulled out idly beyond the *Doria* and began to lift some lobster pots. They stood there watching her as the light went. As she rowed back she saw them standing at the rail. She raised her hand in greeting to them.

Thorne turned away. "She's a saucy so-and-so, I must say."

*　　*　　*　　*

For the next two days he and Rigo worked without interruption. They finally cleared the baulks from the forward hatch and twenty of them lay alongside, lashed into a raft. On the second night, with the fore-deck free of baulks, they rigged the acetylene lamps on the bridge works and got the hatch covers off. The hold was partly flooded with water.

He and Rigo went down on a rope ladder and found themselves standing, above the water, on a pile of water-sodden sacks which were stacked above the main cargo. Up above the lamps spluttered and hissed and the grey and indigo shadows leaped and twitched about the hold. The water a few feet below them washed gently to and fro with the small motion that was still on the *Doria*. Rigo took out his knife and slit one of the sacks. A yellowish, pulpy mass oozed from it and a sour smell rose into the air.

"What is it?"

Rigo picked up a handful and rubbed it in his fingers.

"Flour, señor."

"We'll have to clear it all out and dump it overboard before we can start work."

There was a rope-work loading net folded over part of the sack pile and using this and the deck hoist they began to get the sacks up. It was a filthy, wet job. The sacks were heavy with water and one or two of them had split. As they were lifted a pulpy shower of evil-smelling flour cascaded to the deck. They worked stripped, for the night was warm. In an hour their arms and bare torsos were caked with the stuff. Under the strong lights that pushed the night back in a wide circle from the bows of the *Doria* Thorne had the impression that he was on a stage, mercilessly lighted and constantly watched. From the Villa Ermano he knew that this night work would provoke interest.

Twice during the evening Kate brought them out coffee. She hung around for a while, but there was nothing she could do to help. Eventually Thorne called to her: "There's nothing you can do, darling. It's late—why don't you turn in?"

She nodded and went off.

By midnight they had all the sacks out of the hold and stacked in an untidy mass close to the port bow. A dirty, rank-smelling seepage of flour and water drained from the pile. The back of the job was broken. In the morning all they had to do was to manhandle the sacks overboard.

The two of them, tired and filthy, climbed down on to the baulk raft and, stripping right off, washed themselves down. Thorne dived in and swam out into the dark water. Rigo followed him and for a moment the surface was alive with phosphorescence. Looking back he could see the *Doria*, bulky and brightly lit against the near cliffs.

When he went into the captain's cabin on the bridge the oil lamp was still burning and Kate was asleep in the starboard bunk. It was a warm night and the light blanket covering her had slipped from her shoulders. As he pulled on his pyjamas he heard her mutter once in her sleep.

He looked down at her. She was curled on her side, her head resting on one arm. Her hair was loose on the pillow and above the low neck of her nightdress he could see the smooth line of her breasts. He pulled the blanket over her and then turned out the light.

Lying on his own bunk in the darkness, he listened to the sound of her light breathing. He was tired, his body stretched with fatigue, and there was a physical peace in him which he knew promised deep sleep. . . . But sleep wouldn't come. He lay in the darkness and in his mind, hearing her breathing, he saw another Kate. Slowly, against his will, the imagery became a bitter disturbance in him. The darkness was full of her, the brown arms and the soft swelling of her breasts, the shadowed moulding of her body, smooth and sweet running in lines of beauty . . . and with her was the shadow that during the day he could fight away. But tonight it wouldn't go. . . . It was in the cabin, unmoving, haunting his mind, vivid in his thoughts and fancies. It was like a poison in him, stretching his body to a tenseness . . . a bitter, jealous agony which he didn't want and hated himself for entertaining. But he was powerless against it. It provoked in him a frustration that left anger far behind, stirring a savageness and self-pity which he despised but could not conquer. . . . Someone else . . . somewhere, just once . . . but someone else. . . .

He got up, throwing back his blanket and left the cabin. He went up into the stern. Rigo slept under a little awning in the bows and he did not want to disturb him. He leaned over the stern rail, smoking, and fighting with himself. . . . This was the worst time he had known and he had to ride out a storm of jealousy and torturing, vivid thoughts.

There was no sound except the occasional slap of water alongside and somewhere very faint the call of an animal on the cliffs . . . a goat or a sheep. He leaned against the rail for a long time, unmoving, feeling his arms go stiff, his fingers clamped against the mahogany runner . . . not moving, letting the pain bite into him. Slowly the storm passed. . . .

* * * *

He was up early the next morning and went over the side for a freshener. Dressed, he felt in a better frame of mind. From the galley came the sound and smell of frying. Rigo had put out a couple of night lines and had been lucky. Kate was already busy on the fish.

She put her head out of the galley and called, "Five minutes!"

He saw her, her face bright and full of life, and suddenly the thing was gone. This was morning, things were moving. . . . What did he expect? There had to be the bad times, but they would get fewer and fewer.

He went down on deck, but as he made his way towards the galley he saw the Ermano boat coming out. Guido was rowing and a uniformed figure sat in the stern.

Kate coming out of the galley at this moment joined him and saw the boat.

"A visitor?"

"Looks like it."

Guido pulled alongside the ladder at the stern and the visitor came aboard. Guido stayed where he was, smoking.

Thorne knew the visitor. He was Colonel da Lapa of the Guarda Civil, a fresh-complexioned man of about fifty with a cherubic, baby-face made a little grotesque by a stiff moustache. He had dark wet eyes that looked as though they would smudge if he blinked.

He came up the deck to Thorne, holding a long cigarette holder aloft in one hand like a magician's wand. For all his bulk he seemed only to tap the deck boards with the tip of his toes as he walked. He bowed, smiling, to Kate.

"Good morning, Colonel," said Thorne. "You're a long way from Regano."

"Good morning, señor. I visit my district posts once a week. Last night I was in Puerto."

Regano was the town, about five miles inland, from which Puerto Regano took its name.

"And this morning, out here—very early."

The Colonel nodded and he looked around at the decks of the *Doria*.

"How on earth did they get her in here?"

"They could have been drunk. Can I offer you some coffee?"

"Thank you, no. I'm going back to have breakfast with Señor Manasco." He fitted a new cigarette to his holder and, walking towards the bows, went on, "You know Señor Manasco, of course?"

"Of course. He's refusing to let me use his road to get this cargo out."

"He has the right. The road is private property."

"But the cargo is almost public property. They want it for the new barracks and so on at Palma."

"It's an interesting point. But no concern of mine. You gave up your Tangier interests some time ago, I believe?"

"If I ever had any."

"Quite. There's a lot of smuggling around this part of the coast."

"I'm only interested in this cargo, Colonel."

The Colonel was looking down into the open fore-hold. The water had a thick scum of flour over it. Thorne knew that he hadn't come to the point of his visit yet. The Colonel had a mind like a corkscrew. He was known to be tortuous and obscure in his methods. Everyone respected him. A lot of people had found themselves in trouble because they had been unable to recognise a hint when he gave it.

"An interesting man, Manasco. Powerful, too. Not only in business, but in politics. The betting in Palma is that you won't get this stuff out in time—or at all."

"What do you think?"

"Well. . . ." Da Lapa shrugged.

"We shall get it to Palma," said Kate firmly. "You'll see."

Da Lapa smiled "I hope I do, Señora." He shook his head. "I don't like waste. It would be a pity if the cargo rusted away out here."

"There'd be no trouble at all if it weren't for that young man who brought you out here."

"Kate." Thorne put his hand on her arm gently.

"Well it's true!"

Da Lapa looked from Thorne to Kate and for a moment his face was full of sympathy. "I'm afraid, señora, I bring you more trouble." He looked then directly at Thorne. "You've made a bad enemy in Señor Manasco. I would advise you to settle with him."

He went up to the pile of sacks, picking his way carefully through the thin coating of sludge on the deck which was drying rapidly in the sun.

"Not on his terms," said Thorne sharply. "What does he think he is, a little king?"

"That's what he thinks, and that's what he is, señor." Da Lapa prodded one of the sacks with the point of a highly-polished riding boot. "It's a pity about this flour. It could have filled many a belly. What are you going to do with it?"

"Dump it overboard. It's no use to anyone."

The Colonel shook his head. He was looking past Thorne, to the beach and the Villa Ermano. "I can't allow that. The sacks will rot and split and all this stuff will be washed up along the beach. You can see what a mess it will make."

"The only thing I can see is that you've got out here pretty smartly to tell me that."

The Colonel shrugged his shoulders. "I have a duty to the public. This beach is used by tourists in the summer—we can't have it fouled with rotten flour."

Kate said, "The winter storms will get rid of it before then. And anyway—what tourists can come here? Manasco's closed his road."

"He will change his mind by next season, señora. And anyway the holiday people come round in boats."

Thorne didn't say anything. He knew what had happened. Manasco had a copy of the *Doria*'s cargo manifest. He knew the flour was aboard. He was going to make every delaying difficulty he could. Last night when the hatch covers had come off he must have watched them working, bringing up the sacks. He wondered how Colonel da Lapa had felt when he had the telephone call early in the morning. . . . Only a man like Manasco could have stirred him into such quick action. Maybe it was that which he sensed in the Colonel's manner, some resentment at being one of Manasco's pawns. When the string was jerked he had to dance . . . and da Lapa wasn't a man who liked to dance to other people's bidding.

"What do you want me to do with it?"

"It must be taken out beyond the mouth of the bay and dumped in the open sea."

"That'll take me days. I've only got the motor-boat."

"I realise that. I believe too, from the cargo manifest that there's more flour stored in the other hold. You'll have to dump that at sea, too."

"Blast Manasco!"

The Colonel smiled. "That's exactly what I said at six o'clock this morning. But one can't deny that the man has a strong sense of his public duty. The tourist trade is very important to us. . . ." He walked aft towards the ladder.

The Colonel paused at the head of the ladder. "I wish you luck, señor. Perhaps by some miracle you will bring this job off."

"You, I gather, don't believe in miracles."

"They don't happen very often, señor. And, even then, it is hard to tell which come from God and which are created by man himself."

He went carefully down the ladder and Guido helped him aboard. Watching them pull away Thorne was left with the impression that whenever Manasco needed a miracle and the Colonel's help to pull it off, he would get it.

Drinking coffee with Kate and Rigo, he said, "There's about thirty sacks up there. We can't get more than four or five in the motor-boat at a time. We'll have to manhandle them aboard. If we used the hoist and anything slipped a sack would go right through the bottom. It'll take days to clear them."

Kate grinned. "The boat will look like an uncooked pancake before you finish——"

"Damn the boat! It's the waste of time that counts."

He was angry, and the anger stiffened his stubbornness against Manasco. Well, there was nothing for it but to put his head down and go boring away.

They started after breakfast. The sacks, heavy with water still, had to be taken up on their backs, carried the length of the deck and then down the gangway to the motor-boat. A wet, floury slime trailed behind them. By the time they had three aboard the deck and the gangway steps were slippery and treacherous. Going down with the fourth sack, Rigo slipped and fell. Kate, watching, gave a cry of alarm. The sack hit the bottom of the ladder and burst in a pudgy mess. Rigo, falling, had just time to twist himself outwards and miss the stern of the motor-boat. A foot to the left and he would have broken his back on the boat.

He came back up the ladder, dripping with water. He

was grinning but his lips were tight. The fall had scared him. Nick sent him into the galley to get a glass of *fundador*.

"We'll never shift it this way," said Thorne grimly. "One of us will get smashed up." He walked back to the bows and the mass of sacks. He lit a cigarette and leaned over the side. On the beach Guido and Juana were running about in bathing costumes, throwing a large red ball to each other. The dog, Eduardo, was with them, barking and leaping. The noise of their laughter did nothing for Thorne's mood.

Kate came up alongside him.

"We could wait until dark, Nick, and then dump the lot over."

Thorne shook his head.

"Manasco would like us to do that. Then he'd get the Colonel to arrest us. That would be a fine delay——"

He stared down at the lashed timber baulks alongside. When he had first lashed them up he had considered the idea of towing the raft around to Puerto with the cargo on board but had quickly rejected it. Once loaded there would be little freeboard. Any kind of sea would wash over it. If once the cargo began to move and they lost trim there would be trouble. In addition the motor-boat would never be able to tow such an unwieldy arrangement against any current or wind. Just ferrying the stuff ashore was one thing, but to take it out to sea . . . no. Looking at it now he saw no reason why they shouldn't shift the sacks on it. It was not far out to the mouth of the bay. The trickiest job would be tipping the sacks overboard—and who cared if they lost trim? The sacks had got to go into the sea, anyway. A couple of trips would clear the sacks they had brought up from the forward hold. If he hadn't been so angry he would have thought of it before.

He turned to Kate, smiling. "All right, old girl. I think we've got an answer to Colonel da Lapa." He raised his head and shouted aft for Rigo.

*   *   *   *

He and Rigo went down on to the raft and checked over the lashings that held the timber baulks together. They strengthened some of them. There was going to be more strain hauling the raft out to sea than there would be just ferrying stuff to the beach.

Then they began the hard and dirty work of loading. The slimy, bursting sacks were manhandled into the hoisting net and then hauled up on the deck boom and swung outboard. The sacks were then lowered to the raft and he and Rigo went down and cleared them from the net for the next hoist. The afternoon was well on them before they had the raft loaded, but Thorne reckoned they had enough time to run it out and unload before darkness came.

They ran a couple of tow ropes from the motor-boat to each forward corner of the raft so that the strain would be taken up steadily and the raft not allowed to swing too much.

"All right, Kate," he said. "This is where you can do some real work. You get in the motor-boat. Rigo and I will be on the raft. We'll cast off and pole her away from the side. The moment we're clear and moving you start the motor and take up the strain. Head straight out and I'll tell you what to do when we're free of the bay. O.K.?"

Kate nodded and went down to the motor-boat while they dropped to the raft.

"Start the motor, but don't put her in gear until we're free and moving," Thorne shouted. He watched her swing the crank and the engine came to life.

"All right, Rigo."

One each end of the raft they slipped the lines holding her alongside and began to push her out with a couple of planks. Slowly the heavy raft began to edge away from the *Doria*. When there was a three-foot gap of water between the raft and the *Doria* Thorne turned and gave Kate the signal. He watched as Kate put her into gear. The engine note rose and the tow ropes began to lift from the water. Kate turned and looked anxiously backwards. Thorne waved her on. Kate opened the throttle.

"Not too much. Take it slowly!" Thorne shouted.

Kate turned again and shouted something to him but he could not hear her above the engine. The raft jerked as the full strain came on the ropes and it began to move. But before it had any real way on it there was an ugly grating noise from the motor-boat and the engine began to race wildly.

Thorne ran forward to the edge of the raft. He saw Kate look helplessly back at him.

"Shut off the engine!" he shouted. "Rigo——" he turned, but Rigo had anticipated him. He was in the water swimming with a line from the raft to the gangway. He climbed on to the ladder and bracing himself began to haul the raft in. Thorne picked up one of the tow ropes and pulled the motor-boat towards the raft.

"Shut off that bloody engine!" he shouted above the din.

Kate bent down and cut the engine.

"For Pete's sake, what the devil did you do?"

Thorne jumped aboard.

"But I didn't do anything, Nick. Only what you said."

"Something's up. She wouldn't race away in gear like that. Not with this load."

Five minutes later, with the raft firmly alongside again, they knew the worst. Rigo straightened up from the engine and he shrugged his shoulders dejectedly.

"What is it?" asked Thorne.

"The propeller shaft. Broken, señor."

"To hell with it!" Thorne snapped angrily, and then he saw Kate. She was watching them from the gangway steps. She looked miserable and near to tears. Catching his eye she said:

"Nick, I'm sorry. But I didn't do anything you didn't tell me to. . . ."

Before Thorne could answer, Rigo said, "It would have happened anyway, señora. Towing that water-logged lighter the other day must have opened up some flaw in the shaft. . . ."

"That's right," Thorne said. Kate's eyes were on him and he knew how she felt. No matter how annoyed he might be, it was nothing to do with her. He gave her a smile. "It's all right, Kate. Don't worry about it." He turned to Rigo. "How long will it take to fix?"

"Can't tell, señor, until I've opened her up. We'll have to beach her, too, to replace the shaft."

"Everything happens to us. Can you check it here?"

"Yes." Rigo began to ferret in a locker for his tools. "If it is a shaft, I can go back when it's dark for a new one. Tomorrow she can be beached."

"How long will it take to put a new shaft in?"

"Two hours. Six if we run into trouble. I'll have to go to Palma for one."

"That's cheerful. Well, there it is. . . ."

Kate was at the head of the steps as he came on deck. He took her arm and grinned ruefully. "This will make good news for Manasco."

"Nick, I feel awful."

"You don't have to, darling. If I'd been in the boat the same thing would have happened. Forget it."

And he wanted her to forget it. The whole thing was maddening enough without having Kate blaming herself unnecessarily.

"But I *was* in the boat. That's what's so bloody."

He put his hands under her armpits, turning her towards him and shaking her gently. Unexpectedly, there was a great tenderness and affection in him for her, so great that he was telling himself that he didn't care a damn about anything. Everything in the world could go wrong, but he would beat Manasco. Just that. He would beat Manasco and the thought was a swift intoxication of the spirit. He laughed at her. . . .

"Sure, you're clumsy and ham-handed on a boat. And things fall to pieces in your hands. But I don't care. I love you. And what's more we're going to beat Manasco. We're going to beat the tar out of him. And then, guess what?"

"Nick. . . . What's come over you?"

"Pigheadedness. I don't know. Call it what you like. But when we beat Manasco, I'm going to take my cut of the profits and my share in the business and we're going back to England—for good."

"Nick . . . you're. . . . To England?"

"Yes. Just that. So whenever you feel Manasco or the fates are against us, just think of that. It's a wonderful tonic."

She didn't say anything. He saw her eyes blink from the tears behind them. Then she reached up and kissed him. The next moment she was making for the cabin.

Half an hour later Rigo came aboard to report that the shaft had fractured a few inches inboard of the propeller sealing glands. That meant the boat would definitely have to be beached for the repair.

"Also, señor, I shall have to go to Palma to get a new shaft." They were sitting, the three of them, in the galley drinking coffee.

At the mention of Palma Kate said, "Why don't I go with Rigo? I can drive him down to Palma and back in our car. It'll save time. I could pick up the mail down there, too. There are various odds and ends of clothes we both need."

"I don't want you going down that valley in the dark. What about the dog?" Thorne frowned.

"The dog's kept to the house at night now," said Rigo. "It would be quicker for me to go to Palma by car than bus."

Thorne argued against it for a while, but he could see that this was something Kate wanted to do because she felt it was a definite help. Finally he gave way to her. She could sleep the night at the Margarita and they could both be off early in the morning.

As he rowed them ashore in the dark, he said to Rigo, "You keep away from the road going back."

"Don't worry, señor. I'll look after the señora."

On the beach he held Kate for a moment, his arms round her, and kissed her. Rigo was ahead waiting.

"Look after yourself, darling."

"I'll be all right, Nick dear."

She left him and he watched the two figures slide away into the darkness. He turned back to the boat, smiling. She wanted to help, but he guessed too she was anxious to get the mail . . . there would be letters from Julia. And clothes . . . they had come up here in a rush. A woman always wanted a stack of clothes, even to muck about on a boat.

*　　*　　*　　*

He was on deck, thinking about turning in, when he heard a rowing boat coming out. The strokes were slow and easy, and after a while he saw the drip of phosphorescence from the blades. . . . He leaned over the side and watched it crab around the raft and then come into the gangway.

Juana came up the steps, hesitated a moment and then, seeing the glow of his cigarette, came down the deck to him. She wore trousers and a sweater of some dark colour and in the gloom all he could see was the oval of her face. She came up to the rail and leaned against it a yard from him.

"What do you want?" After the disappointment of the motor-boat there was an apathy in him. It was late and he was too tired to show any feeling.

"Nothing."

"Just a social call?"

"Why not? I was bored. I wanted someone to talk to."

"You should carry a white flag. And anyway, the rest of your people mightn't like you to fraternise with the enemy."

She laughed. At this moment her manner was so devoid of any antagonism that he began to suspect that the girl with the shotgun, the girl with the dark defiance in her eyes sometimes found her part too intense. . . . Now and again she had to revert to this; a pleasant creature, young enough to overplay her moods . . . anxious to be considered adult;

someone whose company any man would welcome. Almost as though to prove him right, she said:

"Sometimes the people you fight are more interesting than the people you fight with. Anyway, they bore me tonight. They play chess together or talk business."

"So you came out here and risked being dropped over the side."

"You would do that?"

"Given the right circumstances."

"I might like it." And then when he didn't answer, she went on, "Where's Rigo and your wife?"

"They're around."

"I don't think so. I saw you come to the beach and they went off."

"I wonder you didn't set the dog after them."

"If I'd stopped them, I couldn't have come and talked to you. What is the matter with the motor-boat?"

"That's why you came?"

"No. I told you I was bored. But, naturally, I am curious."

"There's no harm in your knowing. The propeller shaft is broken."

"Bad luck."

He turned at that, facing her. She sounded as though she meant it.

She was close enough now for him to see the smile on her face.

"You didn't expect me to say that?" she asked.

"I never know what to expect from you. You have your own rules which you don't publish. I should have thought you would have been delighted."

"So I am—for us. But also it is bad luck for you. One can have sympathy for the matador and the bull."

"Which am I?"

"Oh, the bull."

"Thanks."

Just for a moment she almost giggled. Then, and he

could sense the direction she gave herself, she went back to being serious.

"You have strength. Yes, and intelligence, but you do not accept the idea of being killed . . . beaten. That is why, in many ways, I like you."

"You do? I should never have guessed it." He smiled to himself. What was she? Nineteen; perhaps twenty . . . it was a time when life could be serious; but when, to borrow from her metaphor, you had it by the horns, confident of your own powers. She wanted to impress him—and she was, touchingly, but hardly in the way she imagined.

"Yes, I like you—tremendously; even though I'm against you. Stubborn and wilful. You have no chance to win by yourself and yet you go on. . . . It is a wonderful thing to be like that, to believe that you can take the world in your bare hands and crack it apart. No woman ever believes that. . . ."

He smiled again in the darkness. He liked that. The 'No woman' bit. That's what she wanted to be, almost was . . . a queen out here, among the young men of her set. If she'd already had love affairs, and he thought it likely, then they would have come from this desire to be a woman, from a curiosity about being grown-up.

In this moment of darkness, with the night wind sliding over the still waters, she was showing a new aspect of herself and it attracted him. Given training and the right handling, he thought, she could have been turned into a reasonable creature.

"I don't know," he said keeping the amusement from his voice. "Cracking the world apart is quite a job."

"Very few men believe they can. But the ones that do. . . . Well, they are dangerous for themselves and other people, particularly for women."

He laughed. "Don't get me wrong. I'm not a world cracker."

"I don't think you know what you are." She paused and he could see she was watching him.

Then, with a touch of spirit which he had known before, she went on, "I think you're laughing at me."

"No," he lied. "What you say is very interesting . . . very. But don't you think you ought to go? I want to turn in."

"And if I don't go?" There was now a touch of coquetry, the dark ripple of a new understanding between them, in her voice.

"I'll drop you over the side."

She turned to move back along the deck. For an instant—and no man in the world, and maybe not Juana herself, could have said whether it was deliberate—her fingers brushed across his hand on the rail.

"I'm going," she said. "Some other time, perhaps, you'll have to drop me overboard."

He heard her laughing as she went down the darkness of the gangway to her boat.

Chapter Eight

HE was up at daybreak and rowed the motor-boat ashore, towing the skiff behind him. Driving a crowbar into the sand above the water mark as an anchor for the block and tackle, he hauled the boat out of the water stern first. There was nothing else he could do until Kate and Rigo returned.

Knowing that the *Doria* might rise and shift a little when they began to take the cargo out of her, he climbed along the southern flank of the bay and inspected the four rope hawsers that had been run out from her and made fast around rock pinnacles on the cliffs. They were secure and showed no signs of chafing.

Small lizards scattered over the hot rocks before him, and the wind made a gentle scything noise in the dry fronds of the bamboo growths that sprang up between the loose rocks. Looking back from the cliff he could see the Villa Ermano bathed in sunshine. There was the flash of a white tablecloth from the courtyard and he made out Manasco breakfasting alone. Beyond the villa was the long sweep back of the valley. He raised his eyes to the hills; the only movement on them was the slow pattern of grazing ponies and sheep. Above the grey tumble of crags that closed about the narrow gorge at the end of the valley there was an emptiness of sunworn blue sky. Watching it he saw the black fly-shape of a seaplane rise in the sky from the base at Puerto. Its drone was lost in the hum of insects around him. He sat there, tied to idleness, and was conscious of time running from him as though it were his energy and his life. Seven days had gone already and still they hadn't touched the cargo.

Knowing that to sit and think about it would do no good he went back to the beach and rowed out to the *Doria*. He wrote a letter to Julia in England. He covered the margin of his daughter's letter with small drawings to illustrate his doings aboard the *Doria* . . . and finished feeling a different man. For a time he had been in a child's world. Turning over the currency of his love for Julia made him feel solid and more splendidly endowed than he had done for a long time.

Towards midday a motor-boat came into the bay. In it were Johnny Manchester and Rigo. He stood at the bottom of the gangway and caught the boat as it came alongside. Kate wasn't with them.

"Where's the señora?" he asked.

Rigo handed him across Kate's suitcase.

"She brought me back from Palma. I've got a new shaft. She's stayed behind at the Margarita."

"What on earth for?"

"In Palma your partner told her he was going out to Porto Cristo to look at two lighters he heard about. He's going to phone her later today and let her know if they're any good. She thought you would want to know about them as soon as possible. My father can bring her out later, or tomorrow."

Johnny Manchester nodded silently in agreement. Then he looked towards the beach. "You are wasting your time, señor," he said.

"We'll see, Johnny," said Thorne.

"We shall, señor. All Manasco has to do is sit there and wait for you to admit it."

When Johnny left after a glass of *fundador*, Thorne pulled Rigo to the beach with his tools and they got to work.

After a time Rigo said, "You must not misunderstand my father. He wishes you to win—but he does not see how you can. Also, tonight we must not use the deck lights—he is taking the air."

"That's all right. If we get this fixed, we can take the first load out this afternoon and clear the rest tomorrow."

"Also, this evening, I shall work with him. They are a

man short." Rigo was stripped to the waist and wearing a pair of dirty canvas trousers. His mind and his hands were on his work, combining in that absorbed concentration which belongs only to people who love and understand engines, "Also, señor, there is something else . . . about us."

"Yes?"

Rigo, squatting on the stern boards, looked up and a smile flashed across his brown face as he raised a greasy hand and brushed back his dark curls. "You and I, we begin to make people talk. In Regano and in Palma. I do not think Señor Manasco likes it because he is not a man who wishes to be talked about."

"Whose side are they on?"

"Ours mostly, señor. But they will do nothing about it. Still, they are betting . . . it is something even that odds can be found." He straightened his back for a moment, flexing his shoulders so that the muscles slid under the skin like the imprisoned run of waves under an oily sea. "Even in Palma now they know my name. 'Rigo,' they say, 'the son of Johnny Manchester is with the Englishman.' My father, of course, is angry. It is not right, he thinks, for a man's name to be in too many mouths. . . ."

Thorne smiled to himself, liking the thrust of simple pride in Rigo, and knowing that he was lucky to have him.

From the far side of the beach by the spring came the sound of voices and laughter. Juana and Guido came down from the house with the dog. Thorne saw them go into the water and swim out, the dog going with them. They played about for a time and then came back to the beach. Guido went up to the villa with the dog, but the girl, a wrap over her shoulders, walked across the beach. When she was ten yards from them she dropped the wrap to the sand and sat down on it.

Thorne gave her a *buenos dias* and she nodded. Lying back on the wrap she put her hands behind her head and stared up into the sky. She lay there, long brown legs and arms sprawling, naked except for a flaring red scrap of bathing suit, and her silent presence was a provocation and embarrassment. Every time their eyes came up from work she was there.

It amused Thorne. He could appreciate the impulse that had brought her here . . . the need to exercise and prove her powers, to enjoy the disturbance she imagined her presence would bring to them. But with Rigo it was different. Juana made him clumsy, and angry. There was a frown on his face and he muttered when a spanner slipped and cursed when some part resisted his manoeuvring. Once he stopped work and stared angrily across at her.

"It is not right," he said loudly, "for a woman to show herself like that. It is forbidden by law."

Juana staring at the sky showed no sign that she had heard him.

Thorne touched his elbow. "Don't let her get you down. Forget her."

"How can a man forget what is beneath his eyes!"

Rigo spat.

For a second there was the faintest sound of laughter from the stretched-out girl.

A belt, thought Thorne, a flat leather belt, like the one his father had used, that would take the arrogance from her. Last night she had been amusing, touching. But as she lay there, idle, beautiful, charged with disturbance, Thorne felt she was a nuisance. She was making Rigo angry, and that was bad for their work. He decided he must do something about it.

He walked across to her.

She smiled up at him blinking her eyes in his shadow, and one leg came up, powdered with sand and flexing easily.

Pleasantly, he said, "Will you do me a favour?"

"You? But, of course."

"Then go away."

"Why?" The word was well-fed, plump and wrapped with a purr of satisfaction.

"Because—as you know—you're taking our minds off the job."

She sat up, looked from him to Rigo and then, still smiling stood up. He bent down and picked up her wrap and handed it to her. She didn't say anything. She took the wrap from him and her eyes were on him in the way they had been for a time at the end of their first meeting by the gate on the roadway, going over him, cataloguing the points of interest. He knew how she felt; warm with confidence in herself, her strength and the pleasure that came from the acknowledgment of her power. He had seen his daughter look like it when she had finally badgered him into buying her some frivolous present.

She turned and walked away.

As he came back, Rigo said, "I would not have believed it." His voice was full of respect.

* * * *

It was early afternoon before the motor-boat was finished. Without stopping for food, they took the raft tow lines aboard.

This time there was no mishap. The strain came up on the ropes and slowly the raft began to move out behind them. The sea was a little choppy but did no more than run a thin flood of water over the top of the timbers to wash away the loose flour sludge that had seeped from the sacks overnight.

Gradually they moved down the narrow gullet of the bay. As they met the open sea Rigo turned the boat's nose up into the wind which was blowing steadily from the north-west. He let the engine idle until the raft closed up astern and then Thorne jumped aboard. It was impossible for the two of them to work on the raft. While they did so it would have drifted before the wind back on to the coast behind them. Rigo kept the motor-boat going, beating up into the wind then easing off and letting the raft drift back some way before taking her up again and so maintaining their position.

Thorne began to slide the sacks overboard. Most of them sank at once but some that were split, spewed their fine mud of rotten flour. The sea was marked with a long stream of yellowish sediment, a light band against the gun-metal blue of the waves. As the raft lightened and found a new buoyancy it pitched and swung. Twice he slipped in the mess on the timbers and went over the side, but he wore only a pair of khaki shorts and there was no danger. It took him two hours to clear the load and at the end of that time he was exhausted. As Rigo wore the raft round and headed for the bay, Thorne flopped on the wet timbers and lay stretched out, his muscles aching. The flour was caked upon his body and clung between his fingers, clamping them together, and he smelt as though he had spent his whole life paper-hanging. He sat up and saw Rigo grinning at him.

"All right, Rigo," he shouted. "Your turn with the next lot."

But they didn't get far with the next lot. It was another hour before they had the raft back alongside the *Doria* for the second load. They would have time, Thorne reckoned, before the light went to clear the rest of the sacks from the fore-deck and have the raft loaded to run out first thing in the morning. Dumping the load at sea in darkness was too dangerous and, anyway, Rigo that night was going off to help his father with the smuggling run.

The first netload of sacks went over without trouble. But on the next load as they winched the net up from the deck the meshes tore away into a great hole and the sacks thudded back on to the deck. The net ropes, lying so long in the flooded hold, had rotted. It was nothing that couldn't be repaired and Rigo soon had some lengths of rope cut and was busy repairing the loading net. By the time he had finished the sun was down. They gave up and went over the side to clean the filth of flour from their hair and bodies.

With darkness Rigo took the skiff and rowed ashore. They had both eaten in the galley. Thorne watched him row away and then went up to the captain's saloon.

Kate hadn't turned up, and now that it was dark—and he knew Johnny Manchester was working that night—he guessed she would stay over at the Margarita. He couldn't really believe that Domingo would have any luck with the lighters. Still . . . you never knew.

He put a bottle of whisky on the table, and with the oil lamp lit, stretched out on the bunk, feeling as though he had lived most of his life on the *Doria* and saw little prospect of ever moving away from it.

There were some moments of solitude when it was a positive relief to drop your defences. Perhaps it was a good idea, so long as you kept it to yourself, to examine your weaknesses and now and again to take out the dusty little bundles of hopelessness for an airing. What was he doing out here really? Kate hadn't come back. There weren't going to be any lighters. He knew that. There was only the road. And how the hell could he ever get to use that? And yet here he was sweating away and, except for moments like this, never facing the fact that one day soon he was going to run slap up against a brick wall that no amount of pushing would knock down. He wished now that he hadn't said anything about going to England to Kate. That was a flash of wildness in him . . . the trouble was that she might build on it. It would be like her, too. He'd only said it because just then he had known how cut-up she'd felt about the propeller shaft . . . because he'd wanted to give her something else to think about. He reached for his glass, took a sip and coupled it with a silent toast to Manasco's damnation. . . . Damn him. He held all the cards. Idly, he wondered what his father would have done in a situation like this? He could guess. . . . *If you can't win by fair means, my boy; then do the other thing. But always be polite. Never forget you're a gentleman.* The old cynic. It could be that the old boy had enjoyed his many failures, liked to stand alone on the bridge and go down with the ship—and then swim ashore in the dark.

Somebody said, "Good evening."

E

Surprised, he slid his legs off the bunk and turned. Juana was standing in the cabin doorway.

Frowning, he said sharply, "What are you doing here?"

"Visiting. Don't look so cross."

He groaned to himself. He was in no mood to deal with her. He saw the rôle she'd cast for herself tonight, and he knew she would overplay it. Last night he had been amused. Tonight he wanted to be alone and enjoy a slight touch of dejection about his own affairs. . . . Damn the girl.

"I don't know that I want to be visited. And don't tell me that you rowed out here in that outfit."

"Of course." She smiled. "I only had to pull the skirt up above my knees a little." As she spoke she pulled at the tight green skirt sketching a demonstration, and before it fell he caught the flash of her nylons and the shapeliness of her legs. "Do you like it?" She swung around gently so that he could see the dress.

He had to admit that, however, she might play the part, she looked it. *Femme fatale* . . . some conception of herself concocted from too much cinema, or too much imagination and time on her hands . . . but she was certainly looking more woman than girl. It was a close-fitting green silk dress that seemed to make her taller, that gave her a dignity and a maturity which she needed. Her arms and shoulders were bare, and her hair was held with a half-circlet of some sparkling diamanté band, and from the embrace of the dress' bodice her breasts curved in a beautiful brown smoothness. "Do you like it?" she repeated.

"Yes, I do," he said truthfully, "but it's not what I would recommend for salvage work. Also, I think you should go back."

"But I've only just got here." She came across to the cabin table, moving slowly like a cat, smiling, and obviously enjoying the physical rhythm of her legs and body under the gown. He caught the fragrance of her scent. He and

Domingo Peroni had a small line in cheap cosmetics and he knew this was well above their class.

She put out a hand and touched his glass.

"Is this whisky?"

The movement brought her head forward and he saw the gloss laid on her hair by the cabin light and for the first time noticed that she had a white Spanish shawl held in one hand.

"Yes," he said. He didn't feel strong enough to cope with her. If she were bored at the villa why didn't she find someone else to plague. In Puerto there was a reasonable café society . . . why didn't she find a young man there to fascinate? He didn't feel that this was his evening to fascinate easily. "Why don't you go home? Your uncle would give you hell if he knew you were out here."

"Would he?" She picked up his glass. "Can I taste it? I've never had whisky."

"Look," he said deliberately. "I don't want to be rude, even though you're a Manasco. But I don't want you here."

She drank a little of the whisky and then made a face. "It's terrible. How can you drink it?" She put the glass down and he saw the mark of her dark lipstick on the rim. With the movement of her arm with the glass, she came round the table and sat at his side. "And don't keep telling me to go home. Your wife isn't here and Rigo is with his father tonight. Do you know why Rigo is helping you?"

She picked up his cigarette case and helped herself. He found himself holding a match for her.

"Because," he said harshly, "he doesn't like living in someone else's pocket. Like me he doesn't take kindly to being kicked around." What did he have to do? Throw her out. And the girl was a fool anyway. She had a brand new armament of women's weapons from Nature and she was playing around with them without a thought of safety. A man could start off by being amused or annoyed . . . but that neck and bosom, the long, shapely legs and the body that belonged no longer to a child could make the blood hot.

Juana laughed. "If he said that he's a liar. I'll tell you why. We were children together. Rigo, Guido and myself. Always together, swimming, fishing and boating. Then we grew up and he thought it would be the same. . . ." She looked sideways at him, her eyes sparkling, the dark red mouth for a moment partly open and touched with provocation, ". . . he thought we could share other things together. He wanted to make love to me. So he had to be told that he was a fisherman's son and sent away. That is all—and for that he hates all the Manascos. Simply because he hates the truth about himself."

Thorne leaned back against the bunk. He really was angry with her now. "You've no idea how pleased you sound," he said and he didn't disguise the hint of contempt in his voice. But it didn't touch her.

"If I'm pleased, it's because I'm here with you." Her hand dropped on his. Somewhere at the back of his mind a voice was crying furiously, "Somebody ought to teach her a lesson."

"You talk too much," he said sharply. "What are you looking for, trouble?"

"Trouble?" She gave the word a new meaning, and she laughed. "If you call it that. I like talking to you. I like being with you. If it's the truth, why shouldn't I say it?"

"You don't even begin to understand what truth is. The truth about yourself. Everything is a wonderful game to you. Now—we've had our little dose of philosophy—will you please go home?"

"When you're cross I like you even more. That's the truth. Whatever you feel is the truth. . . ." She looked in front of her, absorbed by her own romantic convictions, deep in her part. "Whatever you feel. Whatever you want. That's what truth is. That's why I'm here. I want to know —what is the truth about you, Nick?"

He didn't know whether he was more weary or more angry. He was between something. *What is the truth about you, Nick?* Even in a third-rate film it was a speech that would fall with a thud. . . . And yet, oddly, somewhere it touched him, somewhere far away it amused him and brought back a flash of liking for her.

"The truth about me is that I'm sleepy and want to go to bed."

At once he knew he had done no good. Her face softened, came close to him and he could see the moist shine on her lips.

"You're tired," she said gently and she raised her hand and laid it flat against his cheek, caressing him, and her other hand came out and took one of his. He felt the movement of her fingers against his skin, on his face. And her other hand was warm in his, small, curled, and moving gently. Abruptly he was aware that his fingers were entwined with hers, mastering hers. . . .

He stood up suddenly, gripping her by the arms and pulling her up, too.

"You're being a fool," he said. "You're asking for trouble. . . ."

"You're shaking me. . . ."

"You want to be shaken," he said roughly. "You want the nonsense shaken out of you." He dropped his hands from her.

She stood close to him and he saw her body stirring with her breathing. She smiled and in a quiet, submissive voice said:

"Why do you pretend you don't understand? There's nothing wrong about it. It doesn't matter what there is between you and my uncle. That has nothing to do with me. I have my own life to live. . . ."

He was angry then, the fury in him flashing into the open, shocked into violence and confusion.

"Go away! Go home—you're crazy!" He began to pull at her arm, but even as he shouted she moved to him. The warmth of her body was inside his arms and her mouth for a moment clumsily on the side of his face, and then on his lips. The anger which had wanted to reject her was unexpectedly an exultant traitor in him and he was crushing her, feeling the movement of silk and flesh under his hands. He wanted to push her away but she clung to him, her mouth now soft and seeking against his; and the power of her lips on his, the sweetness of her body in his arms loosened a response in him which he could not subdue. His hands were on her bare shoulders and she raised her head and smiled at him and her body stirred with a long sigh. He saw her eyes blurred with emotion and her lips parted as she called his name.

He wanted to push her away, to throw her from him, but his arms held her. He felt her hands move about his neck and his lips came down to hers. As they kissed the cabin seemed filled with a great silence, holding them immobile, locked together. . . . And then into the stillness, beating through to him, forcing itself upon him came a distant laboured throbbing. Suddenly his mind was cleared by an anger, swift and comprehending.

He flung her away from him. She staggered back against the table and dropped awkwardly to the floor. He looked down at her, cramped against the table, a heap of green silk and brown flesh, the yellow lamplight gleaming on the long length of her nylons as her legs sprawled across the floor.

"You clever devil," he breathed. "You——"

He stepped over her and ran for the door. The noise he had heard was that of a motor-boat labouring seawards. And he'd thought she was an impressionable girl playing with fire. . . .

Behind him he heard her shout something, but the words were lost to him.

*   *   *   *

He raced along the length of the deck to the stern. The motor-boat he could hear was no part of Johnny Manchester's smuggling party. It was too early for that.

At the bottom of the gangway the Villa Ermano skiff was tied up. But the timber raft and his motor-boat had gone. Far down the bay he could hear the labouring noise of the engine. For a moment he thought he could make out the dark bulk of the raft against the star-sprinkle of light on the water. While Juana had been with him others had cut the raft free and eased her out. When they were well free of the *Doria* they had started the motor, keeping her throttled right down until they judged there was no danger of being caught.

He jumped into the skiff and slipped the painter free. He pulled her round with a great boil of water under the blades of the oars and, bending his back to it, sent her racing towards the sea. She was light and she was fast. The motor-boat and raft couldn't make much speed—but already they were well on their way down the bay. Once at sea he knew what would happen. The raft lashings would be cut and the great timbers drift away on the current. But worse than that, the motor-boat would be piled up somewhere on the coast. Another raft could be made from the timbers over the after-hold, but another motor-boat . . .! He swore savagely as he pulled. He could imagine the scene next morning. . . . Manasco and Guido blank-faced at his protests. Was it their fault if his raft and motor-boat had broken free from faulty moorings and drifted out to sea and destruction? *Mala suerte, señor.* And now clear out.

Like hell, he would!

The running ripples of the sea smacked at the bows of the skiff with impatient hands. Above the suck and knuckly drive of the oars against water and rowlocks he heard the thin, lonely cry of a seabird somewhere over on the far cliffs. Two lights showed shoreward. The pale slip from the *Doria's* saloon and a brighter light from the villa. He kept position by them. Through a light drift of cloud a few stars weakened the flat black metal of the sky. The chafe of the oars rubbed rawness into his palms and the muscles of his shoulders cracked each time he came back for his stroke. Ahead of him the engine noise rose higher. Looking round he saw clearly for an instant the black loom of the raft a good three hundred yards ahead. Like a cold hand on his hot face he felt the sudden touch of the seawind as he cleared the point of the bay. At the same time he heard the engine sound die. The silence put new energy into him. The drive of the skiff, biting now into a slow swell, drove cold fans of water back from the bows over his shoulders.

They didn't see him until he was almost on the raft. He swung into it broadside, shipping his port oar. He recognised Guido and the manservant from the villa. They were at the corner of the raft furthest from the motor-boat, cutting away at the lashings. One great timber on the outside of the raft was already free except for the lashing at the fore-end.

The manservant shouted a warning to Guido and came across the wet timbers to prevent Thorne boarding. He came cautiously, awkwardly across the slippery baulks, a knife in his hand. As he reached the edge of the raft Thorne rose in the skiff which bumped alongside and, grabbing an oar, swung it in a low arc. It crashed against the man's thigh and sent him rolling across the timbers.

Thorne jumped aboard and lurched across the swaying platform towards Guido. The young man saw him coming but went on cutting away at a lashing until Thorne was within three yards of him. Then he straightened up and knife in hand came for him. He was shouting and swearing and his face was twisted into ugliness. He jumped at Thorne, striking wildly with the knife. It was all so inexpert and abandoned that it was almost with reluctance that Thorne hit him. But hit him he did to avoid the knife. He slapped him brutally on the side of the face, saw the knife jerk from the right hand and fly into the darkness. As the young man fell he knew that Guido was drunk. For a second, before the sea air shredded it away, the odour of brandy was about him.

The pitch of the raft threw Guido forward. As he slid over the edge into the water, the manservant shouted something from behind Thorne. He turned to find the man rushing at him, knife raised. As the blade flashed downwards Thorne sidestepped and smashed his fist into the side of the man's face. He swayed backwards and fell, spreadeagled against the small pile of sacks in the centre of the raft. The knife was still in his hand.

Thorne went forward and stood over him.

"Throw the knife away," he ordered. "Throw it away, or, by God, I'll come in and smash you!"

The man hesitated and then with a slow movement he pitched the knife into the sea.

Thorne turned. Guido in his fall had slid over the edge of the raft and was now clinging to the end of the great timber which had scissored loose from the after end of the raft. The timber baulk began to swing back towards its fellows. As the gap closed there was danger that Guido could be crushed between them.

"Señor, please. He is——"

"I know. Drunk."

Thorne went to the edge of the raft and waited for the timber to swing in. He stopped it with his foot and bent down and caught Guido by the shoulder. The young face turned up to him was frightened and absurdly pathetic.

"I should let you crush and drown," said Thorne contemptuously. "You know why, don't you?" He shook him, holding him still half in the water. "You lied to your uncle, didn't you? You started all this trouble because you haven't got the guts of a louse!"

"Señor, he doesn't know what you say . . ." the man-servant pleaded.

Guido's face was white, his eyes closed.

"He knows. He just won't face it!"

Suddenly Thorne was too tired and disgusted to bother with him. He dragged the boy out on to the timbers. Guido lay there, panting, his face hidden in the crook of his arm.

"Keep an eye on him," said Thorne to the servant. He went forward, hauled on the tow rope and brought the motor-boat alongside the raft. He climbed aboard, started the

engine and brought the raft around, heading back for the
Doria, steering by the distant villa light. He didn't bother
about the Ermano skiff. If they wanted it they could search
for it tomorrow.

He looked back once or twice. Guido was sitting up now
and the servant stood alongside him.

When they were almost abeam of the *Doria* he cut the
engine and beckoned to the manservant. He came shambling
forward and stood a few yards from him on the end of the
raft.

"All right," said Thorne. "Get over the side, both of you,
and swim ashore. He can manage it now."

Momentarily, the man began some protest, half words,
half gesture, but Thorne, hard with contempt for them both,
cut him short.

"Get over, or I'll come across and sling you in."

He watched the man go back to Guido, heard Guido's
voice rise and then saw the man urge him forward. A moment
later he saw them slip into the night sea and heard them
going back in a splashing, clumsy progress towards the
beach.

He had a little trouble manoeuvring raft and motor-boat
alongside the *Doria*, but finally it was done. As he stood on
deck making the last line fast to the deck rail he thought he
heard the sound, away in the darkness towards the beach, of
oars against rowlocks. Johnny Manchester's party, he told
himself.

He went forward to the captain's saloon. He was tired
and against his anger there was not even a flush of warmth
from his victory. At the cabin door he remembered Juana.
He had taken her skiff. There had been no way for her to get
off the *Doria*.

He jerked open the door. She stood in the centre of the
cabin. There was no smile now. No fear, either, for there
was nothing of Guido's weakness in her.

In a steady voice she said, "Yes, it was to help Guido
that I came aboard. That's how it began——"

"I don't want to listen!"

"But you must. Everything's changed. I didn't know it would but it has. If you wanted it now, I'd help you, even against my uncle——"

"Get out!" She had courage, she had a whole heap of things; she had too much perhaps, but he wanted none of her.

"But Nick—you must see——"

"Out!" He jerked his head to the door behind him.

"Don't be so angry, Nick."

"What the hell do you expect me to be? Get off this boat."

"How—in the motor-boat? There's no skiff. I saw you come back."

"I don't care a damn how. Swim!"

She drew her head up, a movement that reinforced all the arrogant strength in her, and coldly she said, "You will take me in the motor-boat." It was an order, intimidating, wiping away all suggestion of guilt or shame.

He was on her so quickly that she had no time to defend herself. He caught her wrists, spun her round and then she was in his arms as he lifted her from the ground. She fought and struggled, swearing at him. He carried her through the door and to the deck. She tried to bite at his shoulder, but he smothered her against him. Clamping his arms about the kicking, leaping protest of her body he went steadily up the foredeck until he stood in the high flaring bows. The struggle between them now was silent except for the driving sound of her breath as she fought against the binding pressure of his arms. A shoe clattered to the boards as she threshed with her legs. Then, as he shifted his arms, bracing himself to lift and drop her, he felt the fight go from her. Her face came back from his shoulder and she was suddenly laughing, the vibration moving through her body and into his. Before he could avoid them her lips came up and kissed his.

He jerked her from him over the rail, conscious for a

second of the wide flung shawl, and the flesh of legs bared from her worked-up skirt. Her laughter was killed by the sound of the splash.

He turned away from the rail and stood there for a moment, his eyes shut against the fatigue in him.

When he opened them it was to see Kate standing on the deck a few yards from him, her figure outlined in the light from the saloon window.

"Kate," he said in surprise. "How did you get here?"

"After I got Domingo's message—the lighters are no good by the way—I walked out."

"You shouldn't have risked that."

"It was quite safe. Our boat was on the beach, so I rowed out. Things seem to have been happening."

"Yes, they have. . . ."

"Our friend Juana appears to have taken a liking to you. Is that the only way you could get rid of her?"

"Yes." He smiled, going forward and putting his hands on her shoulders and kissing her. "Yes, it was. . . . That girl is strictly from the devil."

His voice was abruptly harsh and he saw Kate look quickly at him.

PART TWO

Chapter Nine

LYING on her bunk Kate watched the moving reflection of sunlit water break and shimmer in mother-of-pearl patterns on the ceiling of the saloon. From the other bunk came the heavy breathing of Nick sleeping. It was a good sound to hear, reassuring and familiar, touching a tenderness in her.

She turned on her side. She could see the hunch of his shoulders and a small tear in the red-and-white striped pyjama jacket below the arm. His hair was tousled against the pillow, and a patch of sunburnt neck showed above the rumpled pyjama collar. Through the window the first sun rays were on the hills. The tight growths of green running down the gullies were like stubble against the grey-gold rocks. Except for Nick's breathing there was a lazy silence everywhere.

She sat up on the bunk, hugging her arms around her knees. A stub of cigarette marked with lipstick caught her eye from the ashtray on the table. The lipstick was dark, much darker than she used. She got out of bed, found her handbag and began to run a comb through her hair. She smiled to herself as she remembered Nick tossing Juana overboard. She deserved it, too. Nick had told her how the girl had come aboard and kept him in talk so that Guido could get away with the raft.

She realised suddenly that Nick was awake and watching her. He grinned, the long, hard face breaking into familiar creases around the eyes and mouth. For a moment she managed to see him dispassionately; just as a man, and an attractive one, too . . . that hard, self-contained assurance, and the sudden flash of a smile. Sun-bitten, a feeling of strength about him; not a man to be overlooked.

"You look pretty serious," said Nick lightly. "What are you thinking about?"

He reached out with his hand and pulled her down alongside him, slipping his arm round her waist and squeezing the flesh of her hip.

"Breakfast," she said.

"Good. . . ."

"It's a pity about the lighters. . . ."

"Never mind," he shrugged.

"Domingo said they just wouldn't have stood up to being towed around."

"That's why Manasco didn't bother with them. You know, Kate, you shouldn't have come up that valley alone at night. Lucky for you it was a smuggling night and the dog wasn't out."

"I wanted to get back." She smiled. "I'm not trusting you alone out here with girls like Juana."

Before Nick could answer there was a shout from the shore. Through the forward sweep of glass Kate saw Rigo standing on the beach.

"It's Rigo."

"I'll go and fetch him," said Nick. He swung himself off the bunk and stripped off his pyjama jacket.

She followed him to the sunlit deck and watched him go down the gangway to the skiff which she had brought out from the beach the previous night. He pulled away strongly from the *Doria* and raised his hand to her for a moment. She turned and went towards the galley.

*   *   *   *

The day passed uneventfully. During the morning she rowed the skiff ashore to fetch fresh water. As she went in Juana came down the beach and swam out. Looking back Kate saw the girl lying on her back, floating just abreast of the *Doria*.

As Kate came back Juana swam round to the starboard

side of the cargo boat and climbed out on to the rocks at the foot of the cliff. She sat there for half an hour sunbathing and watching the work going on aboard.

In the afternoon, when the last of the flour sacks from the forward hold were towed out to sea, Kate took the wheel of the motor-boat. This meant that both Nick and Rigo could work on the raft, pitching the sacks overboard. This saved time and she was pleased that she should be doing something to help directly in the job.

The next morning Nick said he had to go to Puerto to pick up some pieces of shaped angle-iron which Rigo had asked his father to make. They wanted them to fit up the raft so that they could haul it to and from the beach when they began to unload the cargo.

Anxious to help, Kate said, "I could go, Nick. It would save you a lot of time."

"But can you handle the boat?" he asked dubiously.

"Of course. The sea's quite calm. It's no more than driving a car. I handled it yesterday with the sacks, didn't I?"

"Well. . . ."

"It would save time, señor," said Rigo.

"All right—but you keep an eye on it all the time," warned Nick.

Nick stood at the bottom of the gangway holding the boat's painter, ready to let go. With the engine ticking over gently she looked up at him and nodded. He smiled and winked at her, standing there in dirty old trousers and a grease-marked singlet.

"And keep well clear of Cabo de Perada if there's anything like a wind going. Going round you want plenty of sea-room."

She waved, moving away from the *Doria*, smiling to herself. No man completely trusted any woman with anything that held an engine.

Going out she looked back to see them already at work on the great timber baulks over the after-hold. The previous evening they had decided to clear the covers of the timber and dump the flour from the after-hold before they started in on ferrying the cargo from both holds to the shore.

It was pleasant going round. She had nothing to do except steer and this left her mind free for thought. She found herself comparing her attitude and Nick's toward this job.

Normally Nick kept his business affairs to himself. She had no head for that kind of thing. Over this job, until now, she had simply gone along with him. He might talk about breaking down brick walls, but she knew he was not fool enough to charge headlong at one. What had he got in mind? So far as she could see he could never succeed. This was cold, hard logic. He would get as far as having the cargo on the beach—and then what? He must have asked himself this question. She would have done, and then, finding no answer, would have argued that there was no point in going on. It was like mixing up a cake in the kitchen, getting it all ready for the oven, and knowing all the time that there was no oven, no way of baking it. What on earth was Nick going to use for an oven? So far she hadn't asked him, sensing that he didn't want the question asked by anyone yet. It was really illuminating to stand back and look at Nick as other people might look at him, and decide that he was crazy . . . butting his head against a brick wall. He couldn't be such a damn fool. . . . Surely some part of his mind had faced this problem and found an answer, no matter how wild, something that at least for the time being kept the question quiet?

She anchored in the little harbour and got a boy to row her ashore. She picked up the angle-irons from Johnny Manchester, did some shopping, and then had lunch at the Hotel Margarita. After lunch she called Domingo Peroni in Palma. There was a chance he might have found some other lighters. He was out until three, the girl in the office told her. She waited around, filling in the time by writing a letter to Julia. At three she called Domingo again. She told him how things were going at Agua Gelida. Now and again she heard Domingo sigh, and when she had finished, he said:

"Well, Kate, we shall lose our money. I blame myself. If I'd known it was Manasco's toes I was going to step on! People talk to me down here as though I'm off my head."

"Nick will think of something."

"I hope so. If Nick wants more money, let me know."

Back at the motor-boat she found she couldn't start it. She tried for half an hour and then gave it up, wishing she understood more about engines. In the end she got herself rowed ashore again and went round to Johnny Manchester's garage. He wasn't there. He was at Regano, the island town five miles away.

"He will be back soon," said his wife, and she brought out sherry and cake for Kate. But it was gone six o'clock before Johnny got back. Kate was full of impatience. It was over a two-hour run back and she could never do it before dark now. She knew that Nick would be worried. Johnny walked down to the harbour as though he were a tree, dragging a great trail of roots behind him. She wanted to take his arm and hurry him along.

Rowing out, he said, "When you came in and went ashore—did you switch off the petrol?"

"Did I have to?"

Johnny grinned. "But of course."

"But on a car you don't."

Johnny laughed. "On a boat with a gravity feed supply you have to switch off the petrol separately . . . like a motor cycle."

"Then they should have told me!"

"It is difficult for a man to foresee everything where a woman is concerned."

The engine was flooded with petrol. Johnny cleared it and soon had the motor going.

"You would like me to go round with you? It will be dark soon."

"No, thank you, Johnny. I can manage."

There was the light at the end of the cape and she only had to run down the coast until she saw the deck lights. She knew they were going to work on that evening.

It was dark by the time she was round the point and running down to Agua Gelida there was a sea going which sent the spray inboard, soaking her. Her jumper and trousers were soon wet through and she was cold and unhappy.

It was a relief when she saw the deck lights of the *Doria* marking the entrance to the bay. As she came in she saw that they were working on the timber baulks. She throttled the motor back and the sides of the *Doria* were black cliffs in the shadow of the flaring arc-lamps.

Nick ran to the rail and shouted:

"Keep off!"

A timber was balanced on the rail and they were just about to drop it over. She circled away. The timber dropped with a great crash into the sea and jets of gold and black water spouted into the air. Rigo came down the gangway as she brought the motor-boat in. He slipped into the water and swimming to the baulk began to unship the rope from its end. Nick followed him down the gangway and caught the bows of the motor-boat.

"Where the hell have you been?"

His voice was hard, releasing his anxiety with a furious note.

"It's all right, Nick. I got held up——"

"Damn it, you've had us imagining all sorts of things! And then coming back in the dark. . . ."

He twisted the painter round the steps, making it fast with an angry jerk. He reached out and helped her aboard, his fingers gripping her arm.

"I'm sorry, Nick."

"You don't know enough about boats or this coast to be out in the dark!"

She ought to have known that the anger in him was from

anxiety; but meeting it, full of relief herself at getting back, acknowledging now that she had been frightened out there, she resented it.

"What were you worried about—me or the boat?" And the moment she had said it she wished she hadn't.

"Don't be a damn fool, Kate." He pushed her up the steps ahead of him. "Go and get changed. You're wet through."

At the top of the steps she halted, looking back to him. His anger was quick and meant nothing. Of course he'd been anxious for her. She wanted to say something to put herself back with him. But he was standing by the boat still, looking towards Rigo. She heard him call:

"All right, Rigo. Shove her out so that she lies in line with the others off the stern. We'd better make her fast, too. I'll throw you down a lashing."

He turned and came swiftly up the steps and she saw the sweat gleaming on his shoulders and neck. He paused by her. For a moment his smile showed and a hand touched her bottom in a swift pat. "You're wet through. Go and get changed. And we're hungry. I'll bring the stuff up from the boat."

He was by her and hurrying into the stern to throw a lashing down to Rigo. She went into the saloon and began to strip, shivering and feeling miserable. Nick's anxiety had been open and frank, but she saw now that she too had her own anxiety and it could betray her. She was over-anxious for things to be right between herself and Nick and she was too quick to resent any suggestion that they weren't. Rubbing herself with a rough towel, feeling the warmth coming back to her body, she told herself scornfully that she ought to have her head examined. *Me or the boat, which were you anxious about?* From a girl of nineteen full of the need always to hear—*I love you. I love you. You mean everything* —it would have raised a smile. But in a woman of her age, married as long as she. . . . Well, it was sheer sloppiness.

There was a step behind her. She swung round to find Nick standing inside the door. He grinned, then reached out and picked her up, bundling her nakedness to him so that she could feel the warmth of his body and smell the clean work-sweat on him. His face came down so that his lips were hard against her breasts. She laughed and struggled and he dropped her on to the bunk, throwing a blanket at her.

"Me or the boat . . ." he mimicked her. Then, in his own voice, he said as he moved to the door, "You get the supper going, and afterwards I'll show you."

*   *   *   *

In the middle of the following morning she went ashore to fill the two water cans. She rowed in close to the spring outlet so that she would not have far to carry the cans. The morning was golden and the air warm and a soft lacquer of faint heat haze lay over the hills. The beach was empty.

She filled one can and, leaving the other under the outfall, she carried it back to the boat. As she came back she saw the manservant from the villa standing on the small cliff above the spring.

He watched her come up to the spring, a plump, thickset figure, his shadow hard-cut across the damp yellow sands.

"Señora Thorne?"

"Yes."

"The compliments of Señor Manasco. Would you be kind enough to come up and have a glass of sherry with him?"

She didn't answer right away. Why should she go to Manasco? If he had anything to say to her he could come and find her. But as she thought it, she knew that it was a reflection of Nick's attitude, masculine and stubborn. She was on Nick's side, but that didn't mean she couldn't be herself. Both these men had taken a stand dictated by pride. Where did she stand? She put up a hand and touched her hair, which was drawn back for working convenience into a ribbon-tied knot at the back of her head. And with a touch of inner amusement she knew she had her pride, too.

A man's appearance meant nothing. Nick would have strode up covered in grease and wanting a shave and been unworried by the thought that he might meet Juana in the courtyard. For her, appearance was a weapon, and she knew that if Juana were there she would want the girl to concede, no matter how reluctantly (in fact, the more reluctantly the more telling), the fact that Señora Thorne even out here had something which men couldn't overlook. Nick would have laughed like a drain if she had said that to him. But she didn't care. Well, no one could fault her blue-and-white striped beach trousers and the loose blue jersey.

She nodded and climbed to the top of the slope.

Both Juana and Guido were in the courtyard. Guido was stretched out on a rug reading a magazine, his heels in the air. Juana sat on the edge of the fountain and she was grooming Eduardo the black Alsatian with a steel comb. Little clumps of loose hair lay on the paving stones alongside her. Juana gave her a little nod as she passed.

The servant led her into the house, through a long cool hallway and then down a narrow flight of steps to a thick oak door. He knocked. A voice called to them to enter.

It was a long room, cut, Kate saw, from the soft rock of the hillside, and full of green gloom and golden cones of light over a billiard table. Manasco was at the far end of the table where he had been playing by himself.

He came forward, like some old dwarf priest, she thought, the cue in his hand his rod of office, and this room, cut into the hill, a cave where the elaborate rites to the gods of money and power were carried out by him alone. He offered her sherry or coffee and she decided for sherry.

As the manservant went out, Manasco lifted his glass of Tio Pepe to hers and they drank. Over his glass he was watching her, missing nothing and building up, she guessed, some impression which she would dearly have loved to share. What was more fascinating than knowing how other people saw you?

He said "I should have understood if you had refused

to come, señora. But I am glad you did." His free arm waved towards the long, leather-covered bench that ran the length of the room. As she sat he offered his cigarette case.

Kate said, "Somebody has to behave in a reasonable manner around here." But she was careful not to let too much ease and friendliness slip into her voice.

He laughed, lighting her cigarette and then stepped back and leaned against the table.

"It's a woman's point of view. And one I applaud. I am anxious to be reasonable. Do you like living in Spain?"

"Not particularly."

"You'd like to go back, maybe . . . to England?"

"Yes."

"It is understandable." Before she was really comfortably on terms with the shift in the conversation he twisted away from it and started a fresh line. "I asked you here, because through you I wish to thank your husband for looking after Guido the other night. You heard about it, of course?"

"I did. But why not thank him directly?"

"He's a difficult man to thank . . . to approach, even."

"You're as much to blame for that as he." She thrust and to herself was saying, *Don't wriggle little man. Come to the real point.*

"I admit it. We are both loyal, both proud and both stubborn. We oppose one another but it doesn't alter the fact that we respect one another. Some people would find that incongruous. Guido, for instance. He has much to learn."

"He's a small, bad-tempered boy who breaks windows and runs."

Manasco smiled and shrugged his shoulders. "In time he will learn to break things and stand. Your husband intends to ferry the cargo ashore?"

"Yes."

"And after that?"

She chose bluntness, knowing it would draw him unless

he was so tortuous he should decide that she was lying to
cover Nick's plans.

"I do not know."

"I am not surprised. There is nothing he can do after
that. You recognise that, of course. That also is why I
asked you to come and talk to me. I am willing to make him
a fresh offer. I will buy him out, covering every expense
he has incurred so far."

Kate stood up.

"No profit?"

Manasco stirred, raising the cue delicately and half
turning to put it on the table. With his face from her he
said quietly, "No profit."

As his face came back, dark-shadowed by the great cone
of light behind him, Kate smiled. "Señor Manasco," she
said, "you know my husband will never agree to that."

He came forward and filled her empty glass and the
shadow of a bow accompanied his handing it to her.

"Men change their minds, señora."

"Why bother to make an offer? According to you Nick
can never succeed. All you have to do is wait."

"It could be, señora, that I wish to be kind . . . to you
and to him."

"It could be, too, that you are a little uncertain of
yourself. You begin to wonder whether he might not
succeed?"

"It is impossible." Manasco smiled.

Kate put down her glass. "That remains to be seen."

Manasco's blue eyes blinked behind his glasses.

"Think about it, señora. On the whole women are more
sensible than men. You have influence with your husband
obviously. You might be able to persuade him not to cut off
his nose to spite his face. For his sake, and yours, I advise
you to try."

Kate began to move towards the door. "You know I shall
tell him about this?"

"Of course. Perhaps he will see how hopeless his position

is. I really want to help him. I shouldn't be taking this trouble to try and spare him from making a fool of himself otherwise."

Her hand on the door, Kate said firmly: "That could be. But I think that you are frightened of him—that you think he might beat you."

Manasco bowed, and smiled.

"You are very wrong, señora. I am frightened of no one. My bank balance is too big."

"Lucky man." She was surprised at the sudden tartness in her voice.

Manasco moved slowly towards the door. "A woman has influence with a man who loves her. She should use it for his good when the moment comes."

He sounds, Kate thought, just like some doddering old family doctor, telling me not to worry, that the pain will pass, that in a week I shall be back to sparkling health.

"I can find my own way out," she said.

•"Thank you for coming, señora."

Crossing the courtyard towards the gate in the wall that lead to the beach, she saw that Guido and Juana were still by the unicorn fountain. As she came up to them, Juana lifted her arms, stretching them slightly against the warm languor in her body, and her breasts were drawn up, bold and firm against the silk sun-top and her bare torso was suddenly hard and flat like polished marble. With a gentle insolence she said to Kate:

"Take my advice and persuade him to give up."

The arrogance of this household was too much for Kate.

"Take my advice, and mind your own business," she said vulgarly, and walked on, for the moment wonderfully appeased.

Chapter Ten

WHEN she told Nick, he said, "He tries everything, doesn't he? The big weapon and the little one. Did he really think you could talk me out of it?"

"It was a chance, I suppose."

He was leaning over the rail, watching the motor-boat gently grinding its fenders against the rusty steel plates of the *Doria*. He turned and looked solemnly at her.

"Do you want me to give it up? Do you agree with him?"

"This is your department, Nick. It's nothing to do with me."

"But you think I'm crazy?"

"No. I think you're stubborn. Also, I think you believe in miracles. At least. . . ."

"At least, my foot. You're right. I'm crazy and stubborn. But so are a lot of people. And a lot of them come through. I'll tell you what I think. . . ." He looked out over the bay, at the faint wind pluming the tips of the eucalyptus trees by the villa, " . . . he'll try everything. Because he's not sure. Generally, when he runs into trouble, he's got an answer. Money, wire-pulling, politics, some hold, some way of getting under a man's armour. But this time, it's happening on his doorstep. It's so damned outrageous, that he's wondering whether I haven't got a trump card."

"And have you?"

He grinned. "The Lord knows. . . . I haven't sorted my hand out yet."

"And if you find you haven't?"

He laughed, the long body stirring, the brown hands spread strong on the broad teak topping of the rail; "Well, I'm the son of my old man. When he didn't hold good cards, he palmed a few into his hand."

"Now I know you're crazy."

He creased his eyes up against the drifting smoke from his cigarette, and his face was suddenly fined down, skin and bone stark with the turn of hard feeling inside him, a face abruptly hawk-wild and defiant.

"Yes, I'm crazy because I object to being stepped on. Don't you worry, Kate. I'll do this if I have to crack the world apart with my. . . ."

He stopped, gave her a look and jerked his cigarette away.

"With your hands?"

"Yes."

Kate laughed. "I like you when you're stirred up." But she could see that something had come into his mind which had increased the hardness in him.

He went on: "Keep away from Manasco. Battles are lost because men make the mistake of regarding their enemies as humans. We had a sergeant in the Commandos who used to knock that kind of pap out of new boys in five minutes." His voice was sharp, almost menacing.

*   *   *   *

It was a new aspect in Nick. It kept coming back to her during the next two days. Don't regard your enemy as human. It was all right in a military manual. But not in Nick. Not with all the hardness of feeling that he had put behind it. He was a friendly, warm man. Even when he was cheated in business his reaction was more often amusement than anger. She had no conception of Nick as a ruthless person. But he clearly was about Manasco. He was going to beat him, and that was that. And she guessed that to himself he had already said he didn't care a damn how he did it.

Discovering this stranger in him disturbed her. She tried to forget it, but it was there at the back of her mind; and although she watched herself she knew that it was making her anxious and a little uncertain. She fancied that he resented that she had let herself be talked to by Manasco. Just for a moment she had been in the other camp. Maybe it was all nonsense, but it had its effects. He seemed to be irritable and more quickly roused by the small things that went wrong.

On the evening of the second day after she had talked with Manasco Nick came into the saloon late. They had worked under the arc lamps, and he was tired.

"Well, that's the last of the timber overboard. Tomorrow we can start shifting the flour from the after-hold."

He flung himself down on his bunk and pulled out his cigarettes. Kate struck a match for him. She fixed him a whisky and sat by him. They were silent for awhile and then he said suddenly, "What are you thinking about?"

Without knowing why, she said, "About you working so hard . . . and I was wondering. . . ."

"Wondering what?"

"About the cargo. About what you're going to do with it once it's on the beach."

"That worries me, too."

"But what will you do, Nick?" She wanted to know, wanted to share the difficulties with him, to help . . . but she knew at once she had said the wrong thing.

He sat up and frowned.

"I told you—something will turn up. I'm too tired, anyway to think about it now. The future can bloody well look after itself. . . ."

He lay back again and stretched out, shutting his eyes.

"Do you want some hot water for washing?"

"Not tonight. . . ."

Three minutes later he was sleeping and she took the burning stub of his cigarette from his lips. She sat there for a long time looking at him. There was trouble inside him, something was working up . . . and all she knew of it at that moment was that she wanted it to come . . . wanted to get it over so that they could really start moving together again. When it did come she prayed that she would handle it right. . . .

The next morning when the first load of flour sacks from the after-hold were aboard the raft she was given the job of manning the motor-boat on the tow out to sea. Once clear of the bay she kept the nose of the boat up into the wind, the motor just turning over. It was a pleasant morning, the sun warm on her face.

There were a couple of terns ahead of the boat. She watched them in their neat black jockey caps, hovering fork-tailed and then diving like slivers of light to the glassy surface of the sea. They came back, thrown up immediately as though the sea were rejecting them and there was the violent coruscation of the fish shoal under the mirror of water, splintering away in a maze of broken silver.

She kept her hand on the wheel, sensing the tug of the cumbersome raft behind. She didn't look round. She knew what she would see: Nick and Rigo on the raft, stripped down to bathing trunks, covered in flour and wrestling with the unwieldy sacks; Nick and Rigo, looking like a couple of savages, even their eyebrows oddly clogged with flour, whitening their hair like bad make-up for an old man's part. . . . Her eyes were on the terns, clean, beautifully trim, unencumbered birds. Beyond the birds was the long line of grey cliffs and the breakers like a cut-paper frill about their feet. . . .

The engine of the motor-boat suddenly coughed and then stalled. She looked round, jerked out of her reverie. She saw Nick and Rigo come to the forward edge of the raft. It was very close to the motor-boat.

Nick called, "What's up?"

Rigo pointed to the tow-rope and said something she couldn't catch. They dived in and came swimming towards the motor-boat, following the line of the tow. They both dived again, close to the stern. Nick's head and shoulders came up and his right hand grabbed the gunwale.

"For the love of Pete, Kate—what are you dreaming

about? You've got the bloody tow-rope fouled around the propeller."

"I'm sorry, Nick. Anyway, you don't have to swear at me."

"For heaven's sake don't be touchy. That's what you're there for—to keep an even strain on the tow. There's a knife in the locker. Hand it down."

She got the knife and handed it to him and watched him go under with Rigo. He was right. She mustn't be touchy. She was doing a man's job. He spoke to her like a man. He would have bloodied and blasted his best friend. It meant nothing.

Rigo came up, blew a spurt of water into the air like a whale and grinned at her. "It's all right. No damage."

They cut the tow rope free from the propeller and Nick handed her up the loose end.

"Make it fast, sailor," he said. "A bowline, as I taught you. Sorry about the swearing. For 'bloody' read 'blessed'." He winked and was away, swimming with Rigo to the raft.

Kate turned to the crank of the motor and swung it. The engine came to life and she took the wheel, looking back and seeing the tow lift in the water. Two brown bodies rolled aboard the raft and work began again. She turned away.

Suddenly the whole thing was clear and simple in her mind. So simple that she couldn't be sure that it hadn't been there all the time but for some reason she had refused to see it. This *Doria* business, Manasco, Nick's crazy plunging ahead without an answer to his final problem of getting the cargo to Palma were all concerned with her. With her infidelity. She didn't like the word, but she used it firmly.

For herself, acknowledging her mistake, still loving Nick and wanting nothing else ever now except his love, she knew that time was the cure. She had to sit it out, patiently and with understanding. She had been weak . . . stupid. But Nick had been wounded. That was the difference.

Time would help Nick, too. But he needed more than

that. In any marriage where this happened . . . and God knew it happened to enough . . . there was no copybook answer, no inflexible right or wrong way of handling it. Each person had to find his own answer. And for the one with the deep wound, it could take many forms. Some men would have thrashed her. Some would have smashed the furniture. Some would have found another woman and eased the violence with a moment's angry passion. And some would have sat it out, content with Time. . . . Each one had to find his own solution. And she felt that Nick had found it here. He wasn't a wife-beater, or a furniture smasher. But there was too much violence in him to let him be content with Time. He had to smash something, to let the fury and bitter strength flood from him. Right to his hand had come Manasco and this job. It was hopeless and it couldn't succeed. But that was what he wanted. The more hopeless it seemed, the madder and more savagely he could attack. He didn't care whether he won. He just wanted to fight; to fight until he fell back exhausted with all the violence scoured from him . . . and then Time could begin to work. Time and patience, these must be her allies.

* * * *

Working in the galley, washing up after the evening meal, she saw them every time she swung back towards the open door. They were leaning on the rail amidships, their shoulders hunched. There was something about this close communion of men who worked together that for a moment touched a fibre of jealousy in her. Their voices, with a laugh now and again, rose and fell and seemed to shut her out. All the flour had been dumped, the decks washed down and now the after and forward holds were open, ready for the main cargo to be lifted.

She heard Nick say, "It'll be easy to rig the raft as a ferry. We'll fix a post, upright, on one side with a small roller and then fit an endless rope. . . ."

His voice died away and idly she wondered what on earth an endless rope was.

"The lower bridge supports will make a fixing this end for the block and tackle. Ashore we'll have to anchor it well up the beach. . . ."

"How many loads, you think, señor?"

"Can't say exactly. Maybe a dozen to each hold. Maybe more."

"And off-loading at the beach?"

"I've had a look at the stuff. There's little that we can't manhandle. If there is we can use log rollers."

"And after that, señor?"

Kate paused, standing just inside the door. Here was Rigo asking the same question. She waited, wondering what Nick would say.

"What would you do, Rigo?" She heard the lightness, the comradeship in Nick's voice, and saw his big shoulders lift as he flipped his cigarette end out over the sea.

Rigo laughed and said, "I should pray to Santo Rosario del Aurora to tell me. I have a feeling he does not like Señor Manasco either. . . ."

Santo Rosario was the local saint . . . Kate had a swift memory of the dawn processions through the town on his day, the bobbing paper lanterns and the freshness of voices raised in the cool sea air which whipped at the white aprons of the priests and the scarves about the women's heads.

"But you, señor? You have some idea . . . some plan?"

Nick didn't answer for a moment then he said deliberately: "In a way. . . . In a way, Rigo. But I want to think it over to myself for a while. Don't you worry about it."

"I don't worry, señor. If you win or lose I do not stay in Puerto. If you feel there is a way, I am content. . . ."

She came out of the galley and Nick turned to greet her.

"Finished? Good. I'm just going ashore to pick a spot for our block and tackle anchorage tomorrow. Like to come and stretch your legs?"

F

He already had his arm around her, leading her aft to the gangway.

"We'll go for a stroll out along the cliff."

On the beach he spent a few minutes picking his spot for the morrow and then they walked in silence across the sands in the direction of the spring. From the courtyard of the villa came the sound of a gramophone and the chatter and laughter of people.

"Party of some kind," said Nick. "I saw the cars coming up the valley a little while ago. Let's walk along the top." He took her arm and helped her up the small cliff bank.

"They didn't invite us," she joked.

"No. But I'll bet we're the reason for it. This thing is causing a stir in Palma. Manasco's friends have come up to have a look at the situation. . . ."

Some men, she thought would have had a touch of pride in their voices, knowing that they stood at the centre of attraction, that they had caused the situation . . . or at least enlarged it. But nothing could have been more casual than Nick's voice. He didn't care what went on in there.

Just for a moment they paused by the open grill-work door in the courtyard wall. She had a glimpse of young men and women dancing, drinking; a long white-clothed table stacked with bottles and by the fountain Guido jiving with a girl, throwing his body about . . . young, modern, contorted and somehow the whole thing discordant and wrong in this place. Juana she could not see. She put out a hand and found Nick's arm as they moved on.

Behind them the gate opened, and a voice called to them. She turned with Nick. Colonel da Lapa came towards them.

"Señora . . . Señor Thorne. . . . *Buenas tardes*."

A nice, pink-scrubbed man, she thought; crinkling with fresh linen, and with a kind of bright, leather-hard masculinity. She glanced at Nick and saw the shadow of a smile about his lips. They knew each other well, respected each other . . . but between them was the clash of bluntness against subtlety.

"You've taken the flour out to sea, I understand?"

"Yes, colonel. That was the order."

The Colonel made a little flourish with his cigarette holder. "Good. It was an annoyance—for you. But there . . . we cannot always foresee the troubles that lie ahead. Not always." For a moment he looked over his shoulder towards the wall gate. As his eyes came back to them Kate had a feeling that he suddenly wished he had not come out. Being here he had to follow up the impulse which had made him open the gate.

Nick said: "We're keeping you from your party, colonel. Unless there are any more orders?"

In other words, don't say it if you don't want to, Kate thought.

The Colonel touched one side of his black moustache and frowned, and then as suddenly smiled.

"Yes, Señor Thorne, I have another order. But you are at liberty to disobey it, though not without some penalty I imagine. No one must go aboard the *Doria* except you, the señora here, and Rigo." He bowed to them and turned away, the highly-polished riding boots picking their way over the rough ground with a dancing *tap*, *tap* that made him look ridiculous.

"What on earth did he mean by that?" asked Kate as they walked on, following the line of the wall up the cliff side.

"I don't know . . . but he doesn't talk just for the sake of talk. It's not in his nature. It's what he said, a warning. Don't let anyone come aboard."

"If a man wants to help you and I should say he does— why can't he talk plainly?"

Nick laughed. "Oh, my innocent! All these years in Spain and you haven't learned that! He's the law; Manasco is the money-bags, and I'm the tea-leaves. You throw tea-leaves away. He did talk plainly. *Don't let anyone else aboard.* In fact I'm surprised he was as plain as that. He really must hate Manasco's guts."

"That's not hard!"

"Well . . ." he was smiling now. "What a spitfire."

He put his arm round her and they went on, walking slowly across the short sheep-bitten grass, the dusky evening a velvet intimacy about them.

Coming back, the music from the villa was loud and the darkness alive with laughter and cries. As they neared the gate in the wall someone came through it and for a moment, caught in the long shaft of light, Kate saw a great sweep of white lace. She had the impression of some great white moth swinging and dancing, trapped by the hard beam of light. Then she saw that it was Juana and in the same moment Nick put his hand on her arm, stopping her. They stood in the shadows, watching. Juana was dancing by herself and singing gently. Kate could see the gleam of her parted lips, the rise and fall of her naked shoulders and arms and the wide swaying circle of skirt as the girl swung round. She danced in the patch of light like some happy, beautiful ghost. She moved out of the light towards them and momentarily the air was traced with her perfume and soft with the noise of the lace dress whirling about her. Kate saw the sparkle in her eyes, the long moulded sweep of an arm, and then the girl was back in the light and someone was shouting to her from within the courtyard. She hung there for a moment and then dropped in a low curtsey to some invisible partner.

"Well . . . she's feeling happy," said Nick quietly.

Something in his voice made Kate look at him quickly. He was smiling, a gentle, amused smile. Quite suddenly, almost with a shock that she hadn't spotted it before she realised that Nick liked the girl. . . . It was all over his face.

"Don't be an ass, Nick," she said brusquely. "It was all an act."

"Yes?"

"Of course it was—for your benefit. She's got a crush on you. I'll bet she'd been waiting there for us to come back. It's the kind of hammy trick a girl like Juana would think of."

Nick laughed. "Well, it was a good piece of ham. I liked it. And anyway," he looked sideways at her, one eyebrow cocked, "it's not my fault if I'm so attractive. Women go crazy for me—how else could I have got you?"

"I didn't have to do that kind of thing. Who does she think she is? Pavlova?"

His laugh rolled through the darkness.

She lay on her bunk now, long past midnight thinking about it. Distantly she could hear the gentle wash and drag of the sea on the beach. Once she heard the pad of bare feet along the deck and knew it was Rigo. For a young man he was a bad sleeper. He had a mattress under an awning up in the bows and often at night she heard him moving around. . . . Tonight maybe the lights and the music from the villa had disturbed him. And let's face it, she thought, they've disturbed me. More than they should have done. That damned girl had a nerve. The more she thought of it now, the more she wondered she hadn't realised it before. Juana was the right age, a woman but still full of a young girl's fancies. . . . It was a dangerous age. Once they got their teeth into a romantic idea they took some shaking off. Nick mightn't see it; but she did. The girl was building up some picture of him . . . that wonderful business of spending your days dreaming and having imaginary conversations with a man you'd probably spoken to no more than twice in your life. No, Nick wouldn't see it but she did. And she realised now that the girl was always hanging around; swimming out to the *Doria*, sunbathing on the cliff rocks, coming down to the beach when he was there . . . kissing him even as he threw her overboard.

And hell, it was perhaps too naïve to say that Nick didn't know what was going on in the girl's head. He was no fool. Rowing back in the skiff she had known his eyes were on her and that he was conscious of some of her thoughts. It was ridiculous that a small thing like this could make her jealous. But it did. And he knew it. She wondered now whether his silence and once a slight chuckle in the darkness as he rowed weren't all saying. . . . *It hurts, doesn't it? Jealousy, I mean. A little thing like that—so unimportant. But it hurts. Now imagine how I feel about Ray Asherton.*

Could Nick say or think that? Pettiness for her pettiness? Not normally. But things weren't normal. She'd hurt him . . . dear Nick . . . hurt him so much. . . . It was odd, after ten years so close together, to have to admit that there were great reaches of knowledge between them still unexplored. Maybe it was always like that . . . always something new to discover about yourself and those close to you. Certainly about yourself. Oh God, why had she? Why had she ever got into this? She must have been crazy. To do it to Nick, to herself. . . . What demon had stirred in her flesh?

She turned over, pressing her face into the pillow, suddenly possessed with a nameless, crushing black fear in this moment of loneliness, and feeling her weakness free tears behind her eyes. . . . Then she turned back, staring at the dark bunk timbers, angry with herself though the tears were still wet in her eyes.

Chapter Eleven

HAVING no head for mechanical things she found that half the time she had no conception of what they were doing. Told to heave on a rope with Rigo, she pulled wondering why . . . and to her surprise a hundred yards away by the beach the clumsy raft, unloaded, would begin to move out towards the *Doria*. She did this and she did that, ordered and directed and sometimes sworn at by Nick. Once as she fumbled at a rope's end, unhitching it from a rail, it slipped from her fingers and the long length sloping out to the raft fell into the sea. He looked at her, grinned, and rolled his eyes.

She picked up a lump of wet sacking that had come adrift from the packing round a window frame and threw it at him. He caught it, tossed it back and then took a header over the side to get the rope. He went in, just as he was, in shirt and trousers and then came back, dripping like a Labrador, and went on with the job, oblivious of the wet material clinging and drying around his body.

Savages, she thought indulgently. Only by courtesy did they inhabit a woman's world. And she knew she was admiring them both. They were doing a job and nothing stopped them. Grease, water, filth . . . she watched Rigo sink under the scummy surface of the water in the forward hold to get a fastening round a batch of window frames. He came up, the surface oil on the water running in iridescent globules over his face and shoulders. She watched Nick carry a lavatory pan, festooned with protective strips of wet paper. He carried it inverted over his head like a Horse Guard's helmet. He made a rope fast and lowered it to Rigo on the raft, shouting some joke in rapid Spanish slang which, happily, she couldn't understand. Rigo roared with laughter on the raft.

When they came in to eat, they paid her the courtesy of washing their hands, but they smelled to high heaven of stale bilge and rank flour.

Lavatory pans, wash-basins, flat layers of light steel door and window frames . . . she watched them all pile up, and then she would haul on a rope with Rigo or Nick and slowly work the raft ashore. Then the man with her would take the skiff and row ashore to help unload. At first she had taken the oars of the skiff, but in a few journeys had realised that both Nick and Rigo watched her slow strokes with impatience. When they rowed it might have been a race, the oars driving into the water, the bows lifting with an eager, onrushing surge at each stroke.

The stuff began to pile up on the beach. The first day five loads, and the second six. There was nothing above water in the foward hold now. Rigo and Nick took turns in going under carrying a rope with a hook to make a quick fastening. Then up it would come, as they both bent to the double-handled winch, dripping with water and filth, a narrow crate full of windows. If the rope or the crate broke and the load crashed back their language was enough to sear the hairs off her head. At night she boiled gallons of water for them in the galley copper and they stood on deck stark naked—warning her she came out at her own risk—and scrubbed each other down, shouting and laughing and often with enough energy still for horse-play. When she heard them go over the side she would come out, carrying towels and fresh clothes and leave them at the head of the gangway and then go forward to the cabin and set out the drink and the glasses. That was the best time, the two hours before sleep, when they talked and drank—and they drank she noticed with the same gusto they were putting into everything else. As they talked the moths came in brittle, quick drifts around the oil lamp with now and then the bump of some night beetle smacking hard against the glass shade. Rigo had brought out a guitar with him and sometimes he would play and sing . . . *flamenco* songs, *sardanas* and sometimes just plain bawdy dialect songs, she guessed. And now, she saw a different Nick; saw a part of him she had never seen before. He sang as well, and would get up and dance, smacking his hands and stamping and his wild eyes going out across the dark waters. It was as though now they were on the last lap a growing intoxication of spirit was working through them.

And all this, she thought, as though they were getting somewhere. But what would happen when all the stuff was piled on to the beach? There weren't many days left in which to meet the contract date for delivery in Palma. What good would the stuff be just sitting on the beach when it should be on the new barrack site?

The third evening after they had begun to ferry the cargo ashore, Rigo was going off for the night to help his father.

Kate took them their hot water for the nightly scrub down and as she stood waiting in the galley, she heard them talking. There was the usual laughter for a while and then it died away. She heard Nick say:

"Johnny's working tonight?"

"Yes. There is a small load coming in but it will not be until very late, almost the morning. Because of the moon."

"You're going from here to Puerto first?"

"Yes. It is some time since I have seen my mother. And the Manascos do not let their dog roam the nights we work. To them it means nothing if I use the road. The only thing they won't let along will be the stuff from the beach."

"Blast them, don't I know it."

"You wanted something from Puerto, perhaps?"

Nick didn't answer at once. She heard him grunt as he swilled himself down and the shake of his wet hair as he towelled. Then he said:

"Yes. I want you to phone Domingo Peroni at his home. Tell him I'd like him up here within the next two or three days sometime. He can hire a boat and come round."

F*

"Certainly, señor. My father would bring him. Is that all?"

"No. Do you think you could bring back with you a couple of shotguns and some ammunition?"

This time it was Rigo who was silent for a while before answering. Then in a quiet, self-contained voice, he said: "If it is necessary, yes."

"It's necessary," said Nick.

"Then I will bring them."

From the way Rigo spoke Kate had the feeling that he was with Nick, knew what was in his mind and, if it had to be, was prepared to go along with him. Well, Rigo might have guessed but she hadn't, and there was a spark of anger in her that Nick should reveal more of himself and his plans to Rigo than he was prepared to do with her.

When Rigo was ready to leave, she went to the gangway with him.

To Nick, she said, "I'll row Rigo ashore. You go and have a quiet drink."

Rowing Rigo ashore she kept her eyes on his face. Fresh scrubbed, the dark skin shining and his curly black hair limp for a while with water, he looked very young. Knowing she was watching him there was an embarrassed, serious look on his face.

Half way to the beach she said, "I heard Señor Thorne ask you about guns."

"Guns, señora?" He said it stupidly as though he didn't understand her.

"Yes, guns, Rigo. And don't look so damned dumb. You know he did."

"There are quail along the cliffs, señora. Maybe . . . for the pot."

She ignored this. "What does he want them for? You've got some idea."

"Señora. . . ."

"Come on, Rigo. Tell me."

"Señora. . . . How should I know? For hunting, I imagine."

"Nonsense." She rested on her oars.

"Señora, I don't know. He just asked for them. That is all I know."

And that, thought Kate, is all she would get. In Spain women kept their noses out of men's affairs. That was how Rigo felt. And come to think of it, maybe that was how Nick felt.

"All right, Rigo. Keep it to yourself. I'm only a stupid woman!"

She saw him smile at her anger, saw the flash of his white teeth and the glitter in his dark eyes.

"You are not stupid, señora. Also, I would like to say that you are a very beautiful woman. This I say with respect, señora, for you and the señor are my friends."

The anger went from her at his simplicity and directness. Dear Rigo . . . and bless his heart. It was about time somebody told her that she was beautiful.

But standing by the boat on the beach, watching him disappear into the darkness she suddenly knew that he hadn't been so simple. Bless his heart, indeed . . . and she'd fallen for that. The woman begins to ask awkward questions and the man to avoid them tells her she is beautiful and she forgets her questions.

She walked up the beach, not caring to go back yet. She skirted a great pile of cargo that rose dark and cumbersome against the sky and then, from the corner of her eye, saw something white stir up on the low cliff edge. She might have ignored it, thinking it was a sheet of paper. But it stirred again and there was no wind this evening.

She walked up the bank and saw Guido crouched in the shadow of a low tamarisk bush. A foot from him was the anchorage for the running tackle that worked the raft ferry. One of the ropes was cut.

She stood over him and very slowly he came to his feet. He wore a white shirt with his initials on the pocket. She could smell the strong pomade on his sleeked black hair. His thin face had the petulant sullenness of a schoolboy caught in mischief, and he was too late to hide behind his back a broad-bladed bowie knife.

She looked at him and then at the rope.

"You're lucky," she said sharply, "I'm not the señor. He'd have given you a good hiding! And personally I think that's what you want."

"Don't you dare talk to me like that!" But he couldn't get the force and defiance into his voice that he wanted.

"It's time someone did. You started all this. What good do you think cutting a few ropes is going to do? It's an irritation—no more. You're just a buzzing, annoying mosquito and one day someone will smack you flat with their hand. Why don't you go home to bed, boy, and learn some sense."

She saw the insult bring a flush to his face, saw the lips tighten and somewhere deep down she was even sorry for him.

"Be careful!" Even the anguish in him was pathetic, and the movement with the knife was childish, half-hearted. His weakness, although she didn't want it, fed the strength and anger in her.

"Go away," she snapped. "You're no good to anyone, not even to yourself. And put that knife away before you hurt yourself."

The anger in her was wonderful, like a large whisky on top of an empty stomach.

To her surprise he did put that knife away, slipping it slowly into his trouser pocket, but his eyes were on her and she saw that something was with him . . . something that was putting aside all the hurt he had suffered.

In a low, calm voice he said, "You're right, why should I bother? You won't win anyway. . . . You can't win. That husband of yours—you think he's a wonderful person, don't you? You think he can do anything!" He was restless with excitement.

"He's a better man than you'll ever be." She began to turn away, but his voice caught her and made her swing back.

"Oh, he's wonderful. That's what you think. He's just making a fool of you. Ask him what he and Juana get up to any time you are away. Ask him! I've seen them——"

She brought her hand up and smacked his face with all her strength.

He staggered back and gave a long gasp of pain. She fought her anger, breathing heavily against the disgust and nausea in her.

"You dirty-minded little. . . ."

She looked around, possessed with a frantic desire to find something with which she could strike. She bent down swiftly and picked up a large stone. But she never threw it. He was running, shuffling away through the bushes and she could hear the whip of the branches against his clothes.

She dropped the stone. Then slowly she turned and walked back down the beach.

*   *   *   *

She rowed out slowly, stopping now and again to let the skiff drift, knowing she must have time to calm down. And there were two people in the boat, two people she knew well. The Kate who had smacked Guido's face, wanted to pummel him with a stone because of his nastiness . . . and a Kate who was elderly and aunt-like, full of wisdom, experience and hard to touch emotionally.

One said, "I wish I could have killed him!"

And the other, "You're asking for trouble if you pay attention to the angry remarks of a dirty-minded, vindictive boy."

"He's nearly twenty."

"He's a snotty-nosed schoolboy, my dear. And no truth in him. Now calm down."

"As though Nick would——"

"All right," the other sighed; "I see you're determined to bring it up. So let's have it frankly and get it out of the way. She's an attractive girl and there could have been opportunities. And, let's face it, dear—you've given Nick cause to feel that a *quid pro quo* might not be out of place. But do you believe it?"

"No, of course not!"

"Then forget it. And for God's sake do something to your face before you meet him. It looks like a boiled beet-root."

"Oh, shut up being so smug."

"That's better."

Back on board she found Nick in the saloon. He was sitting at the table, working something out on a piece of paper. She guessed he was figuring the number of ferry loads to clear the cargo. When she told him about Guido—suppressing everything except that he had cut a rope—he grunted, and said: "He's a nuisance. Still, I think I'll have Rigo sleep ashore from now on. That boy could do a lot of damage to the cargo with a sledge hammer." He looked up at her. His eyes narrowing against the hurricane lamp light above him, she saw the deep net of crow's feet wrinkles at their corners.

He went on: "I don't know why, but I've a feeling that Manasco is waiting for something. He's got a big card to play yet."

"He's played his biggest card already, Nick. You can't use the road."

"Oh, that——" he brushed it aside. "I don't mean that. There's something else. That's what da Lapa was hinting at."

"But the road, Nick, is the really big thing."

"Not necessarily." He smiled. "I know it worries you. But you must have guessed that I'm not such a fool to have gone on without having some idea how to meet this road snag." He leaned back, tapping the paper with his pencil. His head was cocked characteristically, the way she'd seen him hold it a hundred times when considering some deal, talking aloud but less to her than for the benefit of getting things clear in his own mind. "By taking a few risks, we can use the road. I've though about it a lot. Domingo's coming up in a day or so, and we can all go into it then."

"That's a particularly irritating thing to say. You must know it just makes me unbearably curious." Without meaning to, she sounded cross.

"Sorry—but that's the way it is." He put out his hand and touched hers and smiled.

"But I've got a right to know. You tell Rigo far more than you do me."

"I don't, you know."

"But you do. What about these guns? What on earth do you want guns for?"

"Shotguns—for hunting. I thought you'd like some quail for the pot." He grinned and she knew he would never tell her anything.

"Liar. . . ." But she said it affectionately and his grin broadened, and his hand tightened on hers.

Lying on their bunks in the darkness, they talked for a while before sleeping; about Julia—worrying a little on a calm level because from her last letter they had learned she was in the school sanatorium with sinus trouble; small talk with the intervals growing longer as sleep advanced. Kate lapsed into a lazy state of listening and throwing in a word now and then to keep the talk alive . . . pleasantly relaxed and secure, hearing him in the darkness and knowing she had only to stretch out her hand to touch him across the narrow cabin.

Nick was saying. . . . "It's easy to understand Manasco's point of view. Yes, easy. Even though Guido isn't his son. He's the nearest he's got. Manasco wants to show him how to open oysters . . . how to be like him. When you've got power you have to accept a big slice of pride with it. . . ."

Much later as though her brain was tuned only to pertinent phrases, she heard him say between brackets of silence:

"What did you do with the ear-rings? Send them back?"

She was suddenly alert, lying there very still. The words had come casually, as though he had long forgotten the whole thing and now only a wayward memory prompted them, and she knew it was important to answer in the same terms.

"I sent them back," she said, turning over under the blanket.

"With a letter?"

"Just a note."

"Oh. . . ." For a moment she heard his breathing and she thought, it's all right, this is just the clearing away of rubbish from his mind. Then he said, "Did you get a reply?"

"No."

"Oh. . . ." His breathing was even in the darkness and she waited, but nothing more came and after a long time she suddenly realised that he was sleeping, that there was to be no more, and she was glad and full of a sharp pleasure and relief. This was how it had to begin to be, referred to without emotion, brought up now and again only to be dropped deeper into the past. And now, too, she felt that she was a fool to have even considered what Guido had said. She didn't have to worry about Juana . . . if Nick liked her, was amused by her, there was nothing wrong in that. Still. . . . Then with a sharp, inner exclamation of exasperation she shut the thing from her mind.

Chapter Twelve

SHE woke towards morning and heard the slow beat of a motor-boat coming into the bay. That was Johnny Manchester with his *contrabandista* friends. Someone, Johnny or Manasco, or maybe someone farther back, must have the civil guards well organised. There never seemed to be any trouble about bringing the stuff in. That was a part of Spanish life she had never been able to get used to . . . the giving and taking of bribes. Some insular, britannic indignation worked swiftly in her at the very thought. Her father, visiting them once, had got into trouble over his car with the police and Nick had fixed things for him. She recalled the old man's indignation and Nick's easy dismissal of the whole thing. "Look, they don't want to prosecute you for a piddling accident. Grease a palm—life's easier. If you make them take action it can be long-winded and very expensive. . . ." Johnny or Manasco must be greasing a palm or two.

While she was cooking breakfast Rigo shouted from the beach and Nick went ashore for him. When he came into the galley with Nick for breakfast she said nothing about the two shotguns she had seen him bring aboard. She fried eggs for Nick and Rigo, thinking that in a day or so she would have to go to Puerto to lay in more stores.

After breakfast they repaired the rope which Guido had cut and went to work. Half-way through the morning the Ermano skiff was towed into the bay by a strange motor-boat. The night Guido and the manservant had taken the raft it had drifted down the coast and had run ashore and been damaged. Sometime after the motor-boat had left Guido and Manasco put off in the skiff and came rowing out. They went right around the *Doria*, keeping at a fair distance.

In the middle of the afternoon Kate took the *Doria* skiff and rowed ashore with the water cans. There were two large piles of cargo on the beach now. She was surprised that the forward hold could have contained so much. By the evening, she knew, they hoped to have cleared it.

As she waited for the last water-can to fill, Juana came out of the villa wall-gate and walked across to her. She side-stepped down the broken, sandy slope, pushing her way through the feathery bamboo growths.

"I was in Puerto this morning for our mail. I collected these for you."

She held out three letters to Kate. Kate had arranged for letters to be forwarded from the flat to the Margarita.

"Thank you." She shuffled the letters in her hands, look-ing at the inscriptions. The top one was from Julia, the stamp stuck on a little askew, the childish writing cramped up, waiting for the release and fluidity which a few more years would bring; and the one below was from her father. The last one was post-marked Madrid. She slipped the three letters into the pocket of her jumper.

Juana said pleasantly, "Other people's letters are always fascinating."

"I suppose so." Kate watched the water splashing into the can. It was only half full.

"One's from your daughter?"

Kate didn't answer. She just looked at Juana.

Juana laughed. "I know from my uncle that you've got a daughter at school in England. He makes it his business to find out things like that."

"I wonder he doesn't start a detective agency. Think of the fun you'd have." She kept her voice steady but she blamed herself at once for giving way. Why did she bother with this girl?

"I think he already runs one. The other letter is English too. That would be your father? He's a doctor, isn't he?"

"He's an ear, nose and throat specialist. Your uncle can

probably tell you what his practice is worth, and also, I should think, the make of his favourite cigars."

The can was full now and she picked it up, turning away down the beach. She heard Juana move behind her. Looking over her shoulder she saw that she had picked up the other can and was carrying it. Kate ignored her, dropping her can into the bows of the skiff. Juana came up close to her and lifted the other can in. She put a hand on the bows of the skiff and said, "I'll give you a push out."

"Don't bother."

Kate ran the boat out and jumped in. It drifted, rocking a yard from the beach edge as she sat down and began to get the oars out.

"Three letters to read." Juana was smiling, the breeze from the water ruffling gently the skirts of a white linen dress which Kate knew had never been run up by a local dressmaker.

"Which will you read first?" Juana asked. "The one from Madrid?" Kate couldn't miss the significance in her voice.

Her left oar well raised, she dropped it suddenly so that it hit the water with a fat smack, the blade only a foot from the beach edge. A spray of water fanned upwards over the linen dress.

"Oh, I'm so sorry," called Kate sweetly, and began to pull away from the shore. Juana, laughing, shook the water from her skirts and turned away to the villa.

Back on the *Doria* Kate went into the cabin. Nick and Rigo were working in the hold. She pulled out the three letters. She turned the one from Madrid over. Asherton's name was written on the back, following American custom, but she could not tell whether the letter had been opened. But that meant nothing. Something told her that a girl like Juana would have had a lot of practice in opening other people's letters.

She read the one from Julia first. Her sinus was better. Because she was tall she was going to be one of the Three Wise Men from the East in the Junior School Nativity play this coming Christmas. She would have preferred to have been a shepherd because they had less to say. Kate smiled. She was going to spend Christmas with her grandfather. This was long arranged. And then, reading her father's letter, he wanted to know if they were coming over for Christmas. If it was only a question of cash. . . .

Nick came in before she could open the other and she put it in her pocket for later. He saw Julia's letter on the table and picked it up. "Mail? How did you get this?"

"Juana was in Puerto this morning. She brought it out."

He looked at her, and grinned, "She's getting helpful."

"She didn't do it to help," said Kate. "Probably read them first."

He looked up from the letter in his hand. "Oh, I don't know. You're too hard on her. She can't help being a Manasco."

"I wouldn't trust her a yard!" snapped Kate. "And anyway I don't see why you have to stick up for her."

Nick frowned. "What's the matter with you? You been having a fight with her?"

"Of course not. I just don't like her. And I can't think why you do—except that it flatters you because she's obviously interested in you—" she broke off, wishing at once that she hadn't spoken.

Nick shook his head, and then grinned irritatingly. "All right, she's what you said she was." Then he frowned suddenly and put his hand to the table. "Feel that?"

"Yes. What was it?" For a moment the deck had moved slightly under her.

"Now we've lightened the forward hold she's settling a bit. I think Rigo and I had better check the mooring hawsers. She'll move more when we start emptying the after hold." He went out of the cabin and she heard him calling to Rigo.

When he was gone she sat on the bunk and read the letter from Ray Asherton. It was a long letter and he said most of

the things she had known he would say . . . a man not wanting to shut the door on the past. She tore the letter up and
going to the galley dropped it on the stove fire.

But burning the letter did not dispose of the images
it had created in her mind. They were there, dulled but
waiting, and for the moment all they did was to increase her
impatience against the inevitable creep of time . . . and
impatience made her clumsy. Only a few minutes ago she
had been clumsy about Juana. She could recognise it as it
happened and yet stand powerless to do anything about it.

Rigo slept ashore in the fishermen's shelter now. But
he didn't go ashore until past ten o'clock for the two of
them had worked under the deck lights until they were
ready to drop.

Nick came into the cabin and flung himself down on the
bunk. She fixed a large whisky for him and he lay there,
staring at the bunk boards and sipping his drink now and
again. She'd seen him tired like this before, tired sometimes
from physical labour and sometimes from the fret of business
ups and downs. Stretched out flat, a whisky at hand and
asking only for her presence and the quiet murmur of her
voice. She was a good hand at talking, small, inconsequential
stuff that he didn't have to listen to carefully. . . . And she
did it tonight.

To take his mind off the *Doria* she talked of Julia and
England, and thinking it would please him to have something to look forward to she told him of her father's
hope that they would spend the Christmas with him and
Julia.

"Of course we will," said Nick. "With this job pulled
off we'll have the money."

"Even if this doesn't come off we could go."

"I don't see how? We'll be broke."

She laughed. For a moment he sounded so pessimistic.

"Oh, Nick. Don't be so grim. We'll manage somehow. We
always have."

"Not this time. The cupboard really will be bare."

"Whatever happens we can spend Christmas in England. Father's offered to pay——"

She stopped talking as she saw his head come round swiftly. He frowned at her.

"I don't want him to pay."

"Don't be an ass, Nick. Why shouldn't he pay if he wants to?"

"Because I won't take charity."

She didn't say anything. Whatever she said, she knew would be wrong. He was tired and touchy.

He looked at her waiting for her to say something. When she didn't, he slipped his legs off the bunk and sat up. He drained his whisky and stood up. He was obviously expecting her to say something and she didn't know what to say. But she knew, too, that silence was probably worse than saying the wrong thing.

He stood against the table. She saw the way his fingers were splayed against the surface, saw the dark rims of grease under the nails, recognised the drag of fatigue against the tall, strong frame.

"Of course you'll pull it off, Nick, darling."

He made a sudden irritable movement of his hand.

"You don't believe that. You know you don't. Well, I do! I'm going to do it! But I don't want to be jollied along. You don't have to do that!"

"I'm not. Why do you think I'm here if I don't believe you'll do it? I want to help, that's all. Don't you want me out here?"

"Don't be ridiculous. Of course I do."

"Well, I sometimes feel you don't." Her own temper was rising now and before she could stop herself she said sarcastically, "Maybe you'd like to be left alone out here for that Juana girl to moon over——"

"Oh, that's it, is it? Well, you're a good one to talk after that business with Ash——"

"Nick!"

He stopped. For a moment she thought everything was

going to come right. But he suddenly went on, his voice tight and angry—

"Bloody hell, to everything. I'm going on deck for a smoke."

He went out. Two hours later he came back. She was in bed. She heard him move in the darkness of the saloon, but he said nothing.

She lay there knowing sleep would be long in coming. It had been a stupid quarrel, arising out of nothing, and she knew she ought to have kept her temper. Why on earth had she ever mentioned Juana? A year from now, she thought, we'll laugh about it, understand it . . . but that was ahead. This was now. The bloody unshakable now.

* * * *

The next morning it was difficult to tell whether he was still in a bad temper, or upset at his outburst and waiting for the right moment to smooth things out between them. He came into the galley a little before Rigo for breakfast. As she stood at the stove cooking, her back to him, she debated with herself the wisdom of making an overture. She could apologise, make some remark to lead him in, but there was a little core of stubbornness in her which refused to melt. Why should she be the first to speak? The first to say *I'm sorry*. It was an old situation—but this time with new dangers. She stood there briefly lecturing herself, knowing she was going to speak. Then Rigo came in and the moment was gone. And that, she thought, was what could happen. One's best intentions messed up by the smallest things.

The men ate their breakfast and were quickly out on deck to begin work on the after hold cargo. Washing up, she could almost hear Nick's thoughts. *O.K. Of course, I said too much. But why should I always be the one to apologise? What I said was the truth, anyway. Why should I have to feel bad because I dragged it into the open?*

She threw down her dishcloth and went out on deck quickly. The whole thing was too damn silly for words. She stood at the edge of the hatch coaming and looked down. How could she say anything now? Both of them, stripped to their shorts, were splashing and sliding about in the filthy water like a pair of sea otters, fighting with a small case that was jammed. Nick looked up and the whites of his eyes glittered against the mask of oil on his face.

"Chuck that rope down, will you?"

He nodded to a rope trailing over the coaming. He said something to the case which slipped at that moment. It was so scurrilous that Rigo began to splutter with laughter.

Kate walked back to the galley. Beginning to wipe a plate she felt a sudden sense of frustration. She looked at the plate in her hand and hated it from the depths of impatience in her for things to be right . . . from the longing in her to be wise-headed, calm and capable of handling this sensibly. She threw the plate against the iron front of the stove and breathed a deep sigh of relief. That was better. And that, she knew, was what Nick was waiting for a chance to do; to smash something, to explode in a sudden outburst of fury. Well, the sooner he did it the better. Smash Manasco . . . burst . . . do something . . . but do it quickly so that they would only have time to face.

As she collected up the broken pieces she smiled to herself. When a man smashed something he walked away and left it, but a woman found herself down on her knees picking up the pieces.

Nick's voice behind her said, "Breaking things up?" He sounded genial, composed, and smiled at her, a big, dirty, happy-looking man, extending a great warmth of feeling to her as he came across and squatted on the floor helping her with the pieces.

"It slipped from my hand."

"Naturally. . . ."

He tickled the back of her neck and she couldn't tell whether he had seen her smash the plate or whether he was believing her. One thing was clear; there was no irritation or bad temper in him.

He stood up, scratching at his ruffled hair.

"I was a bit snappy last night," he smiled. "Sorry about that."

"It was my fault, Nick darling. I should have realised you were tired. . . ."

"Well, it's nothing. Cramped up here. . . . And this really isn't your kind of lark. I'll tell you what, there are one or two things we need from Johnny Manchester's garage; chiefly carbide for the deck lamps. I'll write you out a list and you can take the motor-boat round for the stuff. A break from this place will do you good."

"You really want this stuff? Not just sending me off because you think I need. . . . Oh, well you know what I mean."

"No. We really need it. I wish I could come with you. We could have had lunch at the Margarita and split a bottle of wine. I wouldn't mind getting my elbow on a bar again. However. . . ." His hand came out and teased at her ear. "I'll get the boat ready for you."

If it had stayed like that, it would have been all right. This was the rub and fret of any marriage. But when she got out of the bay she remembered that she hadn't brought with her a letter to Julia which she wanted to post. She had plenty of time, so she turned back.

Coming back to the *Doria* she saw that a skiff was lying at the foot of the gangway and as she got closer she recognised Juana's figure. Standing on the edge of the raft, a yard from the skiff, was Nick and she could see that he and the girl were talking. When she was fifty yards away Juana began to row unhurriedly towards the beach. Nick waited for her on the raft. She was angry at the thought that the moment her back was turned the girl came hovering around. . . . Damn her. She told herself to say nothing. It would be clumsy and stupid to say anything. That was the way trouble could be created.

Nick caught the bow of the motor-boat.

"What's up?" he asked.

"I forgot Julia's letter." She could hear her voice tight and unwilling.

"Oh. . . . I'll get it for you."

He ran up the gangway and she waited for him. Say nothing. She kept repeating it to herself. He came down, holding the letter in his hand and passed it across to her. As she took it, as though some stranger inside her spoke, she heard herself say:

"What did she want?"

"Who? Juana?"

"Yes."

"She brought those. Rather nice of her, I thought. I bet if it only rested with her I could get the use of the road. She knows her brother is a liar." As he spoke he nodded to the raft. In a reed crawl were four or five lobsters.

"They're probably poisoned!" Helpless against it, Kate felt the fury rising in her.

"Can't be," he grinned. "Rigo and I watched her lift the pot, across the bay there."

"Well, we don't want her lobsters!" Kate leaned over the side of the boat and jerked at the crawl, tipping the lobsters into the sea.

"What the devil's the matter with you?"

"That girl is. Every time my back's turned out she comes. Lobsters! She just wants to talk to you. I should think you would have more sense than to encourage her."

Then, seeing Nick's face moving from surprise to grimness, watching his lips tighten, knowing that now he was fighting to hold something back, she wished from the depths of her heart that she had kept quiet. Why, why had she broken out?

In a low voice, stiff with control, Nick said evenly, "I think you're being pretty stupid, Kate. Let's hope that on the trip round the sea air blows some of the nonsense from your head."

He turned and went up the gangway without looking back at her and she heard him call to Rigo on deck. Biting at her lip she took the motor-boat away from the ship's side.

*   *   *   *

Nick was right, of course. She had been pretty stupid. What was it that got into you and made the words come tumbling out, even when you knew it was better not to speak? Nick hadn't put a foot wrong. So far—calming down and going over it now—she had no reason to imagine that Juana meant anything to him. She was just the kind of attractive girl any man would look at. Still . . . and there it was. Always the *still* that sprang from instinct.

She watched Cabo de Perada coming closer; a grey snout with the lighthouse sticking up like a horn on the nose of a rhinoceros.

The wind had got up since leaving the *Doria*, and the sea was lumpy and broken. The fringe of breakers along the cliffs made a booming sound that she could hear out here. Coming along she had been thinking of Nick and hadn't noticed the weather. Now she realised that the sun was gone and a great sweep of cloud pall was being pulled over the sky, wrinkled and grey like a bedsheet long due for a change. Now and again the motor-boat lifted its bows, checked by a wave and then plunged, pluming spray back to her. She was glad as the point came closer. At the base of the lighthouse she made out a small black figure. An arm was raised and she waved back, comforted by the presence of someone else. She had no feeling for the sea or boats, distrusting both and trying always to ignore an old fear of them in her. She didn't like this cumbersome slap of the sea and the steady whistle of the wind.

The moment she turned the point and came into the bay the sea was calmer, running evenly and the wind, blocked by the headland, lost its shrill note.

She dropped anchor in the boat basin. A boy rowed her

ashore and she went along to Johnny Manchester's garage to give him Nick's list. He promised to collect the stuff and take it out to the boat for her. She spent the next hour shopping along the seafront and finally finished up at the Hotel Margarita for lunch.

She enjoyed her lunch—a Spanish omelette, then cold lobster—that would have given Nick a laugh—and salad with half a bottle of white wine. She was feeling relaxed now and taking pleasure in eating food she hadn't cooked from a table sparkling with silver and polished glass. She wasn't really, she told herself, a camping or a boating girl; she liked comfort. She liked convention. Things to be right. Maybe stepping out of line convinced you, she decided, that there really was nothing like the rightness of things being right. How she had ever reached the stage of working in a cabaret in Barcelona she couldn't think. It couldn't have been her. She was a respectable doctor's daughter, tweeds in the leafy lanes of Kent, sitting uncomfortably on a shooting stick at point-to-points and standing by while the men heaved the car out of the mud afterwards.

She took a long time over her coffee and then, feeling luxury about her, responding to it after the *Doria*, she went upstairs and had a leisurely hot bath, borrowing bath salts from the proprietor's wife. Pottering around the bathroom naked she was conscious of being satisfyingly contained and protected. She stared at herself critically, but approvingly, in the mirror. . . . Unhurried, relaxed, talking to herself a little, she lay in the hot bath, her ego expanding like a Japanese paper flower dropped into water.

She came down into the tiled hallway, feeling refreshed and with a pleased self-confidence. Stuck out on the *Doria* made her get everything a little out of proportion, made it easy for her to over-exaggerate things. It was good to get away for a while and see things settle back into their rightful perspective. She looked around at the brightly polished furniture, the coloured Majorcan plates on the walls, the hanging lustres . . . and then in her mind saw the tiny captain's saloon of the *Doria*, and the deck littered with cases. For the first time for some days she felt that right in the heart of things she had no cause for worry.

At the bottom of the stairs the proprietor came round from behind his desk, smiling, and said:

"You are wanted on the telephone, Señora Thorne."

She was turning to go to the telephone when a voice from the doorway into the dining room said:

"Kate."

She half-turned back. Standing in the doorway was Ray Asherton. Against the long windows of the hallway there was a sudden lash of rain and somewhere at the back of the hotel a door banged sharply in the wind. She stood there, conscious of a voice crying protestingly inside her, *Oh, no! Oh, no!*

"Kate," he said again and began to come forward with an uncertain, anxious smile on his face.

The proprietor said, "Señora Thorne . . . the telephone. It is your husband wishing to speak to you."

She turned to the telephone, picked it up and heard Nick's voice come to her faintly as though he were a hundred miles away.

PART THREE

Chapter Thirteen

IT wasn't until he and Rigo broke off for lunch that Nick realised the change in the weather. The sun was gone, the wind had risen and there was a new sound in the bay, the long, whistling hiss of rollers running in from the north-west. This was the time of year when they could expect a few sudden gales. The set of water around the *Doria* had a slow, sullen force in it; bad-tempered and spoiling for trouble, he thought. Now and again a squall of wind and rain drove down the long ridge of cliffs and smacked across the decks in hard, fat drops.

Nick said to Rigo: "What do you think of it?"

Rigo looked at the sky.

"We haven't had a blow for a long time. Can't tell, señor. This could die out in an hour, or come in for the night."

"I'm thinking of Señora Thorne. She'll have got round all right. But I wouldn't want her to come back in this."

"She wouldn't try, señor. Not even a woman would be so foolish."

That's what he told himself, too. No woman would be so foolish, not if she thought about it. But if Kate had her mind full of other thoughts she might not even notice the weather. He looked up at the grey sky and then at the thick lacing of foam around the headland at the bay entrance.

They worked for an hour after lunch, but the anxiety was growing in him. They were hauling stuff up from the hold and piling it on deck and they had to be careful. There was a slight movement on the *Doria*, a gentle see-saw where she was held firmly amidships but pivoted to the force of the seas running up to her. The greasy water in the hold slopped and swirled around them and they had to watch the smaller cases to check them from sliding and falling.

At the end of an hour the concern in him for Kate was too much. He'd just realized that around in the Puerto bay there would be shelter from this north-west wind and Kate might easily be deceived by the calmness—until she got out to Cabo de Perada. There was only one way to stop her. He would have to ask Manasco for the use of his telephone —and risk a refusal. It was not something he relished doing, but for Kate it had to be done.

He climbed out of the hold and called to Rigo at the winch: "I'm going to make sure that she doesn't try to come out."

Rigo nodded and then flipping a brown arm towards the sky shouted, "It shows now. There is more to come."

Going to the cabin to clean himself up a little Nick walked down the starboard side of the *Doria*. The four stout rope hawsers that ran away to the cliffs were dipping and rising gently, but there seemed no great strain on them.

He took the skiff ashore and pulled it well up above the water line. The waves were now washing up over parts of the beach that hadn't been touched for weeks. A great mess of cork and bamboo and other drift rubbish lined the suddy edge of the sea. Now and again a wave licked around the base of the cargo piles from the forward hold.

He pulled the bell at the villa gate and waited, watching the wind sweep at the crests of the eucalyptus trees and billow out the loose bougainvillaea hangings along the balcony.

To his surprise it was Manasco himself who came down from the villa to the gate. He had a thick topcoat drawn around him, and a beret pulled tight down over his head. He looked like some old Tibetan monk, his brown face a lined mask, the skin shining from the rain which hissed down from the cliffs before the wind.

He opened the gate and, cocking his head a little, said "Señor?"

Nick came bluntly to the point.

"My wife took the motor-boat round to Puerto before

lunch. I don't want her to try and come back in this. It's going to get worse."

"Well?"

"I'd be glad if I could use your telephone. To call the Margarita. They'll find her and stop her."

Manasco's blue eyes blinked behind his glasses. Then he smiled and said, "Of course. I will show you where it is." He stood aside and with a little wave of his hand beckoned Nick into the garden. With the movement went a faint laugh. "I never expected you to ask any favours of me . . . but we never know, do we?" He began to move towards the house.

Nick wanted to go quickly across the courtyard and into the house, but Manasco walked slowly, huddled against the wind, shrinking before the loss of sun. As they came into the house he began to take off his coat. Over his shoulder he said: "You've nearly cleared the cargo?"

"Yes. It'll all be ashore in two or three days." He wanted to telephone, not to stand talking, but the old boy had been decent and he controlled his impatience. If the Margarita couldn't find Kate or she had left. . . . He could telephone the Perada lighthouse and get them to signal her back. . . .

"And what happens then?" Manasco rubbed a hand over his chin and the movement of his arm made the brown silk of his jacket rustle noisily in the still hallway.

Nick smiled. "You don't expect me to answer that."

"There isn't an answer. The telephone is down here." He led the way down the hall and without looking at Nick he went on talking. "But you still hope that some miracle will get your stuff to Palma on time? It won't, of course. I can tell you that." He unhooked a telephone from the wall and put it to his ear. He was looking now directly at Nick and his face was wrinkled, serious with the expression of a man who considered a problem with less concern in it for himself than for someone he was anxious to help. "It's a dreadful thing . . . this angry power which takes men, señor. This need to dominate. I've lived with it most of my life.

But for you I think it only happens rarely . . . perhaps now
for the first time? Hullo . . . I want the Hotel Margarita."
His attention came back from the telephone to Nick and he
smiled. "I'm used to winning, Señor Thorne. The need for
it is like a drug."

Nick stirred impatiently. "This is hardly the time——"

Manasco wagged a finger. "They always take ages to
make a connection. I shall win. You know that?"

"We shall see."

"No, I shall win. But the sad thing is that in winning we
lose as well. I admire your courage. I could have liked
you. But you threaten me and we fight. That is the tragedy
of power. It creates victories, but it makes no friends.
Neither among men nor nations. When I have beaten you,
remember this; that I could have been your friend."

A voice spoke distantly, reedy in the telephone. Manasco
handed the instrument to Nick. "Here is the hotel."

As Nick took the instrument the old man walked past
him and down a few steps. A door opened and before it shut
he had a glimpse of the long greensward of a billard table.

*   *   *   *

It was difficult to keep the exasperation from his voice.
Why did she have to be so awkward?

"But there's no point in it, Kate. You can't come round
by sea. That's definite. This weather's going to get worse.
And there's no point in your walking back. It's dangerous.
You never know when their damned dog's going to be loose.
I don't want your throat torn out. You stay there."

"But Nick, I don't want to. I want to come back. . . ."

He listened to her, staring at the billiard room door.
What could you do with a woman when she was like this?
You'd think she'd do as she was told. Here he was, asking
favours of Manasco to use his telephone. . . . Kate must
know that . . . and all she did was put up one long bellyache.

"Look, Kate——" he cut in on her. "I'm telling you what

to do. You spend the night at the hotel. Domingo Peroni's probably coming up tomorrow. The bad weather will be gone and you can bring him out. Hell, I should have thought you would have welcomed a night in comfort at the hotel. You deserve a break, anyway. . . ."

She started in again about walking out and he listened to her voice, thin and distant, and his foot tapped irritably on the tiled floor. What on earth had got into her?

"Listen, Kate," he interrupted her sharply. "I've already had to ask Manasco for the use of his telephone. But if you think I'm going to ask him to keep his dog shut up so that you can come up the valley you're mistaken. There's no earthly reason why you shouldn't stay the night there, and I'm not going to argue with you. You stay—and bring Peroni out tomorrow if he arrives. Is that clear? All right then. No more argument."

"But Nick——"

"Good-bye, Kate. See you tomorrow."

He put the receiver back on the wall hook and turned away towards the hall door. You got worried about a woman. You risked a smack in the eye from a man like Manasco over her and then what did she do? Set up a squawk. Why the hell couldn't she spend a night at the Margarita? It was just what she wanted to buck her up. Well, she was going to stay and that was that.

When he was almost at the door he paused. Damn it, here was Kate getting him irritable and he had nearly forgotten to thank Manasco for his courtesy. He began to turn back towards the billiard room when a door to his left opened and Juana came through into the hallway.

She stopped, a look of surprise on her face.

He said, "I don't want to disturb your uncle. Would you thank him for letting me have the use of your telephone?"

"You came here to use the telephone?"

"Yes."

She made a little mouth, smiling. "It must have been very important."

"It was. And if you'll thank him I'll be very grateful."

"Of course."

She went down the hall ahead of him. With her fingers on the door handle she turned, facing him, her face very close to his.

"Nick. . . ."

He frowned at the use of his name.

"Now look, Juana—don't start anything."

She put a hand on his shirt front, her fingers holding on to one of the buttons lightly.

"Don't look so stern. I only want to be sure that you understand what happened to me that night when Guido took the raft."

"Don't let's go into that."

"But I want to . . . I have to. One moment I was against you and the next I was for you. You know"—she cocked her head a little sideways—"I never thought it would be like this. Falling in love. It embarrasses you, but I don't care. I've got to say it. I don't care who knows it . . . It's a wonderful feeling. . . ."

Nick smiled. "You're young. You'll get used to it after the fourth or fifth time. It's like measles, all the childhood complaints . . . we have to have them before we can call ourselves grown up."

She shook her head. "A little while ago you'd have made me angry by that. Calling me young, a child. But I know now that's only your way of defending yourself against me. You don't want to believe me. You don't want to admit what you really feel."

"I feel that this conversation has gone far enough. Come on—open the door like a good girl and let me go. I've got work to do."

She laughed then and before he could move put her arms around his neck and kissed him quickly. She didn't resist when he took her arms and gently put her away from him. He reached past her and opened the door.

He looked back once as he went across the courtyard.

THE MANASCO ROAD 199

She was standing under the balcony and the wind was dragging at her skirts, shaping her legs and thighs under the thin silk. She waved. He deliberately did not wave back.

He went down across the beach and pushed the skiff out. It was a hard pull back to the *Doria* against the wind and he was glad of the chance to stretch his muscles, to fight against the set of the scud-tipped waves. He made an angry face, spat over the side and pulled harder.

* * * *

They worked right through that evening until about nine o'clock. The wind had risen higher and the whole bay was now soughing and hissing with its noise and that of the smash and seething slide of breakers. The overhead acetylene lights swung and dipped on their cables, fizzing and spluttering, and their movement cut the deck with sharp, dancing indigo shadows. The timber baulk raft alongside heaved and strained as the waves rolled across it. Now and again the squalls of wind came filled with the sharp lash of rain, and sometimes they were full of dust and whirling pieces of vegetation as they swooped off the nearby cliffs.

After the warm blue skies and the weeks of placid sea, there was an excitement and wildness in the storm which found a response in both Rigo and Nick. To the challenge of Manasco in their path was added the storm and, though they need not have worked late, they went on, neither questioning the need.

Manhandling the smaller cases, and using the hoist for the larger ones they cleared the after hold to well below water level. The stuff they took out they stacked on deck on the port side ready to off-load to the raft.

It was cold from the water in the hold and they kept a bottle of Domecq brandy by the winch. Hard work, brandy and a wild night. If a man had trouble on his mind, thought Nick, these would lift it. Laughing, singing and swearing with Rigo he felt a sense of rough happiness in him. It was good to have this to do. It was good to have a fight on his hands. He remembered the evening . . . so distant it seemed now . . . when he had got off the Barcelona plane at Palma. He had been happy then, but a smug, unruffled, selfish kind of happiness. Rubbing along in the old groove. But this was different. He had his teeth into this Manasco situation and he wasn't going to let go.

When they knocked off they sluiced down outside the galley and then had a scratch meal washed down with brandy and water. Coming on deck afterwards to douse the acetylene lights, Nick glanced at the four hawsers holding the *Doria* to the far cliff. The bow hawser was under water as the sea channelled between the gap made by the *Doria* and the shore. There seemed to be more strain on the two after-hawsers. They still dipped and rose with the slight movement on the ship, but every now and again one of them would come up almost to full strain.

He turned to Rigo.

"You'd better sleep aboard tonight. Could be we might have some trouble with those hawsers. You can take the other bunk in the cabin."

Lying on their bunks they talked for a while, but they were both so tired that they were soon asleep.

When Nick woke it was to find the cabin oil lamp still burning. It swung free on a hook near the door. He lay there for a while, coming slowly out of deep sleep. He looked at his wristwatch. It was just before midnight. He was wondering what had wakened him. Outside the bay was full of the sound of wind and water, an angry, raw breathing and panting. The wind was higher. He could tell that by the keener note it played on the funnel stays aft of the bridge. He glanced across at Rigo. He was flat on his back, his mouth open.

His eyes came back to the cabin light. The wick was smeeching a little. Then, held by a stupid, half-awake curiosity, he saw the cracks of the door planking behind the lamp slowly slide over out of vertical, stay for a while and then as slowly come back to an upright position. With the movement he felt himself drawn over against the far side of the bunk. He watched while it happened again. Then it came to him.

He leaped out of the bunk and, pulling on his trousers, shouted to Rigo. Rigo came awake, fuddled, and Nick shook at his shoulder.

"Something's wrong. She's heeling. Come on!"

He rushed out of the saloon and down to the deck. A squall of rain slashed into his face, blinding him for a moment. Under his feet the deck heeled again to port. He saved himself against the side of the galley and then tore down the deck to the stern. The deck heeled again and from the darkness of the port side he heard the crash of cases falling.

Rigo came running up to him with a torch in his hand. The beam flickered aft. The light steadied on a deck capstan to which one of the two after-hawsers had been made fast. The great rope that ran from the ship to the cliff was hanging loose.

"Hawser's gone!" shouted Nick. He grabbed the torch from Rigo. A roaring breaker, known only by its ghostly spume-white crest, raced in from the bay and smashed against the stern of the *Doria*. She lifted and then heeled gently over, steadied and then came back . . . but from the far side came the crash of more cases from the stacks there.

From further up in the stern Rigo shouted: "This one's gone, too, señor."

"Take a look at the cases and see what you can do there!"

Nick turned and ran forward. If all four of the ropes parted then nothing could stop the *Doria* from heeling right over. With the torch he checked the two forward hawsers. They were all right. But flicking the light out along them he could see they were well up over the broken water now. If much more strain was put on them they would go.

G*

He ran back to Rigo, the torchlight picking a path for
him. Two piles of cases had slipped as the deck heeled and
the stuff was all over the place and most of it jammed hard
up against the port rail. If the *Doria* heeled much more the
rest of the deck cargo would slide against the rail and crash
through. There was more than half the after-hold cargo on
deck. If they lost that their profits would be that much
smaller. But worse than that, if the *Doria* heeled too much and
came off the rocks that held her pivoted somewhere amidships she might go right over and then they could kiss the
rest of the after-hold cargo goodbye.

Rigo came stumbling towards him over the loose cases.
Nick grabbed his shoulder and they steadied themselves
against another swing of the *Doria*.

"Listen, Rigo,"—he had to shout to be heard above the
wind—"we've got to get new stern hawsers out to stop this
heeling or she'll go over." As he spoke he began to move
around the after-hold to the starboard side. Down below in
the darkness of the hold he could hear the swirl and slap of
water.

"There's enough slack round the capstans on deck to
reach the cliff, no matter where they're broken."

They got hold of the first broken hawser and began to
haul it aboard. It came in easily with the two of them on it.
Twenty yards of heavy, water-sodden rope. With the slack
that had always been on deck beyond the capstan they had
about a hundred yards of hawser. The gap between the
Doria and the shore was no more than fifty yards. The
second hawser had parted nearer the shore and they had
about thirty yards of it as well as the slack on deck.

As they finished hauling it in, Nick said, "I'll row ashore
with two light lines. When I'm there you fasten your end
of the lines to the broken ends of the hawsers here. But
remember—if she starts to go, you jump for it like hell!"

"But, señor, when you haul on these ropes they'll be like
lead."

"I'll get them ashore. Every time she heels back to

position I can work up the slack. You get the light lines and I'll bring the skiff around to this side and you can drop them to me."

At the moment the *Doria* was only pivoting gently and the two hawsers would hold her, but the danger was that before he could check the swing the keel would grind and break away the holding rocks and then—well, Manasco would have good news with his breakfast.

Because of the seas they'd drawn the skiff up the gangway a few feet and lashed her. He jerked the lashings free and let her run stern first down the few steps. A wave caught her stern and swung her out and he jumped, landing all over the place and swearing. Before he could get the oars out he was swept beachwards almost to the bows of the *Doria*. He pulled round under the cutwater, found calm water for a moment and then began to work up the other side.

In the narrow channel between ship and shore the sea was going like a mill race, broken and angry with the scour over the shallow rock bed. His eyes, accustomed to the dark now, watched the black sheer of the *Doria's* plates on his left, marking his progress against the rust patches. The wind, full on his bows and back, fought against him with the run of the sea. For a while he crept up, inch by inch, towards the stern. Then as the channel narrowed with the bulge of *Doria* amidships he was only just holding his own.

From the darkness above him came a shout. He looked up quickly and saw Rigo's silhouette against the grey sky. A couple of lines came snaking down, weighted with pieces of wood. One of the wood lengths hit his foot, but he hardly felt it. He leaned forward, grabbed the lines and made a couple of quick hitches around the stern thwart, feeling the skiff being swept away as he stopped rowing. For a second or two the thin lines were taut like bow strings. Then up above Rigo began to pay them out fast.

Nick grabbed the oars and began to work across the channel current. He didn't have to be told what Rigo was doing. He would pay out and work his way with the other ends of the lines to the stern. Nick could go ashore where he liked and then walk up abreast of the stern with his end of the lines. Even so, the lines were not unlimited and he crabbed across the dark channel to make the nearest landing he could.

He looked over his shoulder. The shore was only a few yards away. But there was no easy sand here; just a grey jumble of rocks and above them the darker shadow of bamboo and the hard line of cactus spikes. The run of the sea smacked against the skiff, sending spray high over him. An angle of rock ran out and he edged in behind it. Momentarily the skiff hung in a mêlée of disturbed water. He unshipped the lines and wound them round his arm. There was a moment of tangle and confusion and the skiff began to slide out. He met the situation with the only solution he could command. He rolled over the side of the skiff and grabbed at the nearest rock.

As he climbed ashore he saw the skiff ride away towards the beach. Well, they could pick her up in the morning. She would drive up on to the sand and come to little harm.

He stood up, sorted the lines out and then began to work his way over the broken rocks, taking in the slack on the lines as he went. He could feel the tug of the water dragging at them as he went. The throb and vibration along them reminded him of the electric pulse that came into a line when a fish struck. Somewhere out in the darkness he heard Rigo shout. He answered, calling back through the night, the wind full in his throat and a sudden surge of excitement filled him. Hell, he wouldn't care for this as a regular thing, but it did something for a man that months of selling tourists' novelties and other odds-and-ends could never do. And anyway, if the *Doria* did go over, it wouldn't be Manasco who had beaten him. It would be the wind and the sea. You couldn't beat them if they really put their minds to it.

A sharp spur of rock went up fifty feet in his path and he climbed it. At the top he paused to take in more slack.

The light lines were clear of the water now. He saw the faint gleam of the oil lamp from the bridge saloon and beyond it, lost now and again in the slashing veil of rain, a light from the Villa Ermano. They'd all be safe in bed.

And Kate would be safe in bed too. He was glad he had stopped her coming back. She couldn't have come off in the skiff with him. She couldn't have done Rigo's job on the *Doria*. . . . Well, things worked out. He'd never have been able to leave her on the *Doria* if there had been the slightest chance that the whole caboodle might go heeling over for good. And, by God, there was more than a chance it could happen.

He took out the torch which he had shoved into his trouser pocket and signalled his position to Rigo. Then he dropped down from the spur and began to work along the jumble of rocks. The wind had shifted and was running now free into the mouth of the bay. The sea was swinging in, raising great shouldering slopes of water, hissing happily as they came smashing against the rocks in a frenzy of power, the spray and spume sheeting high.

He ducked under the first of the bow hawsers running above his head to a rock up the cliffside. Raising his hand he could feel the tension on it. The other one, ten yards further on went slack as he worked his two light lines under it and then came up, taut and humming for a moment as out in the darkness the *Doria* heeled. He flashed his torch again and saw an answering flicker from the *Doria* and fancied he heard Rigo shouting. The cliff broke back in a deep gullet full of dark, churning water. He dropped in and went across the few yards, splashing and kicking clumsily like a dog, the slack on the lines coiled in a tangle over one arm. A wave took him and threw him up against a rock and he felt the harsh bite of raw stone against the skin of his shoulder.

Twenty yards further on and he was on a wide, creviced plateau of rock, the sea smacking against its lip and sending spray cascading high into the air. The surface of the plateau sang and chattered with the noise of returning water. Rigo's torch flashed again and he saw that he was level with the stern now. He swung his own torch round and examined the ground at the back of the rock platform. A blunt pinnacle of stone projected from the foot of the cliff. It would make a good anchorage for one hawser. The original hawsers had been made fast higher up the cliff but he knew he couldn't hope to drag the heavy, sea-sodden ropes up there. Ten yards to the right of the pinnacle there was another rock outcrop which would take the second hawser. He made the end of his light lines fast around each anchorage and then, holding the pinnacle line went back across the rock platform to the sea. A savage burst of wind and water buffeted into him and for a moment he staggered against the force.

Rigo's torch began to move round in a slow circle. He answered and began to haul in on the light line.

It came easily at first, throbbing with the run of the sea over it in the channel. Then he felt it jerk and more weight go on it and he knew that Rigo had started to pay out the thick hawser attached to the end of the light line. He braced against the pull, dragging the line in hand over hand. It came slowly, the weight growing on it with each foot he won. A large wave burst over the edge of the plateau and knocked him flat. He rolled away, still clutching the line, and cursing loudly in the darkness.

He found a footing and started to haul again. After an age he felt the thick end of the hawser come up into his hand. He strained at it now, hand over hand, and all the time working backwards across the platform towards the rock pinnacle.

Rigo was right, he thought grimly. It was like lead. But lead that had life; alive and kicking and fiendishly unwilling to give way to him. Sweating and straining he went back inch by inch. But when he was half-way across the plateau he felt the hawser resist him, hard in his hands with an unmoving malice. Then slowly it began to pull away from him. For a moment he hung on, feeling himself being dragged back towards the plateau edge and he knew that out there in the wild night the *Doria* was heeling over and taking the hawser with it. He ceased fighting the rope and paid out slack until the hawser stopped moving away from him. Then, with a desperate energy, he hauled in again, fighting to take up all the slack he could and win a few more feet towards the pinnacle. He got the hawser end to within two yards of it when he felt the seaward pull and knew the *Doria* was swinging over again. He went back with the rope, panting and cursing with frustration.

Three times he went back and forth on the drag of the hawser. The rope now had become a personal, living presence which he hated and fought with a bitter anger. His hands raw from the bite of the wet rope, his muscles cracking as he fought the long drag from the darkness, he suddenly felt the rock pinnacle rough against his back and wondered desperately through the mist of anger in his mind whether he would ever get enough slack to make a turn round it. . . . His strength was going. The rope began to work away from him again and he went with it. Digging his heels into the rock surface, he tripped and fell. Holding the rope still, he felt himself being dragged forward. The lash of a breaking wave sent a slither of water over his head and shoulders and he choked for air as he fought his way to his knees.

From the darkness to his right he heard a shout. Then there was the wet slap of feet in the water over the rock platform. Someone went by him and he saw the brief whiteness of face and hands. He was on his feet now and as the *Doria* swung back from her heeling he gathered in the hawser once more. This time it came without so much struggle and he saw a dark shape ahead of him, bending to the rope, straining at its unwillingness with him. He came back now with a yard of slack to spare at the pinnacle, but he wanted more. Twice more he followed the rope back on the heel of the *Doria* and then, with three yards of rope to spare at the pinnacle, he threw a quick hitch round the rock, As the *Doria* out there in the gloom and wildness began to heel again, he shouted a warning to the figure on the rope ahead of him.

He went forward quickly his hands free and dragged the figure down to the rock, shouting, "Keep flat—if the hawser parts we could be knocked to hell."

He lay there, head screwed upwards and he saw the stout rope slide away a little and then begin to rise, slack at first and then tightening. It went up, four feet to the level of the pinnacle fastening and then tautened. The water sprayed from the hemp as the strain went on it and he prayed that it would hold against the sway of the *Doria*. If it parted the whipping ends could sweep across the plateau like steel cables, could cut a man in half. . . .

It held. Slowly the strain went off and it slacked back. He jumped to his feet, a cry of triumph in his throat and reached down. A wet hand found his, and the figure at his feet came up. Juana's face was close to his. Her hands grasped at his arms, and he saw the shine in her dark eyes and felt the warm breath from lips close to his cheek.

"There's another one!" he shouted above the wind.

He raced to the edge of the plateau, flashed his torch in a circle to Rigo and began to haul in on the second light line. They worked shoulder to shoulder, without words, and he knew that without her he could never have done it . . . the hawser would have beaten him, worn him down.

They got the other hawser ashore and this time, because the first hawser was checking most of the heeling, it came without too much difficulty. They got a half turn round the other rock and then, waiting their chance, sweated the rope up more and more and finally secured it. The heeling now was down to no more than an occasional sway that brought the hawsers up tight and made them sing for a moment as the wind broke against them. He knew they would hold. In the morning he and Rigo could go over them together and take up any stretch and slackness.

The wind was still high but the clouds were thinning and it was a little lighter now. He watched the two hawsers rise and hold and dip. He had one arm round Juana's shoulder as she stood close to him. Through the light silk mackintosh which the wind draped and billowed around her he felt her shiver.

"I saw your torches flashing. . . . I'm glad I came," she said.

"I'd never have done it without you," he said. "Come on, you're cold and wet through. . . ."

He turned and taking her hand went to the foot of the rough cliff slope and began to climb it. A few yards up there was a little path that led around to the beach. She walked ahead of him, without speaking. A rain squall broke down over them. He saw the broken shine of water on her coat like quicksilver, and somewhere in his mind there was an exultation running like quicksilver, an intoxication arising from the wild night, from his fatigue and the relief of snatching success from the moment of defeat.

They came down on to the beach by the little fisherman's shelter where Rigo normally slept. She stopped and turned to him, her feet thrusting into the soft damp sand, her body braced to take the drag of the wind against her coat. She put up her hands towards him and the wind took her coat and swept it out like a great spread of wings behind her and he saw that she was wearing white pyjamas under it.

"Nick——"

Whatever else she said was lost in a burst of rain that hissed across the beach. To escape it he put his arm around her and pulled her into the little hut. In the darkness the noise of the rain against the bamboo palisade walls of the hut were like the fretting tattoo of hundreds of nervous fingers. He could hear her breathing close to him, the warmth brushing against his neck.

He put his hands up in the darkness and found hers and with the movement he felt her fingers lock gently into his and then begin to tremble.

"You ought to get back," he said and his voice was rough above the noisy assault of rain on the hut. "You're cold. . . ."

Her hands moved, taking his, and through the pyjama silk he felt her breasts as she pressed his raw palms against them.

"Nick. . . ."

Suddenly there was no strength or will in him to break the power of the darkness and her closeness, made closer by the wind and rain-filled night outside. She came to him and there was salt on her lips and the warmth and softness and trembling eagerness of her skin under his hands.

She laughed and kissed him, and there was nothing that had any place in the darkness, no thought, no word, no memory, except the two of them, impatient for each other, tender for each other. . . .

Chapter Fourteen

HE woke once, feeling the weight of her shoulders against his outflung arm. Half-asleep he reached over in the darkness and his hand, touching her skin, moved caressingly over the smooth line of her waist and found the edge of her flung-back pyjama jacket. He pulled it over her gently, feeling her stir and then draw closer to him, her face seeking the angle of his neck and shoulder. Momentarily, the warm, moist pressure of sleeping lips were against his flesh. Hazily the beginning of thought began to pry into his mind, but sleep and the long, calm ease in his body thrust it away as he half-turned and gathered the softness of her body to him and drifted away to the adieu of the wind fretting at the loose thatching of the hut roof.

He woke again much later, knowing she was awake and stirring. For a moment through half-open lids he saw her. The hut was still. The wind and rain had gone and a pale, pearly light was in the place. Outside a late moon had risen. She was on her knees beside him, her face lifted towards the roof, smiling, and her hands were cupped under her bare breasts, holding them, her body drawn up by some muscular ecstasy. He saw the dark pool of shadow across her stomach under the bold arch of her ribs.

A hand touched his forehead. He felt her lips move lightly on to his mouth and work across it in faint kisses. Then the lips were gone and he heard the rustle of her raincoat and the crunch of sand under her feet. He began to lift his shoulders from the roll of nets, wanting to call her back. But she was already at the door, framed against the pale night, and he made neither move nor sound to stop her. This must end, he told himself, as it had begun, the whole thing belonged to this night and the wildness of the storm. . . .

He watched her in the doorway. She was looking out at the beach, at the moonlit bay and the hills that went with a grey, brutal roughness shouldering to the sky. . . . She turned back, not seeing his open eyes in the gloom of the hut, kissed her fingertips to him and moved away.

He lay there, the harshness of the nets under his bare shoulders, and he knew there were two things he must hold to beyond all others. This must be something locked away from Kate since at no point did it touch her or his love for her. And further, and perhaps more important, it would be useless to try and work it out for himself. To ask himself Why? would lead nowhere. It had happened. But it had sprung from no past, and it must not be allowed any future. It sounded ruthless, shameless, but it had to be that way.

He sat up after a while and groped for his shirt. He found it, a limp, torn rag. He must find the skiff and get back to the *Doria*. He went to the door of the hut and there was the long, bulky shape of the *Doria* motionless on the flat, polished marble of a still sea, and away by the spring the skiff nosing against the sand like a patient horse, waiting. . . .

He moved away from the hut and as he went flung down the ripped and useless shirt. It hit the sand at the base of a pile of door frames. Someone moved from the shadow of the piled cargo, looked down at the shirt and then up at him.

It was Kate. She wore an unbuttoned raincoat, her hands deep in the pockets. Her shoulders were hunched a little and a wing of her fair hair curled low over her forehead.

They looked at one another without speaking, and he could read the hard lines of thought and pain on her face. Momentarily it was the face of another Kate, older, sadder and coldly disturbing.

"Kate——"

She shook her head suddenly, a bitter gesture that stopped his tongue, and he heard her breath drawn in sharply, hungrily, as though she had a desperate need of air.

"I saw her come out," she said. "You don't have to say anything." She spoke low, but her voice was vibrant, shaking with held-down emotions.

He put his hand up, covering his eyes. "The whole thing . . . Kate, it was a madness. It doesn't belong to anything we know——"

"Yes it does! It's part of you, part of us." She turned away, hiding her face from him. "But why talk about it? I did it to you. Now you do it to me——"

"Kate! For God's sake, it wasn't like that!"

"Wasn't it?" She turned back and for the first time the stir of anger was clear in her eyes. "You had to do something, didn't you? You had to let go somewhere. But why should I complain? Is that what you're saying to yourself? After all I started the ball rolling——"

"I won't let you talk like that." He stepped forward and took her arm fiercely. Impatiently, she pulled her arm free.

"Go away, Nick. Leave me alone."

"Don't be a fool, Kate. I'm staying with you."

"No. . . ." It was a sudden cry. "Don't you see . . . only a little while ago that girl walked out of there and everything went upside down. . . . I don't know what I'm thinking or feeling yet."

She began to walk away from him. He hurried after her.

"Where are you going? You can't hang about here all night."

"Don't worry about me. There's nothing here now that can hurt me any more. Let me go."

"But Kate, I must know. . . . What are you going to do?"

"I'm going back to Puerto. I want to think and I want to be alone."

"But Kate, I've got to know . . . about us, I mean."

"So have I, Nick. But I don't know. I can't know yet——"

"But that's not fair. When you told me, I gave you an answer——"

"An answer!" She swung round, the sound of her words

bitter on the night air. "You used words. If that's an answer. But this is the real answer. This, tonight——"

"Kate!"

He reached for her as she moved away, but she avoided him and, without looking back, cried, "Don't follow me! I can't bear it. Just leave me alone. . . ."

He followed her to the top of the rise overlooking the long valley and watched her move away through the myrtle bushes until she finally reached the road. Under the moonlight the small black figure moving down the rough track looked forlorn and lonely. She reached the padlocked road gate and a few moments later was lost to sight.

He turned away and walked back to the beach. What could he do, he asked himself savagely? He was in the wrong. He had to wait. She'd come back, and he would get hell; all sorts of hell, but none of it mattering because underneath they were still Kate and Nick. . . .

There was one oar still left in the skiff. She was half-full of water and he rolled her over and drained her out. Using the oar over the stern he ferried himself out to the *Doria*. It was hard to believe that three hours ago the bay had been churning with sea and wind. . . . Now it was like a tarnished mirror.

Standing at the top of the gangway, he saw that astern on the port side the deck was littered with cases. One of them had smashed open and the white porcelain shards of a washbasin caught the moonlight like ice. But the rail had held and nothing had gone overboard.

Rigo was in the saloon, asleep and snoring. Nick fixed himself a brandy and water, lit a cigarette and went out on to the bridge. He leaned on the rail, smoking and drinking gradually feeling calmer. His eyes were on the valley running back to Puerto. The only thing to do now was to ride it out. She'd be back in the morning . . . or if she wasn't he'd go and fetch her.

*   *   *   *

They checked the hawsers after breakfast, sweating up the slack on them from the deck around the fore and aft capstan. With the sun a light breeze was running, but there was no movement on the *Doria* to worry about. She'd settled a little more and the water was higher in the engine room and holds.

For two hours they worked, off-loading stuff from the deck on the raft. There was little cargo left in the after hold now and they wouldn't touch it until they had made more deck room. While they worked, Nick kept looking towards the beach. Maybe she wouldn't come back on her own. She would have returned to Puerto, calmed down and would now wait to bring Peroni around. He kept one ear cocked for the sound of the motor-boat rounding the point into the bay.

The rope tackle which they used to ferry the raft ashore had parted during the night and when the raft was loaded and ready for the first run to the beach, they rigged a new line and Nick rowed ashore with it to make it fast to the anchorage up on the cliff bluff.

From the beach, he saw Juana come out of the villa side gate and walk along the top of the bluff towards him. She raised a hand and waved and he waited for her by a pile of cargo. He lit a cigarette and watched her come down to the beach. She looked young and fresh, moving lightly, one hand holding the side of her white skirt, drawing the pleats out as though she were showing off its lines. With each step she took towards him he knew that the moment was coming which he would hate, but which had to be met. And he knew that he could never come out of this with any credit.

She stopped a yard from him and the sun was bright on her face as she said, "Nick." He knew that look must have been there as she walked unknowingly past Kate last night. That look, a sword thrust to Kate then, and a sword thrust to him now.

"Juana."

She said, "Nick" again, as though the word were an echo

repeating itself in her mind, and he told himself not to weaken because of the young happiness in her.

He said, "Juana, I've got to speak to you very frankly." He stopped, groaning to himself. God, how bloody pompous he sounded, hollow and false.

She nodded, unsurprised, full of calm and said, "I know what you're going to say. That you will give me the chance to forget it all. But you don't have to give me any chance to escape, Nick. I love you and I know that you love me."

He pulled at his cigarette and the end broke between his lips, the bitter tobacco harsh on his tongue. He jerked the frayed stub from him.

"You've got to listen to me carefully, Juana. I don't want to, but I'm going to hurt you. You're going to hate me——"

"Nick! I told you I don't want a chance to escape. I've got it all worked out. You think because of this——" her hand swept towards the piled cargo and out at the *Doria*, "that it's impossible, but it isn't. My uncle won't fight you when he knows about us. He'll help us. Be with us."

"Juana, you mustn't talk like that."

"Why not? You don't imagine I don't know how things are between you and your wife? Nick, why do you look like that?" Her voice faded and she frowned and, for the first time, he guessed that she was aware that things weren't moving the way she had imagined they would.

"What do you know?"

"That you've had trouble . . . that she doesn't love you."

He stepped forward, taking her by the arms and pulling her towards him so that her face looked up into his and she could not escape him.

"Juana—listen to me. Get this straight. What happened last night was the kind of thing that happens to men and women out of the blue. When you are young, it's part of growing up, reaching out into the world to find yourself. When you're my age . . . God knows what it is. But you must understand this—it has nothing to do with love. You don't love me. You love the idea of loving me . . . you're still looking for yourself. But with me it's different. I love Kate and she loves me and there's no real trouble between us. . . ."

She pulled away from him. He could see from her frown and the shadow in her eyes and the hardening of her mouth that she was hurt and baffled.

Slowly she said, "You don't love me?"

"No."

"You wouldn't marry me?"

"I'm married to Kate."

"And you love her?"

"I said so."

"And you think she loves you?"

"I know she does."

He saw her press her hands together hard as though inside her she fought some effort either to hold back or thrust forward some protest. Then with a scornful laugh she said:

"She loves you. . . . Oh, Nick, don't keep it up. I know she doesn't. I read the letter Ray Asherton sent her. She must have been glad when you telephoned her to stay the night in Puerto. Guido saw them. Your wife and Asherton having dinner together——"

"What!"

He stepped forward, grabbing at her wrist.

"Guido saw them!"

He understood then, and there was a humiliation in him which Juana would never see. He closed his eyes and the warm morning air was arid in his throat. That was why she'd wanted to come back, fought him over the telephone and finally set out in the night. . . . And she had come back to find him—

He suddenly released Juana's wrist and turned away. God, what a mess! What a mess!

She was at his side as he walked to the skiff, and without looking at her he said fiercely:

"Go away, please." He bent to the bows of the skiff and

began to push it off the sand. "I've given you the truth, been honest. You've got to take it. You can hate me, think what you like, but you've got to take it."

He stood ankle deep in the water and she splashed to his side and caught his arm. Her face was angry now and the pride was back, the black flash alive in her eyes and a new, hard set to her body.

"You're going to Puerto? To find her?"

"Yes."

"You're a fool!"

Her hand flashed up and she struck him across the face with all her force. His eyes misted with the shock. He heard her speak words of dark abuse.

"Good," he said hoarsely. "That is what I deserved, and more, and much more."

He got into the skiff, took the oars and began to row and he saw her standing at the water's edge, watching him go, unmoving until he was almost at the *Doria* when she turned and began to walk slowly back to the villa.

*   *   *   *

He didn't give Rigo any explanation. He told him he had to go to Puerto suddenly and hoped to be back that night. Rigo could ferry the raft load ashore on his own and then unload it. For the rest of the time he could get the remaining smaller cases out of the after-hold. Rigo knew there was something wrong, but he asked no questions: not even when Nick took one of the shotguns with him. He meant to go to Puerto down the valley, using the road, and he needed the gun for the dog was often loose by day.

Rigo rowed him ashore. He went up over the cliff bluff and then across the stony fields below the valley wall to the right. When he was well past the house he struck across and found the rough road. There was no sign of the dog. Beyond the padlocked gate, he found a clump of bushes and hid the shotgun in them.

It was gone midday when he reached Puerto. At the
Margarita the proprietor came round his desk with a smile
to greet him.

"Is Señora Thorne here?"

"No, señor."

"But she has been?"

"Yes, señor. She came in early this morning. She changed
and went out after breakfast."

Nick was silent for a moment. Kate kept a case of spare
clothes at the hotel.

"You've got a Mr. Asherton staying here?"

"We did have, señor. He left in his car for Palma, very
early this morning . . . about seven. . . ." The hotel proprietor was looking curiously at him.

"And you don't know where Señora Thorne has gone?"

"No, señor. I am sorry."

Outside, as he made his way to Johnny Manchester's
garage, where he had left his car, he saw that their motor-
boat was still anchored in the boat basin.

He was luckier with Johnny. Kate had come to the
garage around eleven and wanted the car.

"But you know, señor, you ask me to check over the
brakes for you sometime . . . I was in the middle of it, and
she would not wait."

"Where was she going, Johnny?"

"Palma. But she was too late for the bus that goes right
through. I saw her get the local bus to Regano, across the
road there. She would have an hour to wait in Regano for
a connection. Is something wrong?"

"No, Johnny . . . but I'll take the car now if it's ready."

Palma; and Asherton had gone to Palma, too. He drove
the five miles to Regano trying not to think. He turned off
the main road up into the town. The bus station was in the
square. Knowing the casual way the buses made their
connections and the frequency with which they broke down,
there was just a chance that Kate might be still hanging
about. Full of impatience he threaded his way through the

narrow streets and turned into the sleepy, sun-washed square with the tall, baroque facing of the church of Nuestra Señora de los Angeles dominating the narrow-faced houses around.

A handful of children were playing around the porch of the church; two old men were asleep on a bench under a tree, and outside the café a few people were sitting at tables drinking coffee.

There was no sign of a bus or Kate. Nick drove round the square to make his way back to the main road. A blaze of bright-coloured posters caught his eye from the dingy wall of the cinema. As he slowed for the turning someone called to him. Colonel da Lapa came out of the cinema hallway and waved. Nick drew up.

The Colonel gave him a little bow and smiled, holding aloft a couple of paper slips.

"Tonight it is a western film. I am an addict and book seats for myself and my wife."

Even in his own abstraction and worry Nick felt a tinge of surprise. Odd, he had never imagined that da Lapa had a wife.

Nick said, casually, "I suppose you haven't seen my wife about? We arranged to meet here."

Colonel da Lapa looked at his wristlet watch and cocked a thin eyebrow at Nick.

"You are in trouble, señor. You are two hours late. She will be angry with you."

"You've seen her?"

"But of course. As I came down from police headquarters before lunch I saw her. We spoke for a while."

"Where is she now?"

"She said she was walking up to the Oratory. There is a wonderful view from there. Maybe she is up there still. . . ."

"Thanks."

"It is nothing. You are still working against Señor Manasco?"

"What? Oh, that. . . ." Nick laughed absently. There

had been nothing in his mind for hours but Kate. Manasco
was a million miles away. "Oh, yes—we're still at it."

Colonel da Lapa touched the polished, fresh-shaven side
of his face, gently flexing his cheek muscles. "Maybe I
should book seats for the end of that show, too?"

"I'll give you a couple of free ones."

Nick let in the gear and backed away, turning into the
square. He went slowly through the narrow streets and
alleys that led to the foot of the long Calvary steps at the
top of the town. The Oratory was at the top of the steps,
perched on the crest of the hill which rose above Regano.

A few cottages crowded about the bottom of the steps. In
their open doorways sat old women, bent over their sewing.
They scarcely looked at him as he passed. Cypresses and a
low wall flanked the steps and the hillside was terraced for
vines and olives. Little patches of vegetables made a green
brightness against the red earth and over the hot wide
stones there was the thin flash of lizards disturbed by his
hurrying footsteps. Meeting da Lapa had been luck. A sign.
She had to be up here. If she weren't up here, everything
was to hell and gone. If she'd only come up to pass the
time until her bus, he was sunk. He knew that. Not with
any reason but from instinct. If she ever reached Palma, he
was sunk . . . his impatience took him up the steps three at
a time and long before he reached the top he was sweating
hard. Below him the ground dropped away, cut by narrow
valleys, the neighbouring hills and crests bold against the
blue afternoon sky. Regano itself spread out in a maze of
chocolate, red and ochre tiled roofs.

There were a couple of workmen repairing one of the
walls of the tiny oratory. One of them was singing as he
mixed cement with a long-handled, heart-shaped spade. A
little notice by some newly-planted trees read: *Quien troncha
un arbol, corta una vida.* There were more ways of killing life,
he thought than by using an axe. . . . You could die and
still live.

The breeze, cloaked until now by the steep walls and

the dark, sentinel cypresses, swept free over the hill crest,
striking cold against Nick's hot face. She had to be here.
A little path ran out to the right of the oratory, flanked by
young trees.

He stopped, held by a leaden drape that seemed to cloak
his whole body. She wasn't here. Slowly, feeling that he
had to fight for every movement, he lit himself a cigarette.
She was in Palma. Her anger with him had carried her that
far, lasted through the hours, shown itself permanent . . .
and now there was no meaning in anything for him. Not
even any pieces to pick up and patch together. The shabbi-
ness of the whole thing filled him with dejection. She'd come
back from Asherton, refused to stay the night near him . .
and he, Nick, had presented her with a fine reward. He
swore to himself and began to turn back to the steps.

As he did so there was a movement behind an old olive
tree near the wall that guarded the edge of the far slope.
He saw a flash of pale, straw-coloured hair and the swinging
edge of a green skirt. Without appearing to move she was
abruptly in the open, leaning back against the wall and
watching him.

Very slowly he went to her. He stopped, uncertain, when
he was close to her. Her face looked tired, but composed.

"Kate. . . ."

"Hullo, Nick." Her voice was calm, but he knew that
this was no moment to go closer, to touch her.

"Kate," he said quietly, "I'm so glad I've found you. . . ."

She looked down at her hands, spreading them for a
moment against the green of her skirt, and then her eyes
came back to him.

When she didn't answer he went on. "When you didn't
come back, I wondered. . . . Why didn't you come back?"

She looked up sharply. "Because I had a lot of thinking
to do. Because I wasn't in the right frame of mind when I
left you. I've been sitting up here for the last two hours
trying to get it all straight."

"What is there to get straight? It's clear enough, Kate.

I made a damned fool of myself. I love you and I want
you to forgive me. If you can't . . . well. . . ." He made a
hopeless gesture with his hands.

"That would be easy, wouldn't it? We love each other,
so we forgive each other. That's been the whole trouble.
We haven't gone deeper than that."

"I don't understand you. If you love then you can forgive."

"No, Nick—there's far more to it. That's what I've been
thinking about. Why do you think you and that girl——"

"Because I was an idiot. I must have been mad. I could
explain how it happened——"

"Not how, Nick. I know how it happened, or I can
guess. What I want to know is why it happened. Why did
you do it?"

"You don't think I did it because I thought it was a
way of getting my own back?"

"If I did I wouldn't be talking to you now. Last night
in the heat of the moment I thought that. But not now.
But the real reason isn't very different. You did it, Nick,
because right down in your heart you hadn't forgiven me."

"But of course I had!"

"No. Why should you? Forgiveness isn't the act of a
moment. It takes time to forgive. When a man's hurt he
wants to strike back and forgive afterwards. So does a
woman—and that's where the danger is. You tried to forgive
and not strike back. . . . I saw that right from the start. But
I know that it only needed something to touch you off . . .
to release your violence. That's why I was glad when you
decided to fight Manasco."

"What on earth's he got to do with it?"

"He was something to strike. A safety valve, if you like.
But I was wrong about that. Manasco wasn't enough. You
wanted something quicker than that. If Asherton had been
around you'd have gone for him. As it was. . . ." her words
trailed away.

He was silent for a moment, thinking over what she had

said. In the valley below he caught the slow movement of an ox-cart through the olive trees. Was she right? Was he really like that? Only able to forgive if he worked off his anger first. Was that something everyone felt?

"It's not a very pretty picture of myself," he said quietly. "But I see that maybe it's the true one. Only what the hell do we do now?" He stirred quickly, taking a step towards her. "Yes, it is the truth!" he said fiercely. "I wanted to hit something! That's why I came dashing after you. Because I love you. Because I heard that Asherton was at the hotel. I thought you might have gone off with him. I'd have smashed him to pieces, but only because I wanted you back."

"And if it had happened, and I'd come back, and you'd forgiven me . . . what would happen after that? How long can two people who love one another go on forgiving one another? Not for ever, Nick. And that's what I've been thinking about. That's what I had to be calm enough to see. Now I know that this is the only moment when it can be stopped. That's why I didn't even see Asherton. Do you understand that Nick?"

"Yes," he said grimly. "I see that. But I love you, Kate. I'm not letting anything break us up. . . ."

For a moment before she turned her head from him he saw her lips tremble and he heard her say, "I want it to be as it was . . . I can't imagine us not being together. . . ."

She half-turned towards him and he saw the pink flesh-glow of one ear where the sun struck down at the side of her face, and, as she went on speaking, he saw the faint stir of the loose pale hair and was thinking . . . *This is Kate, Kate of all the small and much loved things . . . bath flannels over her body in the bath, the untidiness of newspapers in the flat, the quiet beauty of a woman in a raincoat, waiting. . . .* All the small, real things that must be remembered in any moment of anger or stupidity, whether in her or him. . . .

She was saying, ". . . it's other people who complicate things, and just time and place . . . that girl and then

Asherton turning up out of the blue and the storm. . . . They make it easier for one's anger and pettiness, but if you let go—well, then there's no coming back. It starts to build up. You do this. I do that. I've always known this, but it was hard to remember at the moment. . . ." Her face lifted a little towards him.

There was nothing more he could say. He pulled her to him. She came with a sudden eagerness and there was a small cry in her throat as he kissed her. Her arms went round him, her fingers digging in to him as though momentarily there was a panic in her, a fear of falling away, of being torn from him. He held her trembling body close to him. Then drawing away from him a little, sniffing against the emotion in her, her eyes blinking with the nearness of tears she suddenly pounded her right fist vigorously against his chest and cried out fiercely, "But don't try me again, Nick! Don't you try! I'll cut your throat! I'll leave you! I don't want to have to go through all that again. . . . Do you hear?"

"Of course, I do," he said gently, pulling her back to him. Her head came to his breast and he caressed her hair.

H

Chapter Fifteen

WHEN they reached Puerto they found Domingo Peroni—who had driven up from Palma—waiting for them at the Margarita.

Opposite the Margarita, and across the road, was a little courtyard set with tables and chairs and overhung by tall palms. Meals were served in the open here during the season and it was also used as a landing stage, jutting out into the calm waters like a flat pier. They sat there in the gathering dusk with their drinks.

Nick could see that Peroni was nervous, and he knew why. Time was running out and Peroni wanted to know what was going to happen. He laughed and talked too much and there was a rubbery affability about him which Nick knew could easily harden into stubborn opposition. After his second drink Peroni said directly; "Come on, Nick. You know what I'm here for. Let's get down to business."

Nick sat on the balcony rail. Behind his back the harbour light by the seaplane base was beginning to flick on and off.

"All right, Domingo," he said. "When's the last date that Vargiu wants the stuff at Palma?"

"You've got seven days, counting today."

"Rigo should have a fair amount of stuff ashore today. Another day will clear the lot. That leaves five days after tomorrow."

"It leaves the stuff on the beach. Not in Palma," said Kate gently. She was sitting by Peroni, looking up at Nick.

"We'll take the stuff out by road," said Nick.

"But you can't use the road," objected Peroni.

"The road can be used. We just don't have permission, that's all. So what? We'll use it without permission. . . .

226

No, no"—he lifted a hand,—"let me go on, Domingo.
I've got it all worked out. Twenty lorries will shift all that
stuff in one go. It'll take half a day to load them, but it
will be a quick shift. Better than, say, using four lorries and
taking several days. All you have to do, Domingo, is to hire
twenty lorries. Get them from all over the place and don't
let anyone know what you're fixing up. They can come up
to Puerto in the evening and we'll go through late at night
and have until the next morning for loading. Manasco
mustn't know anything about the lorries. We'll hit him
suddenly and give him no chance to make a comeback. . . ."

Looking down on them he saw that they were both thinking he was crazy. Well, he wasn't. Desperate, maybe. But
then this business called for desperate measures.

Domingo got up and walked a few paces, deep in thought.
Then he turned and flirted up his arms as though he were
scaring off a flock of birds.

"It won't work, Nick. I could get the lorries. But there's
a padlocked gate across the valley road."

"Simple. We smash it open."

"O.K. . . ." Domingo nodded, going with him. "And
then you drive up to the beach. That's a lot of noise. Manasco
hears you and in no time he's on the phone to da Lapa.
In an hour you'd have the police or the military sitting
across the road. No lorry goes out—and you're under arrest."

"And the cargo still on the beach," added Kate.

Nick slipped off the balustrade rail. "We cut the telephone wires that run up the valley."

"And Manasco sends Guido or a servant down to the
Cala Boquer farm to telephone, or even into Puerto. It
delays things a little, that's all."

"If it were left like that, yes. But it isn't. We go in at night
and Rigo and I will go straight to the villa. Everyone there
will be bundled into one room. There's a billiard room that
will do fine. Rigo stays on guard until our job is finished——"

"You've always had this in mind?" Kate looked at him
shrewdly.

"I hoped somthing else would turn up. There's four thousand quid hanging on this job. Manasco's been tough about it. Now I'm going to get tough. We keep 'em locked up for twelve hours. If the dog's loose we'll fix him."

Peroni came back to the table and poured himself a glass of *fundador*. He drank it in one gulp.

"Does Rigo agree to all this?" he asked.

"Yes. He doesn't like Manasco any more than we do."

"Well, it's his own neck." Peroni pouted his fat lips. "All right, I admit that as a plan it would work. But it doesn't stop there. What about when you've got the stuff out and you let Manasco off the hook? I hate to think about it. He's Manasco, Nick. Lawsuits . . . prosecutions for trespass and assault . . . every legal trick in the bag. He'll skin you and me, and it won't be safe for Rigo to stop running until he reaches the Antarctic."

Nick shook his head. "He could do all these things, but will he? If a tuppenny-halfpenny set-up like ours beats him he's going to want to forget the whole thing. He won't want to advertise his defeat. Everyone would be on our side. Anyway, even if Manasco wins a case for assault and trespass, what happens?"

"You spend six months in jail and I sit around waiting for you," said Kate ruefully.

Nick grinned. "You can visit me."

"Be sensible, Nick," said Peroni. "Manasco made you an offer that at any time he'd take over the cargo and pay all expenses up-to-date. I think we should accept that offer."

"I'll see him in hell first! Climb down after all the hard work we've put into this?"

"Of course he can't do that, Domingo," said Kate quickly.

Peroni sighed. "You English. . . ."

"I'm not going to be steam-rollered by Manasco and his money!"

Peroni wasn't looking at him. He was staring down at his fat hands on the edge of the table and Nick saw that they were trembling a little. The man was nervous but that didn't mean he was afraid.

"All right, Nick. . . . We're partners. This is the way you want it. If there's going to be trouble, I'll take my share. After all, I started all this."

"Good," said Nick. "Let's go and have some dinner. Then you can get back to Palma and start on the lorries. Have them up here the night after tomorrow night, round about nine. If it's a clear night we can work through and get away that much earlier the next day."

He took Kate's arm, turning towards the hotel. Feeling her close to him, he was happy and certain of himself.

Manasco was going to have a shock . . . but then Manasco was due for a shock. No man should get so big or so greedy that he wanted the whole melon for himself.

*　　*　　*　　*

They meant to go back to the *Doria* that night. The weather was good and the sky full of stars that seemed brighter than ever since the storm. But after dinner, when Peroni had gone, they sat and talked.

They talked in a way which for them was new and full of small truths and discoveries which only the past years, their love and this recent trouble could have brought to the surface. In every marriage Nick realised there were things which it took a long time to say . . . to come to the point of saying, that is. They had both been under strain; they had both been subjected to a distortion of character which they hadn't expected. Now they were back, but not at the same point; back on the only road they wanted to travel but further along it. But he was sure that Kate, like himself, didn't imagine that this evening of heightened awareness and emotion could live over into the rest of their lives. The truth of their love, and its strength, would go on, up and down, through other troubles and irritations but not—this conviction was sure in him—not to be tried again in the way it had been. Each marriage worked out its own problems, not always by a recognised ethic, but at least by an acceptable understanding. If it didn't, it wasted away. No amount of paint could make a boat seaworthy unless its timbers were sound.

They stayed the night, taking it out of the calendar for themselves and were lovers again. In the morning while she bathed, they sang some stupid song of their own making and she borrowed his razor to shave her legs. He scrubbed her back for her and in the midst of towelling her down found himself picking her up and carrying her back into the bedroom to the wide bed with a great shaft of sunlight cutting across it.

At eight o'clock they were rounding Cabo de Perada in the motor-boat and not until they were running into Agua Gelida bay did they begin to sober up from the happiness inside them.

Rigo was hauling the raft ashore single-handed. He had worked all through the previous day and most of the deck cargo from the after-hold was cleared. Nick pitched in with him and they worked like blacks. There was no sign of life from the Villa Ermano.

By late afternoon they had brought up the last of the cargo from the after-hold. The cases and sack-wrapped bundles were stacked on the deck, black water running from them and drying rapidly in the sun.

"All right," said Nick. "We'll call it a day. We can shift what's left ashore tomorrow. We've got plenty of time to get it all stacked on the beach before the lorries come tomorrow night."

He and Rigo stripped and washed themselves down on deck.

Rigo said, "It is all agreed?"

"Yes, Rigo. Tomorrow night at nine the lorries come in."

Rigo nodded. Then he said, "Last night, I slept ashore. Manasco came to see me in the fisherman's hut. He offered a lot of money if I would tell him what your plans were. It was a good feeling to have Señor Manasco ask me for something—and then to refuse him." He smiled and began to whistle.

Kate came down from the bridge saloon carrying a bundle of clean clothes for them. She dumped them on the top of a skylight and went forward to wait until they were dressed.

A little later Nick heard her call to him and, buttoning his shirt, he walked forward. She was leaning over the bows looking towards the beach.

"We're going to have visitors," she said.

Nick saw the Ermano skiff being run down to the water's edge by Guido. Once it was afloat he got in and, oars out, held it stern-on to the sands. The wall gate of the villa opened and three men began to make their way down to the boat.

"It's da Lapa and a couple of his men," said Nick, frowning. He watched as da Lapa got into the skiff and was joined by the two Civil Guards. The sun flashed on the polished wood of their carbines and on the leather of da Lapa's belt and shoulder strap. Crowded down to its gunwales, the slow beat of oars stirring up white water, the skiff came out like some clumsy water insect.

As they came abreast of the bows Nick and Kate turned and followed them to the gangway. Guido had a little trouble coming alongside. Looking up and seeing Nick watching, the young man's mouth twisted into a smile . . . the kind of smile which told of some secret delight he was hugging to himself. Full of disquiet he waited for da Lapa to come aboard.

The Colonel came up the gangway, his men close behind him. He paused at the top, gave Kate a little bow, and then looking at Nick, slowly brushed the palms of his hands together as though they were dusty. His eyes holding Nick's, he shook his head. There was an elegant sadness in the gesture.

"Business or pleasure?" asked Nick, and seeing the stiff, unrevealing faces of the two guards behind da Lapa, he knew the answer.

"Business, Señor Thorne," answered da Lapa. And then added sympathetically, "I regret to say."

"Well . . . let's have it," said Nick.

"In good time, señor. In good time." Da Lapa's hand went up to his tunic breast pocket and he pulled out his cigarette holder. Very carefully he fitted a cigarette to it and, satisfied that the cigarette was in a straight line with the holder, said to the guards, "Search the ship."

The two guards moved forward. As they passed him Nick said, "What the devil's all this about?"

Da Lapa waved his holder, "Patience. . . ."

He moved away on his own, walking around the cargo piled on the after deck, picking his way carefully. He went right up into the stern, stared out at the mouth of the bay and then turned back. Nick, Kate and Rigo watched him. Although his movements were precise and elegant it was easy to see that underneath he was disturbed.

He came back to Nick and said, "Once I gave you an order and you wisely obeyed it—though it meant a lot of additional work for you. Later I gave you some advice. You should not have neglected it." He glanced at Kate and at Rigo. "More than that I cannot say."

A noise on the deck behind him made Nick turn. Coming down from the bows were the two guards and they carried between them a bulky package wrapped up in old army ground-sheets and bound with rough cords. They settled it on the deck close to da Lapa.

"We found this under a bunk, forward in the crew's quarters, Colonel."

"Open it."

One of them took out a knife and slit the cords, a brown hand jerked at the wrappings, inner cords were cut and more wrapping pulled back. On to the deck spilled a cascade of long, white cigarette cartons.

Behind him Nick heard Kate breathe, "Oh, no. . . ."

He said nothing himself. Two and two made four; looking up he saw the pink walls of the Villa Ermano, the pluming crests of the eucalyptus trees, and he thought wryly that the master mathematician was over there, lounging in the garden sunlight, confident, feeling the power under his hands as a driver feels the power of a great motor throbbing in the smooth black curve of a steering wheel. There must be about fifty thousand cigarettes in the bundle, he thought. Good American cigarettes, and not one packet with a government stamp to make it legal.

Colonel da Lapa bent down, his tunic drawing tight across his shoulders with the movement, and picked up a carton. He held it up, close to Nick's face.

"Tangier . . . Casablanca, señor. Old habits die hard."

Angrily Nick snapped, "You don't believe that! Manasco planted these on me. Rigo slept ashore last night and the *Doria* was deserted. Manasco planted them and then tipped you off. And you know why. Admit it."

Da Lapa shrugged and tossed the carton back with the others.

"I was tipped off, señor. Yes. How otherwise do we catch smugglers? But you know it is not our practice to divulge the sources of our information." He looked around at the tall cliffs of the bay and shook his head. "This ship, this situation . . . it is ideal, of course."

Kate moved up alongside Nick, her hand on his arm, gripping him, "You know this isn't true, Colonel. You know it."

Da Lapa shook his head. "I only know what I see, señora. I do not even judge. That comes later. Señor Thorne—" he stepped aside a little, "I must ask you to come with me." Rigo came forward, his fists clenched, his dark face frowning with anger. "What about me, Colonel?"

"I have no information against you, Rigo."

"Where are you going? Where are you taking him?" cried Kate.

"Señora . . . you know as well as I do. To the *Comisaria* at Regano. He will be held there. Later, maybe, he will have to be transferred to Palma——"

H*

"But——"

Nick put out a hand and held Kate. "Don't waste your breath, Kate." He looked at da Lapa. "Can I have a word alone with my wife for a moment?"

The Colonel hesitated. "Well . . . it is irregular. But, I suppose so."

Nick took Kate's arm and led her forward towards the bows. When they were out of earshot, he said in a low voice; "This is Manasco all right. This is his trump card. But he's not beating me. You go round in the motor-boat tonight with Rigo and phone Peroni and tell him what's happened —and tell him to have those lorries up here tomorrow night. I'll meet you at Cala Boquer at nine tomorrow."

"But you can't, Nick. How can you——"

"I'll be there at nine," he said firmly. "And make sure that tomorrow you and Rigo get the rest of this stuff ashore." He shook her gently. "Nine. I'll be there." He bent forward and kissed her on the cheek and then turned back towards the gangway.

*   *   *   *

They took him ashore, leaving one guard to be rowed by Rigo in their own skiff with the cigarettes. All the way Guido swaying on the oars watched his face and, smiling, said nothing. Da Lapa smoked and the frayed trail of cigarette smoke whirled away over his shoulder.

The police car was parked on the road beyond the villa. To reach it they went up from the beach and through the wall gate, the two guards on either side of Nick and da Lapa behind. Then came Guido and the manservant, who had met them, carrying the loosely wrapped bundle of cigarettes.

In the cool courtyard Manasco and Juana were standing by the unicorn fountain. Juana had one hand on the Alsatian dog's collar. She watched him, her face calm and indifferent. As though, Nick thought, she watched someone of whom she had dimly heard, had been mildly curious about and who now, in the flesh, proved disappointing. For him, too, she seemed remote: a figure from a dream . . . to be remembered only rarely. Manasco, too, seemed withdrawn from the pantomime. He was too old, too wise, to grant himself any obvious pleasure.

Da Lapa said, "Thank you for the boat, Señor Manasco, and for letting us come through."

"It is nothing, Colonel." Then, his eyes on Nick, he allowed himself the first savour of triumph, his voice flat with mockery; "Bad luck, Señor Thorne. . . ."

Nick said nothing. The guards moved on and he followed them to the car. He sat in silence in the back with da Lapa as they drove down to the road gate. Guido rode on the running-board alongside the driver to lock the gate after them. As he jumped off he grinned and waved at Nick and shouted something that was lost in the accelerating note of the engine.

At Nick's side da Lapa said quietly so that the two guards ahead should not hear, "He is young and the young always handle victory clumsily. If he says one word out of place to Manasco he will have his head bitten off. The old man has had so many victories that he no longer celebrates them."

"He hasn't won yet."

Da Lapa pursed his lips, looking sideways at Nick.

"Unfortunately, that is only your opinion."

Chapter Sixteen

THE *Comisaria de la Guardia Civil* was in a narrow street in the upper part of the town. They formally charged him and then he was led to a small room with a stout door, a truckle bed and a tiny barred window head-high from which he could look down over the sloping roof-tops towards the main square of Regano. Beyond the house-tops on the far side of the square the green flanks of a hill rose from the line of the main Palma road. He exhausted the view in two minutes and sat on the truckle bed. Food was brought to him. At eight the electric light came on in the room, and at nine it went off leaving him in darkness. A few moments later a priest hole shutter in the door was drawn aside and a faint light from the corridor outside filtered in.

He lay on his bed, feeling too bloody-minded even to think about sleep. Kate would have let Peroni know by now. He hoped Peroni wouldn't panic and stop arranging for the lorries. If he suggested it, he knew that Kate would jump on him. He had told her that he was going to be at Cala Boquer at nine tomorrow evening and she would accept that. How on earth he was going to get there he had no idea at this moment. But get there he would. Without him Kate and Rigo couldn't manage the Manasco household. The lorry drivers couldn't help. They would only drive up to the beach, load and drive off.

He lay there thinking about Colonel da Lapa. The man was on his side, but he was much too correct to do more than hint it. No matter how much sympathy he had for him, he would do nothing that took him a step outside his duties.

The problem was a very simple one. At least, he told himself, it had to be kept simple. He had to get to Cala

Boquer at nine tomorrow. That meant breaking out of this place. Once he was out it was unlikely that da Lapa would think that he had headed back for the *Doria*. He would—or at least Nick hoped he would—think that he was far more likely to head for Palma, or some place where he could lie up in safety. In fact, come to think of it, da Lapa, knowing nothing of the lorry move, wouldn't expect him to break out at all. Anyway, the smaller the margin of time he could leave himself between breaking out and reaching Cala Boquer the better. There was that much less time in which he could be caught.

All he needed was a chance to get the lorries loaded and away. . . . After that? Well, it didn't pay to think too far ahead.

Somewhere in the town a church bell rang and he thought of the Villa Ermano. They would have finished dinner. Manasco, Juana and Guido . . . everything settled for them.

They woke him at six with coffee and dry rounds of toast. A guard took him down the corridor to a washroom. He shaved with his own razor from the little toilet bag which da Lapa had allowed Kate to pack for him before he left the *Doria*. The guard leaned against the door and chatted. He was a Puerto man. If there was anything Nick wanted he could get it. In his opinion Nick would be sent on to Palma very soon. Rigo was a friend of his. They had played football together. It was a pity that things had gone wrong. A great pity. Between themselves he had made a small bet on it and now he would lose his money. The Señor would be surprised at the number of bets which had been made. But Señor—fancy giving anyone a chance like that . . . such an old trick! Yet difficult to prove. That was the trouble.

At ten o'clock Nick was taken from his cell again and escorted to a room in the front of the building. Here one of da Lapa's lieutenants asked him if he wished to make a statement or whether he wished to consult a lawyer first? Nick said he would like a lawyer, and named a man he knew in Palma. The lieutenant said he would notify the lawyer, and then Nick was taken back to his cell.

He sat there while the hours went by. The lawyer might come today, or tomorrow. Once a man was in custody nobody in Spain considered there was any reason for hurry. Twice during the afternoon he banged on his door and got the guard to take him down to the lavatory. He didn't want to use it, but he wanted to establish the procedure. The layout of the lower floor of the building was now clear in his mind.

In his mind he went over, too, the country between Regano and Agua Gelida. Three hours he reckoned he would want. He worked it out, timing it in his imagination; down the main road towards Puerto—he could steal a bicycle, or a motor-cycle—and then left-handed out to the coast at Calle San Vincente. That was a beach a few miles lower down the coast from Agua Gelida. There was a handful of villas in the place but most of them would be shut up for the season. Then over the southern valley ridge and drop down to Agua Gelida. Rigo would be aboard . . . but everything depended on getting out. He lay on his bunk, hands behind his head, staring at his feet. At a quarter to six he slid off the bed and knocked for the guard on the door. The guard slid back the door hatch.

"Again . . . ?" The guard grinned. "To be locked up—it always affects the bladder, señor. This I have noticed."

"You ought to know."

The man opened the door and Nick moved down the corridor.

"It is the nerves," said the guard behind him.

The guard pushed open the door and stood aside for Nick to enter. It was a moment Nick disliked. This man was Rigo's friend, and had shown sympathy for him . . . but there was no other way. As he drew level with the man he turned and crowded him against the upright of the door frame. His right arm came up in a jabbing uppercut and he hit the man under the jaw. Twice he hit him, hearing his head jolt back against the door. A whistle of surprised breath came warm and garlic-flavoured in his nostrils. The guard fell sideways to the floor, his carbine rattling over the tiles. He lay there without moving.

Nick backed into the corridor and closed the door. Slowly he walked down the length of the passage and up three steps to a half-glass door. Through it he could see an untidy office, the walls hung with notices, and a framed photograph of General Franco over the empty fireplace. By the far window overlooking the street a girl sat in front of a typewriter, her back to him. He pushed the door open quietly and edged into the room. The door to the main hall-way was to his right. He went swiftly towards it. There was a row of hooks by the door and hanging from them were two light overcoats, one with a black beret sticking from its side pocket. His eyes on the girl who still typed away, he reached up and took down the overcoat with the beret. He dropped it over his arm and stretched out his hand for the door handle. It came open silently for a foot and then squealed on bad hinges. As the girl turned round, he moved into the shelter of the half-open door and called anonymously, "*Buenas tardes.* . . ."

The hallway was lofty and lit by a hanging cluster of unshaded bulbs, already burning against the gloom. A man and woman, peasants, sat on a bench halfway down the hall. There was a clerk behind a reception desk near the double doors that led out to the street. Outside Nick knew there would be an armed guard.

Quietly he slipped into the overcoat and pulled on the beret. The clerk was reading a newspaper, his shoulders hunched over the desk.

Forcing himself to show no haste, Nick went down the hall. When he was abreast of the peasant couple, the man rose. He was old, in a black coat and a collarless blue-and-white striped shirt. The brown neck was wrinkled and grained and as he spoke the brass head of his collar stud rose and fell.

"Señor teniente, we have been waiting so long to see the captain. . . ." He held his hands together in the nervous gesture of peasants before authority.

Nick, turning his head from the clerk, said gently, "Patience, father . . . he will soon be free."

He passed on and not until he was by the desk did the clerk look up. Nick raised a hand in greeting and hid his face. The clerk smiled at the familiar coat and hat, and then Nick was pushing through the double-doors. As they swung behind him he thought he heard a shout from somewhere deep in the building.

The street guard was standing at the bottom of the steps, carbine over his shoulder, talking to a small sparrow of a woman in a dusty black dress, a scarf drawn over her head. She chattered away, her voice full of protest and irritation, and her hands sketched gestures under the guard's face. He didn't even see Nick pass down the steps.

Nick turned to the right and made his way down the street, away from the main square, towards the outskirts on the Puerto side. Lights were already on in some of the small shops and the long narrow street was sprinkled with a drifting evening crowd. He kept his head down and walked just off the edge of the pavement to avoid the little knots of people outside the shops. Anxious to get out of the street as soon as he could, he took the first turning to his right into a narrow alleyway. A hand came out and held his arm and someone was walking beside him. A voice he knew well—though the familiarity of it came too late to spare him a moment of panic that started his heart racing—said "Welcome, señor. . . . Keep walking. There is a car at the bottom of the hill."

Johnny Manchester, his hand dropping from Nick's arm, shuffled along beside him, blowing a little at the effort of keeping up even a moderate walking pace.

"Johnny . . . you keep out of this." He didn't want the old man mixed up in his trouble.

Johnny chuckled.

"It was too much, señor. I had to do something. Rigo told me last night about it. . . . All night I thought about it. Must you go so fast, señor?"

"Any minute they'll be after me. Save your breath until we reach the car."

They came to the bottom of the lane. An old black Chevrolet was parked against a wall plastered with lottery and circus bills.

Johnny got in the driver's seat and Nick slipped in alongside him.

"Where, señor?"

"Calle San Vincente."

The car engine roared noisily and they moved off. Nick slumped down in his seat.

"How the hell could you know?" he asked.

"You taught me, señor. Remember in the old days? What was it? Intelligent appreciation? It is a good phrase. . . ." He drove awkwardly, grinding at the gears, forcing his way stubbornly through the narrow streets. Dusk was coming fast and under the canvas hood of the car it would be hard, Nick knew, for anyone to see him clearly.

"From Rigo I know that you want to get out for tonight —though, señor, believe me, even to me, he would not say why. And knowing you, I took a chance. I have been waiting since midday watching the building. It was not difficult. Most of the time I sat and drank coffee. . . . Waiting is not difficult at my age."

"You'll have Manasco and da Lapa on your shoulders if they ever find out."

Johnny laughed and wrenched at the wheel with his root-like hands to avoid a mule-cart. "I have seventy years of trouble on my shoulders. What does a little more matter? Besides smuggling is an honourable thing with us. You know that. Every man, woman and child here is for the *contrabandistas*. Manasco should not have used it dishonourably. Even da Lapa would agree. Some things, señor, are not done."

Nick laughed, and feeling in his overcoat pocket found a black and green packet of *Ideales*. He lit one of the cigarettes and watched the last of the houses fall back. Ahead of them stretched the low walled road to Puerto, the smooth elephant grey trunks of the fig trees framing the evening sky.

"Good old Johnny. God bless you."

They turned left-handed off the main road and began to run out to Calle San Vincente, and they were both silent. There was no profit, Nick knew, in thinking too far ahead. One thing at a time.

The road twisted through a shallow valley, the rough fields scarred with smooth rock outcrops. Once they had to stop while a flock of black goats passed them. Then in the pale, smoky haze of the last evening light they ran out on to the small rond-point above the San Vincente beach. Away to the right were a few villas, but there was no sign of life. Johnny shut off the engine. The sound of the waves washing on the beach flooded into the car.

Johnny said, "You would like me to come with you? I can help, maybe?"

Nick put his hand on the old man's arm. "No, Johnny. Thank you. You've done enough. But when you get back to Puerto if you see my wife you can tell her I'm on my way."

"I will, senor. Also, I should say that I have a friend in Regano who by now will have informed the police that he saw you on a motor-bicycle going towards Palma."

*   *   *   *

It was a long, slogging climb across from Calle San Vincente to the top of the Agua Gelida valley ridge. He did the last half-hour in darkness. It was a quarter past eight when he reached the crest of the narrow-backed ridge. Below him the valley was blacked out except for a faint light from the villa and another, fainter light, from the *Doria*.

Away to his right, smudged by the night mist he could make out the pin-prick lights of Puerto and the distant loom of the Cabo de Perada lighthouse. The moment he began to drop down from the crest all the lights except from villa and *Doria* were blotted out by the far peaks of the other side of the valley.

It was dangerous going in the dark for the valley side fell sharply in deep slides of gravel and sudden breaks in the rock face. He went down as fast as he could and eventually hit the long wall that ran across the valley to the padlocked road-gate. Keeping to the Puerto side of it he went up towards the gate and, after a little search, found the shotgun which he had left in the bushes on the day he had gone after Kate.

By half-past eight he was on the lip of the low cliff above the beach. For over two hours now he had been going steadily, not thinking too much, just keeping one goal in mind, to reach Agua Gelida. Now with the beach below him the thrust of excitement was suddenly stronger in him. He felt hard but calm above it . . . settled now into a steady mental gear which would take him through anything. The high stubbornness of a deep-seated anger and determination not to be outdone. The mood too, of a man who would take risks in defiance of common sense in order not to be turned back.

He went down to the beach, seeing the piles of cargo silhouetted against the night sky at the mouth of the bay. Close to the fisherman's shelter someone stirred in the darkness. Rigo's voice came softly to him.

"Senor?"

"Rigo."

He heard the sand crunch underfoot and a hand came out. Just for a moment Rigo shook at him, the movement full of welcome and gladness. Then the hand left him.

"Ready?"

"*Si, señor. . . .*"

He heard Rigo's hand slap gently against the stock of his shotgun.

"Are they all up there?"

"Four of them, señor. I was up there a little while ago. The dog barked, but he is shut up in a kennel round the back. Since you went they have not bothered. . . ."

"You know the billiard room?"

"I know the house well, señor. It is the best room for us. There is only a door. No window. And it runs back into the hill slope."

"All right. Let's go."

They climbed up from the beach and began to follow the path to the villa. Half-way there Nick halted.

"Is your gun loaded, Rigo?"

"Yes, señor. . . ."

He could hear the edge in Rigo's voice. He broke his own gun and took the two shells out.

"Unload it, Rigo. We don't want any accidents."

In the darkness he heard Rigo unload.

The gate into the courtyard was locked. Rigo gave Nick a boost to the top and then Nick reached down and pulled Rigo up. They dropped quietly into a flowerbed on the far side.

Leading the way Nick skirted the courtyard, the gentle sound of water cascading came from the unicorn fountain on his left. A little coach lantern shone over the main door. Nick stopped below the verandah and whispered to Rigo:

"Slip round the back to the terraced garden and cut the telephone wires. I'll wait for you here."

He heard Rigo move off. The telephone wires ran through the garden on low poles. Standing there, he wondered if da Lapa would think of phoning Manasco to tell him the news.

After a while he heard Rigo breathing at his side. Together they went up to the door. What he was going to do now was as illegal as it could be. Crazy. But that wasn't going to stop him. In his place Manasco would have done the same . . . and Manasco, he guessed, was as ready to damn consequences now as he was. He'd framed him for smuggling. Well . . . he must expect what came. Just the two of them, like a couple of fighting cocks. . . .

He turned the handle of the door gently and eased it open. He slid round it with Rigo following, pressed close up against his back. The hall was well lit, bright-coloured rugs on the gay tiles and a cluster of green and blue lamp lustres hanging from the ceiling. From the far end of the hall he heard voices . . . Manasco and Guido . . . and then the click of billiard balls.

Rigo nudged him and pointed. The door of the billiard room was partly open, a wedge of green baize and a corner of the mahogany table showing. They saw Guido in shirt sleeves, his back to them, leaning over the table.

Keeping close to the side of the hall Nick went forward to the door. He reached it without being seen and looking through the crack where it swung part open on its hinges he saw Manasco and Guido alone in the room. He motioned to Rigo to stay on guard and then drew away. Behind him he heard Manasco say something from the depths of the room. Guido laughed. The balls clicked again on the table.

He crossed the hall to a leather-padded door studded with copper rivets and pushed it gently. He edged round it and it closed behind him with a little gasp of air.

The manservant was sitting at a table, close to the stove. There was a glass and a flask of wine on the table and he was writing a letter. He looked up, elbows crooked on the rough table surface, pen in a clumsy hand and the corner of his tongue showing between his lips.

Nick said deliberately, raising the barrel of the shotgun: "If you shout or make a noise, I'll fix you."

The man's tongue slid back between his lips like a worm going to ground.

Nick tipped his head towards the leather door.

"Move out and go into the billiard room. And remember —no noise."

The man stood up slowly, and absently slipped a piece of blotting paper over his letter. Nick stood aside and then backed to the door, pressing against it with his shoulders.

The manservant came towards him and flattened himself

against the edge of the door frame. Then, as Nick stood away from him, holding the door with his foot, he moved into the hall.

Nick crowded him down the hall. Rigo came a few steps towards them, his dark face serious and took the man's arm. With a sudden jerk, he tugged him backwards and pushed him through the door. There was a surprised shout from inside. Rigo pulled the door and turned the key in the lock.

"Juana," said Nick quickly. "You stay here and watch the front door. I'll find her."

"Upstairs," said Rigo. "Second door on the right. I saw a light there as I went round for the telephone wires. It's her bedroom."

Nick turned. Giving no heed now to noise he raced up the wide run of carpeted stairs. As he reached the first floor he saw a door open ahead of him. A wedge of light struck brightly across the dimly lit passageway.

He ran down to the door, his feet noiseless on the thick carpet. As he came into the light she was standing back just inside the room. He put his hands on each side of the door frame, barring the way, and they faced one another in silence. Behind her he could see a four-poster bed hung with pink and green curtains, a milk-white rug, the sparkle of silver reflections in the triple mirror on a dressing table and, oddly, propped against the uncovered pillows of the bed a long-legged, rather shabby teddy bear.

A blue dressing gown was open loosely over her pyjamas; her face was pink and glowing, and there was a small towel wrapped around her head. She had been washing her hair. Just for a moment he was full of sympathy for her, hating himself.

He said, "The others are locked in the billiard room. You must join them."

Calmly she said, "So that's it."

"Yes."

"And if I refuse to go?"

"I think you will."

"Why?"

"Because you wouldn't want me to carry you down."

She moved, drawing the dressing gown close about her. "No, I wouldn't want you to touch me."

He stood aside and she came out. As she passed him he could smell the sweet shampoo from her hair and she carried herself proudly, not looking at him. He followed her, angry with himself, bitter against the clumsiness of being human.

At the bottom of the stairs Rigo stood aside for her. Someone was banging on the far side of the billiard room door. Nick slipped ahead of her and turned the key, pulling the door back. Guido and the manservant fell back from it. Guido, a billiard cue raised, butt-end held towards Nick, lunged at him. Nick caught the end and twisted it away. Juana moved past him into the room and stood by Manasco.

Nick stood in the doorway, his shotgun held low. Guido and the manservant went back until they were touching the end of the billiard table. From the gloom above the green-shaded lights the four faces floated on different levels, silent, watching him. Manasco held a cigar between his lips, the blue smoke drifting in a thin signal across his forehead. His grip on the cigar gave a bitter grimacing turn to his mouth. He took the cigar from his mouth and the wrinkled face moved slowly to calmness. A hand came up and pushed glasses from his eyes to rest on his forehead. For a second or two the deep-sunk eyes blinked rapidly.

"Congratulations on your escape, señor," said Manasco, and there was the suggestion in the long cavernous room of a chuckle, humourless, and not intended to be shared with anyone.

Nick said, "I have twenty lorries coming up here very shortly. By early morning we shall have the cargo away. Until then you must be kept here. I offer you all my apologies, though I think you will understand that the necessity for this has not been entirely of my making."

"Pretty speech," Guido sneered.

"Guido!" Manasco flicked the word like a whip lash.

Then raising his hands, spreading the fingers wide as though he lifted a weight, he went on to Nick, "You must feel good, Señor Thorne. You have done what you said you would do. Oh, yes, I know well how you feel. But——" his hands collapsed suddenly as though he had dropped the invisible load he carried, "no deal is sound until the cheque is cashed."

Nick stepped back. "Rigo will be outside on guard the whole time, and we shall barricade the door. You have wine"—his eyes rested on the decanter and glasses standing on a small table,—"and it is not cold."

"And a little fasting hurts no one," said Manasco. "Good night, señor."

Nick stepped back through the door, pulled it shut and then locked it. He turned to Rigo. "I don't think they'll try to break out but we'll make sure."

They shifted a heavy chest in front of the door, and Rigo found a couple of planks at the back of the house which they wedged against the projecting iron studs of the door. It was a good stout door and it would take more than billiard cues to batter it down.

*   *   *   *

He reached the padlocked gate across the road just as the first lorry headlights turned distantly out of the narrow gorge which formed the entrance to the valley above the Cala Boquer farmhouse. With the barrel of his shotgun he levered off the padlock fastening and swung the gate wide open.

The chain of lights came lurching and crawling towards him. As the first lorry neared the gate he stepped out into the lights and raised his arms.

Someone jumped down from the cab as the lorry halted and Kate ran to him, flinging herself into his arms.

"Nick!"

His face was against hers, his arms around her, and he could feel her body trembling.

Over her head he saw the other lorries close up. Another figure came forward into the lights. It was Domingo Peroni wrapped in a belted raincoat, his face grey and large under the lights. He cocked his head towards the far villa. "Well?"

"They're all bottled up," said Nick. "We can get to work. What do these drivers know?"

"Nothing. That is, nothing I've told them. But I think they guess a lot—and they don't seem to mind. By the way, I could only get eighteen."

"That'll do."

"Let's get started then."

Kate got back into the cab of the leading lorry. Standing on the running board, Nick led it at the head of the convoy up to the beach.

At the back of the low cliff overhang there was a wide piece of broken ground big enough to take all the lorries. Two lorries were driven up on either flank of this piece of ground to shine their headlights on to the cargo piled on the beach. The plan was that one by one the other lorries should drive up to the head of the small track down to the beach, turn, and be loaded by gangs of the drivers man-handling cases and crates up from the shore. From the eighteen drivers Nick formed three gangs, two on the beach and one on the cliff top loading. They worked hard, needing no driving.

Kate rowed out to the *Doria* and brought back her stores of coffee. She built a fire on the beach and when the gangs rested there was coffee or wine for them. They worked, singing and shouting, their shadows thrown long across the pale sands by the headlights.

As each lorry was loaded it was driven back on to the road and halted. Slowly the loaded convoy began to take form. Nick saw that if this rate was kept up they could be away by nine o'clock.

Once or twice during the night he went up to the villa to see Rigo. Rigo had made himself comfortable in an arm-chair outside the billiard room door.

"Any trouble?"

"No, señor. For most of the time they are quiet. Now and again I hear them talking."

"Have they tried the door?"

"No, señor."

When dawn came they had fourteen lorries loaded and lined up on the road. On the beach now was the heavy part of the cargo which Nick had decided to leave until they had the advantage of daylight.

Nick worked with the men until they had three more lorries loaded and drawn away. Then as they began work on the last lorry Nick said to Peroni:

"All right. As soon as this one's loaded, you move off." He looked down at the beach. There was little more than half a load left for the last lorry. "Take Kate with you. I'm going up to join Rigo. I'll let Manasco out and face him when I see you're well away."

"Nick, I should stay with you." Kate, grubby and untidy from the night stood at his side.

"No, you go with Domingo." He put his arm around her and kissed her.

"There's still da Lapa after Manasco," said Peroni.

"I know. But I've a feeling that da Lapa will decide what to do when he sees how Manasco will jump. Anyway, I can't worry about that now. The main thing is that we're getting this stuff to Palma. That's what we said we would do."

He stayed until they had almost all the load on the lorry and then with a wave to Kate he turned and began to walk up to the villa.

The sun was up now, strong in the clear sky. To his left the bay was dancing with silver chips of light as a strong breeze ruffled the waters. He went slowly, feeling tired, and for the moment lost to all feeling of triumph. He'd done it; been awkward, stubborn, and fought his way through . . . Manasco was beaten. There could be trouble, still. He might spend a few months in jail . . . but in the end he would go back to England with Kate.

Crossing the courtyard he raised his eyes to the slopes behind the house which Manasco had terraced into a garden. Olive and fig trees, lines of pimento and here and there an odd almond tree . . . all neat and orderly. Then along the top of one of the terrace walls he saw a quick brown movement. He stopped. A brownish figure slipped between two trees, crouched and then straightened to pull itself to the top of a wall. It was Manasco.

Nick ran for the house. He jerked open the main door and looked down the hallway. Rigo, sitting in his chair, turned his head. Beyond him the billiard room door was secure. Without waiting to give any explanation, Nick swung out of the doorway on to the verandah. He ran round to the back of the house. He followed the line of the billiard room wall into the sloping hill behind. A small rockery faced the slope. He climbed up it and saw quickly how Manasco had escaped. Somewhere at the back of the billiard room in the ceiling was a small air shaft for ventilation. On top of the rockery was an iron grid about eighteen inches square. The grid had been pushed back. Nick guessed that his prisoners had spent the night widening it from the inside. Manasco was small and could get through easily.

Looking up between the olive trees Nick saw Manasco break from the garden and begin to run along the side of the valley, keeping close in to the foot of the hills, following the line of the telephone poles. He began to run after him, swearing to himself. There was plenty Manasco could still do, and he knew what Manasco's temper would be like. He could phone da Lapa from the Cala Boquer farm and he could borrow a shotgun and hold the convoy up at the narrow defile that formed the entrance to the valley. Manasco would shoot, too. No empty shotgun threat for him.

Nick saw that he had to catch the man before he reached the Cala Boquer farm. He went across the terraced garden and vaulted the boundary wall into the valley. Away behind him to his right he heard the roar of the lorries warming up. Glancing back he saw that the last lorry was lurching and swaying across the rough ground to form the tail of the convoy. The drivers were on his side, but they'd never try to pass an angry Manasco with a gun.

It was a long run to the defile and Nick put everything into it. Loose stones skidded and clattered away from under his feet. The sun smacked hard at his neck and the tiredness in him from the night's work made his legs seem leaden. Climbing the wall that ran down to the road gate he saw Manasco look round. From the spurt the man put on he knew that he had been seen. Manasco began to work down from the slope now towards the road at the defile and Nick angled off after him. He was gaining but not enough. For an old man Manasco was fit, and he ran now with the promise of triumph in him.

Manasco reached the road and Nick saw the brown shape clear against the pale grey jumble of rocks that closed in on the track.

To his surprise, instead of following the road through the defile Manasco suddenly swerved to the left and began to climb up the face of the rocks. They were about a hundred feet high and he went up them like a goat. Momentarily his figure was silhouetted against the skyline at the top of the rocks and then it disappeared.

Nick hit the road fifty yards from the throat of the valley. Behind him he could hear the low sound of the convoy beginning to make its way down the road. The shadow of the tall gorge sides closed over him. He swung off the road and climbed up the route Manasco had taken. As he pulled himself over the top he saw Manasco.

He was sitting on a boulder near the overhanging lip of the defile. A hundred feet below him was the road and thirty feet away the other side of the gorge. His shoulders were hunched over his knees and he was breathing heavily. He raised his head at the sound of Nick's feet on the hard rock. For a moment his teeth were bared as he smiled, the old face wrinkled and brown, and the blue eyes dancing behind the spectacles. Very slowly he pulled himself upright. The sunlight scattered reddish flecks in the short-cut hair. He raised his right hand and Nick saw that he held a revolver.

"I told you Señor Thorne. . . . Remember, I told you. . . ." Manasco's need for breath broke his words. "No deal is sound until the cheque is cashed."

The index finger of his left hand flicked stiffly sideways. A few feet from him a loose coil like a long white worm snaked across the rock and disappeared into a crack six feet from the edge of the fall. The end of the fuse length was already smoking and spluttering quietly.

His voice almost friendly, Manasco went on: "We'd better get off here. It has about three minutes to go. . . ." He raised his eyes and looked seawards up the valley. The convoy was coming down the rough road, the head already near the boundary gate. "They'll be still half a mile away when it happens. And when it does, nothing will go out of here for weeks. I understand gun-cotton, you know. I've used it so much for making my terraces. Now go, and I will follow."

Nick glanced towards the lorries. He could see Manasco climbing out of the ventilator grid, sure of himself, the last card in his hand, slipping into his garage for gun-cotton, even into his study for a revolver. . . . And he thought, I'd have done just what he's done. Although he could find no anger in him against the man, he knew that he was not capable now of turning and climbing down.

He took a step forward.

Manasco lifted the gun a little.

"I'm a serious man, Señor Thorne. I shall shoot."

"We must both do what we have to do."

He jumped forward, reaching for Manasco. Manasco stepped back, away from him, and fired.

The bullet smashed into Nick's left shoulder. Pain went through him. An expanding burst of colour splashed violently across his eyeballs. He twisted round and crashed heavily to the ground. As he lay there his mind and his senses were for one moment wonderfully clear, hearing the rocking surge of echoes from the shot beating free from the high walls of the defile, and seeing Manasco standing over him. Sharp in his nostrils was the acrid smell of the burning fuse.

"I said I was serious," Manasco stepped towards Nick. "Come, I'll help you down. . . ." There was regret in his voice, sadness and the compassion which is stirred by victory. . . .

Nick drew his hand away from his shoulder and his fingers were wet with his blood. The movement sent a stab of pain through his arm. Anger came with the return of pain. He rolled over on the ground, flung his right arm out and caught at Manasco's legs. The man came down in a heap on him and he saw the revolver fall and slide away. He rolled over the man, crushing and smothering him with the weight of his body. He lay on him, pinning him down while he kicked and struggled under him. He reached out for the fuse length. He pulled it to him, holding the burning end, clamping it into his palm and clenching his fingers round it. In his rage, determined to be sure, he seized it in his teeth, biting and tearing at it, all his movements furious with the sharp spur of pain from his shoulder. The fuse parted in his mouth. Spitting the bits from his lips and teeth he fought with Manasco, holding his body over the man, gripping with his legs, beating down the fight in the other. . . . They were both shouting, swearing and twisting. He got his right arm round the man's neck, forcing him down and, with his face pressed against Manasco's back, clung on to him. He stayed like that, fastened to him, and he heard the noise of the first lorry roar into the defile, heard the grind of gears and the high whine of engines as they drew more power for the rise of the road. . . . He counted them, lost count, and waited for the noise of their passing to die. It seemed to him as though it would go on for ever . . . great waves of engine noise dying and swelling

and matching the surge and fall of pain in his body. The
noise faded and a heavy, hot stillness swept across him.
He fell away, conscious only of a great tiredness.

*   *   *   *

Kate was there. Standing by the window, the tufted
crown of a palm tree showing beyond her head outside. The
sun striking into the room made the silhouette of her body
a soft shape under the while silk of her dress. She'd always
been there in the last days when he had managed to break
through. But now he was through and knew he wasn't
going back. His arm and part of his shoulder was in plaster
and there was a dull ache somewhere under the plaster.

He said, "Kate. . . ."

She turned and came towards him, the sun now putting
an aureole of pale flame around her fair hair. He smiled
at her. She put out a hand and touched his face, then
bent and kissed him gently on the lips.

"Darling. . . ."

She drew away from him and reached to the table for
cigarettes and a lighter.

"Here."

She put a lighted cigarette between his lips.

She sat on the side of the bed and looked at him, her
hand moving up and resting lightly on his.

"What happened?"

"Up there?"

"Yes."

"It was three days ago. . . . The bullet smashed a bone.
But there was a broken artery too. . . . You could have died.
We didn't know it then. But he did. . . ."

"Manasco?"

"Yes. . . . He fixed you up with a tourniquet but he didn't
say anything to us. Only to da Lapa who came up the valley
just after the lorries went through."

"Manasco saved my life?"

"Yes. He also saved himself from . . . well, I don't know what charge."

"Where is he now?"

"He's gone. I don't know where, South America. . . . Somewhere on business. He and da Lapa talked after you were brought down here."

"Is he bringing any charges against me?"

"No. He and da Lapa had a long talk."

"What about da Lapa? Is he after me?

"Well. . . . You've got to go, as soon as possible. Out of Spain. . . . That's official."

"Isn't that what we want? We know where we want to go."

"As soon as you're fit to travel."

He shut his eyes again. Da Lapa talking to Manasco . . . he could imagine it; da Lapa, pink-face and polished leather, and Manasco who would be very still, listening and not saying much. But nothing da Lapa could say would make any difference to Manasco. He would have made his own decision already, and the fact that he had gone showed what it was.

He opened his eyes and saw Kate looking at him and he could tell that she was stirred up, near to tears because he was back and she no longer had to go on frightening herself as she must have done in the last three days.

She said, "You're all right?"

He nodded. "Yes, darling." He put out his good arm and slid it round her waist. Suddenly she came down to him her face hiding itself in his chest and he felt her shaking a little with affectionate anger, kissing him and crying too and he heard her saying:

"Oh, you men . . . you men."

His arm slid up and the bandaged palm of his right hand cupped her shoulder and he held her to him firmly.